Praise for *Follow*

"*Follow Me Back* is the perfect mix .... with just the right amount of suspense. An enthralling page-turner from beginning to end."

—Anna Todd, *New York Times* bestselling author of the After series

"Dark and suspenseful, *Follow Me Back* is sure to be the next big thing in YA thrillers."

—Ali Novak, author of the Heartbreak Chronicles and *My Life with the Walter Boys*

"Timely, twisty, and totally thrilling. *Follow Me Back* will have readers wondering about the identity of every online friend and follower they've got. A riveting read that will keep you up late and keep you guessing!"

—Paula Stokes, author of *Liars, Inc.* and *Vicarious*

"*Follow Me Back* is an unforgettable page-turner and a cautionary tale for any fan who's ever wished their favorite celebrity followed them on social media."

—Sandy Hall, author of *Signs Point to Yes* and *A Little Something Different*

ALSO BY A. V. GEIGER

Follow Me Back

TELL ME NO LIES

A. V. GEIGER

sourcebooks
fire

Published by Sourcebooks Fire, an imprint of Sourcebooks, Inc.
P.O. Box 4410, Naperville, Illinois 60567-4410
(630) 961-3900
Fax: (630) 961-2168
sourcebooks.com

Library of Congress Cataloging-in-Publication Data

Names: Geiger, A. V., author.
Title: Tell me no lies / A.V. Geiger.
Description: Naperville, Illinois : Sourcebooks Fire, [2018] | Sequel to:
    Follow me back. | Summary: Tessa and Eric are forced out of hiding when
    pop star Dorian Grey is found alive, intimate photos appear on Eric's
    biggest fan account, and Tessa becomes a suspect in a murder.
Identifiers: LCCN 2017043009 |
Subjects: | CYAC: Agoraphobia--Fiction. | Mental illness--Fiction. |
    Celebrities--Fiction. | Social media--Fiction. | Stalking--Fiction. |
    Singers--Fiction. | Popular music--Fiction.
Classification: LCC PZ7.1.G4475 Tel 2018 | DDC [Fic]--dc23 LC record avail-
able at https://lccn.loc.gov/2017043009

Printed and bound in Canada.
MBP 10 9 8 7 6 5 4 3 2 1

To my mom and dad, with love.

THE INTERROGATION (FRAGMENT 1)

May 1, 2017, 2:19 p.m.
Case #75932.394.1
OFFICIAL TRANSCRIPTION OF POLICE INTERVIEW

—START PAGE 1—

INVESTIGATOR:	Thank you for joining us, Ms. Hart. For the record, I'm Detective Tyrone Stevens with the Los Angeles Police Department. This is my partner, Detective Andrew Morales. Today is May 1, 2017, at 2:19 p.m. This interview is being recorded.
HART:	Why am I here exactly?
INVESTIGATOR:	Just a few questions. Could you please state your full name for the record?
HART:	Tessa Lynn Hart.
INVESTIGATOR:	Occupation?
HART:	I'm a social media consultant.
INVESTIGATOR:	Consultant. Very nice. You're how old now?
HART:	I'm nineteen.
INVESTIGATOR:	And how long have you been in that profession?
HART:	A few months. I started in January.

INVESTIGATOR: What date in January? Can you recall?

HART: January 1.

INVESTIGATOR: New Year's Day?

HART: Yes.

INVESTIGATOR: And what services do you provide for your clients?

HART: Only one client. I run his Twitter… Sorry, can I have a glass of water?

INVESTIGATOR: Are you all right?

HART: No… [pause] It'll pass. Just give me a sec.

INVESTIGATOR: Are you ill, Ms. Hart?

HART: I'm OK now. What were you asking me?

INVESTIGATOR: What do you charge as your consulting fee?

HART: I can't tell you that.

INVESTIGATOR: Ms. Hart, this will all go much faster if you simply answer the questions.

HART: I'm really not allowed to say. I signed a nondisclosure agreement.

INVESTIGATOR: Well, let me ask you this: If we were to contact your so-called client, would he corroborate your statement that he employs you as a… What did you call it again? A social media consultant?

HART:	Are you calling me a liar?
INVESTIGATOR:	I'm simply trying to get the facts on the record.
HART:	Look, I can prove it. I'm not delusional, OK?
INVESTIGATOR:	No need to get defensive, Tessa. We're simply trying to establish your employment history.
HART:	I already told you as much as I can say about it, so can we please move on?
INVESTIGATOR:	I'll decide when we move on.
HART:	I'm sorry. I don't mean to be rude, but you haven't even told me what you're investigating. What division are you guys with?
INVESTIGATOR:	Homicide.
HART:	Oh.
INVESTIGATOR:	Ms. Hart, the Twitter account you say you run… Is it by any chance the Twitter-verified account of Eric Thorn?
HART:	What homicide? Is someone dead?
INVESTIGATOR:	Tessa, did your role as a social media consultant include the tweet sent from the @EricThorn Twitter account on… Andy, what was that tweet again?
INVESTIGATOR 2:	"Sleep with a leech, and it just might bleed you dry." Tweeted January 1, 2017, at 7:26 a.m.

INVESTIGATOR:	That's right. New Year's Day. Tessa, you tweeted that message from Mr. Thorn's account, did you not?
HART:	Like I told you, I signed a nondisclosure—
INVESTIGATOR:	Do you have a copy of the agreement you signed?
HART:	N-no. I mean, not on me. I don't carry it around with me.
INVESTIGATOR:	See, the odd thing is, according to the Twitter records we obtained, someone tweeted that one message, and then there was no further activity on the account for an extended period. In fact, the account with username @EricThorn was completely inactive over the entire month of January. Does that sound right to you?
HART:	Wait. You already have the Twitter records?
INVESTIGATOR:	And then the account resumed activity on... Do you have that date, Andy?
INVESTIGATOR 2:	February 3, 2017.
INVESTIGATOR:	Tessa, what happened on or about February 3, 2017?
HART:	I'm not stupid, OK? You obviously already know.
INVESTIGATOR:	For the record, Ms. Hart.
HART:	February 3. It was a couple days after the news broke.

INVESTIGATOR: What news, Tessa?

HART: It was all over the Internet. There's no way you could've missed it. I was living out of a VW camper van on the other side of the Mexican border, and I still heard the news.

INVESTIGATOR: Tessa, can I ask you to clarify what news story you're referencing?

HART: It started with one little post on Facebook, and then it spread like wildfire. It trended on Twitter for weeks. You'd have to be living under a rock not to have heard about it. I mean, I practically was living under a rock.

INVESTIGATOR: For the record, you're referring to—

HART: Dorian Cromwell, lead singer of Fourth Dimension, spotted by some goatherd in Switzerland…very much alive.

1

DEAD CELEBRITIES

February 1, 2017 (Three Months Earlier)

"AND THIS JUST *in. We're getting word now from sources in Switzerland that the Facebook Live video has been authenticated. The man in the video is, in fact, Dorian Cromwell—*"

Tessa squinted at the tiny image on her phone, straining to make out the facial features of the blurry figure. The thirty-second clip showed a lone man making his way down an icy slope. He had his face tipped down, eyes on the uneven terrain, but he glanced up and raised a ski pole in greeting as the clip ended.

Dorian Cromwell, for real? How could they be so certain? To Tessa, the man looked more like a cross between a hippie and a homeless person, with a scraggly beard and a mop of unwashed hair that hung down below his shoulders. She supposed she could see a passing resemblance to the formerly clean-cut boy band leader, but it was hard to say. A bush of facial hair concealed the whole bottom half of his face. The video was shot from too far away to make out his age or eye color.

Someone had streamed it on Facebook two days ago with a geotag in Munster, Switzerland, and a clickbaiting caption:

Guten Tag, Dorian. #DorianCromwell #VeryMuchAlive

Tessa had noticed the story on TMZ the other day, but she hadn't given it much thought. Just another rumor started by some attention seeker. It happened with Eric all the time too. In the month since Eric's disappearance from Texas, he'd been "spotted" dozens of times by fans around the world. All fake, of course. Those pics were old shots doctored in Photoshop, easily recognizable to anyone who followed Eric's social media half as closely as Tessa always had.

Still, the mere thought of dead celebrities made Tessa's pulse rate jump. She shifted position inside the back of the van, sitting up straight. The thin, fold-down cushion that served as her sleeping surface creaked beneath her weight. At the noise, her eyes flicked to the tinted van window beside her. She'd propped it open a few minutes ago to let in a whiff of the cool mountain air. It was after dusk, and the long shadows of the pine trees cloaked the van's interior in darkness. No one could see her inside. The rational part of her mind knew that—and yet she fought the urge to pull the window closed.

"No," Tessa muttered. She'd suffocate in here without fresh air. She closed her eyes and pulled in a deep breath, counting the beats inside her head.

Eric one…Eric two…Eric three…

Better.

There was no one out there watching her. Tessa had learned to view the lingering sense of dread with clinical detachment. It was anxiety creeping up on her. A quirk of her brain chemistry. Nothing more. Nothing real. The van was parked at the far end of a densely wooded campground in the foothills of a Mexican mountain range. It was quiet here, with only a couple other cars parked near the cabins at the other end of the unpaved lot.

No one was watching. No one cared about some beat-up, old VW camper with Texas plates.

Tessa exhaled slowly, releasing the tension from her lungs. She turned her attention back to her phone. The story about Dorian was turning into more than idle Twitter gossip. Tessa was tuned in to a live stream of U.S. network television, and they'd interrupted the evening news to cover the breaking story. She wished they would freeze the frame so she could study the face in the video. She didn't dare hit Pause, for fear that she might lose her connection to the feed.

The show went to commercial, and Tessa glanced toward the window again. She pulled out one of her headphones to listen for the sound of approaching footsteps, swallowing against the bubble of tension that swelled inside her chest.

Her ears were greeted by the gentle sounds of nightfall. The distant hoot of an owl. The babble of the creek that ran nearby. The breeze stirring back and forth through the tree limbs. Not a human sound in the mix.

Safe.

If only she could make her mind believe that…

Tessa scowled. She knew she should focus on the positive. She would always have anxiety, but she'd come a long way since December. Literally. Her phone's GPS placed her at 543.2 miles from her childhood home in Midland. To think, only a month ago, she'd worried she would never set foot outside her front door.

So much for small steps. Tessa pursed her lips at the thought of her old therapist, Dr. Regan, and the excruciating desensitization exercises she'd prescribed. What a monumental waste of time. In the end, the small steps led nowhere. Everything had changed in one night. One giant leap.

Tessa couldn't really blame her therapist though. She never would have attempted this trip if she hadn't been forced by circumstances. Tessa still longed for the safe cocoon of her childhood home, but she knew she could never go back. Not after what happened there on New Year's Eve. The house itself had become one giant trigger. The mere thought of the rotted, old back deck made Tessa's mouth go dry.

No, her old, safe refuge was lost to her—like an empty womb, and she was the infant who'd been ripped from it and cast out into the cold, harsh world. By dawn on New Year's Day, she'd understood that she couldn't stay there any longer. She knew what she had to do.

A month had passed since that morning. All that blood… staining her hands, her clothes, her mother's hallway carpet…

Then easing the Ferrari down the unplowed, snowy streets, with its owner hidden in the trunk...

And then the frantic flight across the border. Tessa had rolled into this campground by nightfall on January 2, and the journey had taken every ounce of mental stamina she possessed. She'd collapsed after she got here. Taken a double dose of anxiety meds and slept in the back of the van for twenty-four hours straight. But she'd made it. When push came to shove, she was stronger than she knew.

Tessa nodded to herself. She turned her back to the open window and bent over her phone. The live stream cut back to the news studio, and Tessa slipped in her earphones to listen.

"Once again, if you're just tuning in, a spokesperson has confirmed that Dorian Cromwell is not dead. He has been living for the past seven months in an underpopulated region of the Swiss Alps, accessible only by foot or cross-country ski..."

Tessa fought back the urge to shake her phone. The whole story made no sense! Dorian's death couldn't have been staged. They found his body in the Thames. They conducted a murder trial and locked up his killer in a psych hospital. How could he have faked all that?

"—still a lot of unanswered questions." The news anchor paused and pressed in his earpiece, listening. Tessa leaned forward as she waited for new information. *"Right. I'm getting word now that—"*

But Tessa never heard the end of his sentence.

Out of nowhere, the sound cut out. Tessa's head snapped up.

She registered the shadow of a human arm, reaching through the window behind her. She lunged to close the curtain, but not before her gaze locked with a pair of eyes peering back at her in the darkness.

"Oh my God," she whispered, clapping a hand to her heart. "You scared me!"

Her travel companion made no reply. He slid the van door open, with her headphone jack in his hands and a curious expression on his face.

"Sorry, sweet pea," Eric said after he settled onto his half of the double mattress. "You looked intense. What are you watching?"

2

ALIVE AND WELL

ERIC HANDED THE headphones back to Tessa. He stretched out on his side, with his head propped in his hand and his knee forming an upright triangle with the mattress. He recognized it as a classic underwear modeling position—a pose he'd struck so many times that it must have lodged itself permanently in his muscle memory.

He wrinkled his nose and sat up.

Tessa watched his movements, but her eyes looked blank and hollow. Had it been the wrong move, pulling out her earbuds? He could see he'd set her off by the way her face went rigid. In the month since they'd run away together, Eric had learned to recognize that tension at the corners of Tessa's mouth whenever her anxiety level rose.

"Are you OK?" he asked, reaching for her hand. "I didn't mean to creep up." He'd gone out to stretch his legs under the cover of darkness, and he couldn't have been away for more than ten minutes. He'd pulled out her earbuds without thinking—one of those playful gestures of intimacy that people do all the time when they're in a relationship. She must have been too fixated on her phone to hear him approach.

Tessa pulled her hand away, but her face softened. She scrunched her mouth to the side, trying for a stern look. "'Sweet pea,' Eric? Are you still calling me that?"

Eric grinned. "That's your name! It's not my fault you turned out to be nonspherical." He waved his hand with mock irritation toward the long, slender legs that lay beside him, clad in a pair of skin-tight yoga pants, with her fuzzy, pink bunny slippers covering her feet.

A reluctant smile curled her lips. "Um, that nickname sounded a lot less cheesy over DM."

"No good?" He reached over and pinched her knee, gathering the black spandex between his thumb and index finger. "Would you prefer 'snowflake'?"

Tessa laughed. Eric moved to draw her legs toward him, but she swatted his hand away. Her eyes returned to the cell phone in her lap. "Wait. You have to watch this!"

She tucked the headphones into the kangaroo pocket of her sweatshirt and turned up the phone's speaker volume as high as it would go. Eric stifled a groan. What was it, YouTube? He wasn't in the mood for social media. Not now. He finally had the only person in the world he cared about sitting by his side—close enough to reach out and touch her face.

And all she wanted to do was look at cell phone videos?

With a sigh, Eric leaned closer, struggling to make out the tinny voices. They really should have bought a second cell. They'd picked this one up on a supply run into town, but they hadn't wanted to waste the cash on two. It wasn't like they had anyone to call except each other.

"What is this?" Eric asked. It looked like the evening news. He took the phone from Tessa with a tiny pinprick of alarm. His face had been in and out of the cable news coverage ever since his disappearance. Had they found something new? Were they on to him?

"It's not about you," Tessa said, reading his thoughts. "It's Dorian Cromwell. That video of him skiing the other day!"

Eric squinted at the screen. "That video was fake. It barely even looked like Dorian."

She tapped his arm to shush him, and Eric strained to catch up with the broadcast. The silver-haired news anchor was yammering about solicitors and Scotland Yard.

"*I'm joined now via satellite by British legal analyst Horace Killjoy. Horace, what can you tell us?*"

The image cut to a middle-aged man in a business suit, fidgeting with his tie. "*Anderson, from my sources at Scotland Yard, it appears we're looking at an elaborate conspiracy involving a number of key players at DBA Records and possibly extending to one or more members of the British law enforcement community.*"

It couldn't be true, could it? Dorian's murder…a hoax? Eric shook his head, forcing his attention back to the interview.

"*—may be in a spot of legal trouble. It will be interesting to see
how this plays out.*"

"*Could Dorian Cromwell be facing prison time?*"

"*Possibly.*"

"*Is it a crime to fake your own death?*"

Eric's spine went stiff. That part he understood—and it hit
awfully close to home. It was a question that robbed him of
sleep more nights than he cared to admit.

He hadn't paused to consider the legal ins and outs that
morning in Midland when the plan had first taken shape.
Running away had seemed like their best option at the time.
Tessa didn't feel safe in her house anymore—not after being
held hostage there by her stalker. Eric had offered to take her
with him on the road, but they both knew it would never work.
He was trapped in a record deal, contractually obligated to
appear before crowds of people and smile pretty for the camera.
If Tessa went public as his girlfriend, the scrutiny would be
intense. No way could she withstand that kind of attention.
Eric himself found it terrifying most of the time, even without
a history of agoraphobia.

It was Tessa who'd figured out the answer. The whole plan
had started as a joke. At least, he'd thought Tessa was kidding
when she first brought it up. She'd sat cross-legged beside him
on her bed, covered head to toe in her thick flannel pajamas,
when he saw her eyes go wide with a flash of inspiration.

*It's perfect, Eric! You said so yourself. It's only a matter of time
before some copycat turns up and another celebrity winds up dead.*

It had taken him a moment to catch up with her…

Don't you get it? she'd explained, tugging at his arm. *I'm the copycat! They let me walk out of that police station alone with you. No bodyguards. No security. No witnesses. Just some emotionally unstable fangirl with the object of her obsession. You know what conclusion they'll leap to if you don't show up for sound check in the morning!*

Eric shifted uncomfortably. His eyes darted down to the tender skin of his inner elbow. The array of needle pricks had long since faded, but he could still recall the stinging pain. Tessa hadn't been the most competent phlebotomist. She'd never performed a blood draw on her own before—only watched her mother doing them. Eric winced as he recalled the way she'd poked and prodded with her mother's spare equipment before she finally hit a vein.

He still couldn't believe anyone had fallen for it. Tessa Hart, a murderer? She'd taken a pint of his blood…left her house looking like a crime scene…and that final tweet she'd sent from his phone had sounded pretty damned incriminating… But the whole plot seemed ridiculously transparent to him. Could two teenagers with a phlebotomy kit really outwit the FBI?

Maybe.

The authorities didn't know his true state of mind. They didn't understand how trapped he felt by his old life—how badly he wanted out. His parents might have had some clue, or maybe his manager, Maury, but none of them had ever really listened to a single word Eric said.

So here they were a month later, and so far everything had played out as Tessa predicted. She had her face plastered all over the FBI Most Wanted List, and @EricThorn's famous last words had been retweeted 11.2 million times…

But otherwise, they were safe. They were together. And most miraculous of all, they were free.

At least for now.

Eric blew out a tense breath. He returned his attention to the phone.

"—*not a crime in and of itself. However, it appears that Dorian may have continued to receive royalty payments through a Swiss bank account during the time of his sequestration. He could be looking at charges of money laundering or even income tax evasion—*"

That didn't sound so good. Eric looped an arm around Tessa's shoulders and hit the pause button. "Hold on a sec. When was this show broadcast?"

"It's a live stream! Don't pause it!" Tessa reached for the phone, but Eric had his hand over the screen, blocking her. "Eric, you're going to lose the feed."

"I don't understand," he said. "What makes them so sure he's still alive?" He eyed her skeptically, his gaze flitting from her face to the phone and back again.

"I don't know, but they're saying it's confirmed. Dorian's supposed to give a statement any second. Hit Play!"

Eric handed the phone to her, but the image had gone black. Tessa tapped the play button again, and Eric's grip tightened around her shoulders as they waited. At last, the image sprang back to life.

The scene jumped forward to a new location. The camera panned across a long table covered with microphones, all pointed in the direction of an unmistakable face. The young man seated in the center had his hair pulled back in a messy man bun, and the bottom half of his face appeared oddly pale from where he'd shaved his beard—but otherwise he looked the same as ever.

Dorian Cromwell, in the flesh. Alive and well. He cleared his throat, and the camera zoomed in close.

"*Hi, guys. As you can see, the rumors of my death have been mildly exaggerated...*"

"I can't believe it," Eric murmured, but he couldn't deny the evidence before his eyes. Dorian Cromwell filled the screen, reading a prepared statement off a crisp, white sheet of paper.

"*On behalf of myself and everyone at DBA Records, I'd like to apologize to the fans and to anyone else I may have caused undue distress...*"

Eric choked. Undue distress? That was one way to put it. He'd spent the better part of a year fearing for his life because of Dorian's murder. Ever since the story broke last summer, Eric hadn't taken a single step without looking over his shoulder. And none of it was real. Pure smoke and mirrors...and public relations. Just like everything else in his phony, bubblegum-pop existence.

Honestly, he should have known.

Tessa must have seen his expression change. Her hand brushed against his knee. "Eric?"

He tilted back his head. Why did the van's interior feel ten times smaller than it had a moment ago? Eric reached up and grazed the ceiling with his fingertips. "I turned my life upside down because of him. The whole reason I'm here is because of Dorian!"

Tessa pulled his elbow down and inched closer. Her hands ran up and down the length of his forearm to soothe him. "That's not the only reason. There was other stuff too, wasn't there? The followers? The fame?"

"Yeah, but—"

"And it was because of me," she said. She laced her fingers through his and raised her eyes to look at him. "I mean, I thought that was part of it. You ran away with me to protect me. Didn't you?"

Eric's face softened as he heard the quaver in her voice. He clasped her hand firmly. It killed him every time he saw her doubts resurface. If anything good had come out of Dorian's deception, it was the fact that it brought the beautiful girl beside him into his life. He didn't regret for a second the way he'd spent the past four weeks.

Eric dropped his arm to her waist and pulled her toward him, pressing his mouth into her hair.

"Of course it was because of you," he murmured. "So we could be together."

She nuzzled her face into the crook of his neck, and Eric

closed his eyes. She felt so fragile—so thin and slight. It filled him with an overwhelming urge to keep her safe.

The truth was he'd do anything to shield Tessa from the harsh light of public scrutiny. She had more to worry about than celebrity gossip and overbearing fans. Tessa still had a stalker on the loose—another unintended consequence of their decision to run away. The police had locked up Blair Duncan, but they couldn't have held him for long. None of the charges would stick without the victim around to testify. For all Eric and Tessa knew, Blair was out there at this very moment, biding his time, waiting for Tessa to reappear.

Eric gave her shoulders another protective squeeze. His eyes drifted back to the scene unfolding on the phone. Dorian's voice sounded flat, his face devoid of emotion, as he read the statement prepared for him by publicists and lawyers:

"*I would also like to apologize to my countrymen for any alleged legal or financial wrongdoing. I remain a faithful British subject, and I would take this opportunity to beg the Crown for leniency…*"

Tessa tensed in Eric's arms. "He won't really go to jail, will he?" she asked. "It's all spin, right?"

Eric shook his head. "I don't understand. What law did he break?"

"They said something about income tax evasion." Tessa sat up straighter. "You don't think you could get in trouble for that, do you?"

Eric laughed. "For tax evasion? Tessa, look at this place." He gestured around the van's cramped interior. No furniture. No running water. Not enough headroom to stand. "We're basically living in squalor. I don't have any income."

"We sold your car though," she responded. "Does that count?"

Eric dismissed her worries with another low chuckle, but he couldn't deny a sliver of concern. They'd ditched his beloved convertible at a chop shop on the side of the road, traded in for this rusted-out camper van and a trash bag full of cash. Was that income? He'd left all his other worldly possessions behind him. Tens of millions of dollars, abandoned and untouched. The government couldn't come after him for a measly fifty grand—a mere fraction of the Ferrari's rightful value. Of all the worries that kept him up at night, it had never occurred to him that he could be in trouble with the IRS.

"I suppose it's not too late," Tessa said slowly. "It's not April 15 yet."

He looked at her blankly.

"Oh, come on, Eric. Tax day?" She poked him in the chest. "Even rock stars have to file their taxes by April 15."

She did that sideways scrunchy thing with her mouth again. Eric grinned. "My job was to keep my abs tight and occasionally play a guitar. I had a manager to take care of the finances."

"Well, maybe you need to give your manager a call before you end up sharing a prison cell with Dorian."

Eric's smile faded. Call Maury or go to jail for tax evasion? He wasn't sure which option sounded worse…

For now, Eric raised a finger to his lips to hush Tessa.

Dorian's voice had grown more animated. He pushed aside his sheet of paper and leaned into the mic.

"*My only excuse for my actions is that fame itself comes with an astronomical price, not measured in pounds sterling. For years, I have paid dearly. I have been hounded. I have been stalked. I have been relentlessly slandered in the press along with everyone important in my life. I know I'm not the only one who has suffered and sought refuge.*"

Dorian paused and looked directly into the camera. Eric sat transfixed, his eyes locked with Dorian's piercing gaze. He had the strangest sensation that Dorian could see him—that the other man was looking straight through the screen.

"*I'm not the only one. There are others like me. I call on them to come forward and stand with me. If you're out there somewhere, watching this broadcast, then I beg you. Please. I'm in trouble. I need your help.*"

Eric slipped his hand into Tessa's. She let out a gasp, and Eric felt the hairs rise on the back of his neck as Dorian plowed on.

"*You know who you are, but I'll name you if I must. I'm speaking, of course, of Tupac, Michael Jackson, and most recently, Eric Thorn.*"

JUST ANOTHER SNOWFLAKE

3

TESSA HIT PAUSE on the live stream and turned to face Eric. His jaw had dropped open at the sound of his own name on Dorian's lips.

How did he know? Tessa wondered.

Eric must have been thinking the same thing. He looked dazed, but he gathered himself after a moment. He squared his shoulders and reached for the phone. "I have to talk to him."

Tessa grabbed his wrist. "Eric, no!"

"You heard him. He knows I faked it. I have to find out who told him. If my label is onto me—"

Tessa cut him off. "But what if he doesn't know? Maybe he's just guessing."

"Well, I have to find out!"

"But if he doesn't know, then you'll be outing yourself..."

Tessa's voice trailed off. Eric wasn't even listening. He grabbed the phone and swiped through the apps on her display. "Where's Twitter? Do you think Dorian reactivated his old account?"

Twitter? The word hit Tessa like a slap across the face. "Eric, no. You can't!"

He paused, his forehead crinkling. "I'll start a fake account."

"No." She shook her head fiercely. "Talk to him if you want, but not over Twitter."

"How? Call the operator and ask them to connect me to Dorian Cromwell? It's not like there's some magic phone directory for pop stars."

He chuckled, but Tessa only crossed her arms in front of her chest. "Um, have your people call his people?" She grabbed the phone out of his hands and navigated to the keypad to place a call. "Go ahead," she said. "What's the number?"

"What number? Dorian? I told you—"

"No, not Dorian." Tessa raised her eyebrows meaningfully.

Eric's face fell as he caught on. "Tessa, I am *not* contacting Maury! Forget it. No way."

"I know you don't want to, but it's safer."

Eric rose to his knees on the mattress, wiping his palms against the fabric of his jeans. Tessa had come to recognize the expression that crossed his face. Not quite panic. More like a hunted animal, startled by the sound of a snapping twig.

"You don't understand," he said, his words tumbling out in a rush. "I just want to find out what Dorian knows. I'm not necessarily going to do anything about it. But if Maury figures out I'm here, then it's over. He'll tell the label. They'll force me to come back."

"But I'm sure Maury wouldn't do that if you explained the situation—"

"Tessa, you don't know what my record label is like. They're horrible people. Maury shields me from the worst of it, but there's only so much he can do!"

He raked a hand through his overgrown hair. It stuck up wildly at his hairline, and Tessa reached out to smooth it down. Eric caught her hand instead and pressed it against his cheek. She watched the tense lines in his forehead disappear with the touch of her fingertips—and somehow, the sight calmed the worries racing through her own mind.

His voice sank low as he drew her close. "I'm not ready to go back. Maybe in another month or two, but not now. I need more time." He pressed a kiss into her palm, and Tessa felt her resolve melt at the gentle insistence of his lips. "*We* need more time."

Tessa's eyes fluttered closed. "There you go again," she said softly. "Deflecting. Always deflecting."

His breath tickled her cheek as he whispered in her ear. "Is that one like projecting?"

"Deflection," she answered, twining her fingers through his shaggy hair. "That's when you change the subject to avoid a topic that makes you uncomfortable."

Her lips parted, waiting for his kiss. Instead, she felt the glide of cold metal as he removed the cell phone from her hand.

"Guilty as charged." A hint of a smile tugged at the corner of Eric's mouth as he tapped the screen. He found the Twitter app, and a shudder ran through Tessa's shoulders at the sight of the log-in screen. She'd sworn to herself that she would never touch Twitter again. Not after what happened the last time.

Eric navigated to create a new account, but Tessa couldn't bear to watch. She fixed her eyes on her bunny slippers and pulled the air deep into her lungs.

Eric one…Eric two…Eric three…Eric Thorn…Eric five…

The jagged edge of panic loosened its grip around her throat. Not that she felt relaxed. Not by a long shot. Every instinct screamed against the idea of a new Twitter account. But Tessa calmed her mind enough to question the source of her anxiety. Was it based on a real threat? Or was distorted thinking magnifying the danger in her head?

"Trust me," Eric said. "I'll pick a super-secure password." Tessa read over his shoulder as his thumbs flashed across the keypad. She squinted at the string of characters he input. It took her a moment to realize what it was.

Password: TEXASjf97bv

"The license plate number from the van?"

Eric glanced at her sideways. "Totally unhackable, right? No one else could guess that but you and me."

The next prompt came up on the screen before she could respond. Their account still needed a handle. "I'll make it look like a fan account," Eric told her as he typed. "Nobody pays attention to those."

Username: @Snowflake734

Tessa recognized the title of his most recent single, "Snowflake." Eric's label had released it a week before his disappearance. With the publicity generated by the crime, the song had ended up with more downloads than any other single he'd ever recorded.

"Why 734?" she asked. "Does that mean something?"

Eric shrugged. "Snowflakes 1 through 733 were taken," he said with a dry laugh. "See? Just another snowflake. I blend."

He hit Create Account, and the new profile sprang to life.

Just Another Snowflake @Snowflake734

TWEETS	FOLLOWING	FOLLOWERS
0	**0**	**0**

Tessa's stomach did a somersault. She quickly looked away. Her eyes darted toward the window of the van, but night had fallen. It was pitch-black outside. She only saw the pale oval of her own face reflected in the glass, echoing the same expression Eric had worn a moment ago.

Haunted. Spooked.

"Please don't tweet anything," she whispered. "Please, Eric. He could be watching. He's still out there somewhere."

Blair sat in the coffee shop, hunched forward over the table with his phone hidden in his lap. He could feel a crick forming in his neck, but he didn't straighten up. He liked the way the tabletop shielded his screen from the view of nosy onlookers.

Some people… Always inserting themselves into everyone else's business. Maybe Tessa had the right idea, hiding out in her room for months on end. People could be such trouble-makers. Why couldn't they keep their eyes to themselves?

Blair hated logging on from a public place, but he had no choice. He needed the free Wi-Fi. At least the staff here left him alone, as long as he refilled his coffee every few hours.

He inserted his earbuds and tapped the Twitter app open, entering the same search term he input every day.

#EricThorn

He'd been following the news coverage ever since the police let him out of custody. The Texas police had him extradited to Louisiana, but the DA there declined to prosecute. They didn't consider it a priority to press stalking charges when the victim was a murderer herself.

Of course, Blair didn't buy for a second that Tessa had actually offed Eric Thorn. He knew her better than that. She was nothing if not conniving. Blair's biggest mistake in Texas had been underestimating her capacity for deceit. She'd gotten the better of him, and the memory still rankled. He'd have a few things to say when he found her.

She and her *beloved* Eric had obviously faked the crime and run away together. They'd turn up eventually. Blair would be watching when they did. He had new accounts on every social media app in existence, and he spent all day, every day refreshing…and refreshing…and refreshing…

It was only a matter of time before they poked their heads out from wherever they were hiding. Then Blair would get her back. He didn't know what she saw in that talentless pretty boy anyway. Eric Thorn… Blair let out a snort. Someday, he and Eric Thorn were going to have a serious score to settle.

For now, Blair returned his attention to Twitter's current list of trending topics.

Interesting.

A shadow fell across the table, and Blair sensed someone standing on the other side. He leaned farther forward, hoping the stranger would take the hint, but he heard the sound of a girl clearing her throat. With a grunt, Blair glanced up.

"Hey, are you using this chair?" The girl didn't wait for an answer. Wooden chair legs scraped across the floor. Blair darted a glance around the coffee shop, but all the other seats were full. "Are you saving it for someone?" she asked, as she set her drink down on the table.

Blair shook his head. He stuffed his phone in his pocket, and his chair clattered as he thrust himself to his feet.

"Take it," he said without meeting her eyes. He left his half-empty coffee cup where it stood and headed for the door.

He'd come back later. After the lunch rush. No point raising a fuss. He didn't want to draw attention to himself.

And most of all, he didn't want an audience for what he had in mind.

4

COGNITIVE DISTORTIONS

ERIC DISMISSED TESSA'S warning with an absentminded nod. He didn't hit the button to compose a tweet. Instead, he toggled to the trending list. He hated causing Tessa anxiety, but he needed to see what people were saying. Had they believed it when Dorian outed him? Or were they dismissing it as Dorian's desperate attempt to deflect attention from himself?

The trending list popped up, and Eric let out the breath he'd been holding. His name was nowhere to be seen.

Trends for you

#DorianIsAlive
1.2M tweets

#TupacIsProbablyDead
383K tweets

#KurtCobainIsDefinitelyDead

28.9K tweets

"Kurt Cobain?" Tessa asked. "What makes them so sure?"

Eric shrugged. "I guess because he had an autopsy?"

"Well, so did Dorian Cromwell!"

Crap, Eric thought. That was true. How the hell had Dorian pulled it off, anyway?

Tessa reached around him and flicked to refresh the list. Eric's relief evaporated as he saw a new hashtag pop up in the third spot:

#EricIsAliveToo

29.3K tweets

"Dammit!" He shut his eyes to block out the words. When he reopened them, Tessa had already clicked to bring up the Top Tweets.

MET @MrsEricThorn

WE FORGIVE YOU @ERICTHORN! COME
BACK TO US BABY! #EricIsAliveToo

↻ 1.6K   ♥ 3.2K

Eric snarled softly at the screen. He recognized the handle of his old Twitter superfan. Of course it would be MET. She was still up to her old tricks, riling up his fandom into their latest frenzy.

Judging from the retweet count, she wasn't the only one who'd latched on to Dorian's claim.

Wishful thinking, Eric told himself. They didn't actually *know* that he was alive. "What about #EricIsDead?" he murmured. Maybe that was trending too.

He entered the words into the search bar, but the results didn't do much to soothe his nerves.

MET @MrsEricThorn

Does anyone still believe #EricIsDead? Nah.
Me neither. #EricIsAliveToo

↻ 63   ♥ 354

That was the top tweet? Wow, he was screwed.

Eric scrubbed a hand down the length of his face. Obviously, the Twitterverse had arrived at its final verdict. It was only a matter of time before his label hunted him down. He and Tessa were a few hours south of the border, but they might have to keep running. Central America, maybe? He'd heard Costa Rica was pretty nice…

But it was no use, and Eric knew it. He'd be no safer in Costa Rica than anywhere else. He had fans all over the world. All he needed was for one person to spot him and stream a video, and then the game was up.

Maybe it wasn't too late. MET wasn't the only fangirl he knew with a knack for social media. He glanced at Tessa. "You made that #EricThornObsessed thing take off last summer, right? Can you get something going with #EricIsDead?"

"You know it doesn't work that way." She clicked back onto the #EricIsAliveToo hashtag and scrolled through the results. MET had tweeted another one with an embedded video clip from Dorian's press conference. It began playing automatically, and Tessa moved to click it off, but Eric stopped her. Something else had caught his attention—a different part of Dorian's statement. Not his own name. The words that Dorian had spoken just before:

"If you're out there somewhere, watching this broadcast, then I beg you. Please. I'm in trouble. I need your help…"

What was that all about? He had to admit he was curious. Eric took the phone back from Tessa and input Dorian's username.

Dorian Cromwell ✔ @DorianCromwell

FOLLOWING	FOLLOWERS
1,947	**25.3M**

Twitter had deactivated Dorian's account after his murder, but apparently it was never truly dead. It must have lingered somewhere—buried in the bowels of some internal server or hovering in the ether on some cloud. It hadn't taken long to resurrect, with Dorian's list of 25 million followers still intact.

"Look," Eric said, pointing to the checkmark next to Dorian's name. "Alive and Twitter verified."

He tapped the button to Follow. That way, if Dorian wanted to talk, he'd be able to send Eric a private direct message.

Eric knew it was useless though. He wasn't @EricThorn at the moment. He was @Snowflake734. There was no way he'd get Dorian's attention amid the flood of other fans. And he couldn't send a direct message himself unless @DorianCromwell followed him back.

There had to be another way…

Eric hesitated. The phone went into sleep mode, and he stared at his dim reflection in the black rectangle of the screen. His face looked different from before he went into hiding. His record deal had a personal hygiene clause that required daily shaving, but he'd let that go since he ran away. His jawline was fringed with dark stubble. In another week, the growth would be thick enough to call a beard.

The sight of it gave Eric an idea. A fleeting smile quirked his lips. *Maybe*, he thought. *Just maybe…*

He flicked the phone back on and switched it into selfie mode.

Tessa let out a gasp at his side. She slapped her hand in front of the phone to block the camera lens before he could snap a pic. "What are you doing?"

"I have to tweet something at Dorian to show it's really me," Eric replied. "He's never going to get in a message exchange with @Snowflake734."

"But…but…"

"Don't worry," he argued, peeling her hand away from the phone. "I'll delete it as soon as he follows me."

"You can't tweet it publicly, Eric!"

"No one will see it but Dorian. I have zero followers!"

Tessa gave up trying to block him. Her face had gone pale, and she clutched her head between her hands. Eric relented, flicking the camera app closed again. Maybe she was right. Her fears were not entirely unfounded. Eric was worried about his label catching wind, but Tessa had bigger concerns.

"Blair isn't going to see it," Eric said in a low voice. "I promise you, Tessa. I will never let that animal get anywhere near you again."

She drew in her legs and hugged them, resting her forehead on her knees. Eric had to strain to understand her muffled voice. "That's what happened last time. That's how he found me." She looked up. "You started some fake Twitter account, and the next thing you know… *Boom.* There he was in my living room."

Her voice trembled, and Eric locked his arm around her waist to steady her. "That's not going to happen this time."

"If it happened once, it could happen again."

Eric cocked his head, studying her face. "You know what you're doing, right?" He didn't wait for Tessa's answer. Eric clicked off Twitter and brought up the iTherapy app that had taken the place of her former sessions with Dr. Regan. "Distorted thinking," he said with a grim smile.

Tessa craned her neck to read over his shoulder:

15 Common Cognitive Distortions

Eric knew Tessa had the whole list memorized. He didn't pause for her to read as he scrolled past the introduction:

A cognitive distortion is an inaccurate pattern of thought that can lead to false conclusions and negative emotions…

His thumb skimmed down the page, and he muttered the terms aloud as he went. "Personalizing…filtering…catastrophizing…polarizing…" He stopped short. "Polarizing maybe?"

Tessa shook her head. "Polarizing is when you see everything in absolutes. Black or white. Good or evil."

Eric squinted at her.

Tessa's voice gained confidence as she continued. "Like, for example, everyone at your record label is a horrible person? That might be considered a polarizing thought."

Was she making fun of him? Eric grinned, but Tessa broke into a scowl.

"See, that's the problem with therapy," she said. "Dr. Regan would probably say I was polarizing, but some things really are black and white. Blair is evil. There's nothing good about him. It's not a distortion if it's true!"

"No, no," Eric reassured her, quickly scrolling down the page. "I wasn't saying that. It must be one of these other ones." He bent his head back to the phone. "Overgeneralizing, maybe?" He read the definition:

Focusing on an event in the past that had an unpleasant outcome, and assuming the same result will occur over and over again.

Eric pinched her lightly on the arm. "Bingo."

"How is this overgeneralizing?"

He could see her trying to school her face into a skeptical expression, but she couldn't help but smile back at him. They'd always played this game—pointing out each other's psychological weaknesses—from the first day they'd started talking over DM.

He pecked her on the lips, and the smile broke free over her face. She slipped a hand around the back of his head to pull him toward her, but he stopped short of kissing her again. "Overgeneralizing," he said, resting his forehead against hers.

"If you say so," she replied with her eyes glued to his lips. "What were we talking about? I lost my train of thought."

His smile changed into a smirk. "My new fake Twitter," he answered.

Tessa closed her eyes and moaned.

"Listen to me, Tessa. Blair used Twitter to track you down one time, but it's not going to happen again." He placed a finger beneath her chin and tilted her face upward. "Don't give him so much power. He's not some psychic Twitter genius watching every new account that gets created."

"I know, but if he *did* notice it—"

"If he noticed it, then what?" Eric asked. "He still wouldn't be able to figure out your location."

Tessa dropped her head onto his shoulder. Eric's finger hung in midair, but he hesitated. For all his psychobabble talk, he couldn't help but wonder if Tessa might be right. Tweeting publicly hadn't gone so well the last time.

Eric couldn't ignore the knot of tension in his throat. He had the strangest feeling of déjà vu. It wasn't so long ago that he'd set up a fake handle and tweeted out a selfie from an account with zero followers. He'd deleted that tweet—the maiden tweet from @EricThornSucks, illustrated with a shot of him kissing himself in the mirror.

But deleted or not, a picture tweeted could never be *un*tweeted. He'd learned that lesson the hard way. It hadn't taken long for MET to poach that photo and tweet it from her own account. That girl spent every waking moment on Twitter, watching his every move.

And she was still out there.

Tessa was right. He couldn't tweet a selfie. He couldn't take the risk. There had to be a safer way to get Dorian's attention...

Just then, another tweet popped up at the top of the screen.

> **MET** @MrsEricThorn
>
> Andddd this entire fandom is now stalking @DorianCromwell LOLOL. Here's his not-so-secret Snapcode, folks ;) #DorianIsAlive #EricIsAliveToo

She'd attached the image of a white ghost cutout, surrounded by a yellow square. Beneath it was a username:

ShowYouTheDor

THE CURSE OF THE MALE CELEBRITY

"SNAPCHAT?" ERIC'S EYES narrowed. He'd never bothered to make an account himself. That was the last thing he needed—one more social media account for his fans to stalk. But it might not be the worst idea. "That's more private than Twitter, right?"

"In theory," Tessa said slowly. "Everything you share on Snapchat is automatically deleted, so there isn't any record."

"But Dorian would still have to follow me back, wouldn't he?"

Tessa pressed her lips together, thinking. "Maybe not," she said. "I can use this thingy MET tweeted to add Dorian as a friend." She kneeled on the mattress beside him, bending over the phone. A small crease formed between her eyes as she concentrated. Eric couldn't quite follow the stream of social-media-speak that tumbled from her lips. "It's called a Snapcode. Kind of like a QR code. See the random dots around the edges? A lot of celebrities use Snapchat with secret usernames, but the fans find them eventually. I can't believe MET just shared it publicly!"

Eric leaned back and rested his weight on his elbows. He didn't need to know the details. Tessa would figure it out. He brushed his hand idly across the faded coverlet they shared at night, waiting for her to reemerge from whatever fangirlish rabbit hole she'd fallen down.

He had to admit, sleeping with a fangirl had its perks.

Not that they were doing anything other than *sleeping*. Tessa had made her boundaries clear, and Eric could respect that. They'd only been together for a month, and it felt right to take things slow. He'd fallen in love with Tessa's words. Her mind. He could wait for the rest.

He glanced at her heart-shaped face. A lock of brown hair had come loose from her braid and dangled by her cheek. In a different mood, he might have reached out and brushed it back behind her ear, but he didn't want to distract her.

"Got it!" A triumphant grin spread across her face. "Done."

"What? You made us a Snapchat?"

"Yup, we're Snowflake734, and we added Dorian as a friend. Now we can send him a Snap." She flashed the screen in Eric's direction. "If he notices it, we can open up a Chat."

Tessa pointed the phone at Eric's face, but he held up a hand to stop her. He could only imagine the flood of other accounts adding ShowYouTheDor at this very moment. They needed a pic that would grab Dorian's attention, and Eric knew exactly what to do. He clutched the collar of his T-shirt with one hand and peeled it over his head.

The phone blocked most of Tessa's face, but he could see the way her eyes went round. "Um. OK. Why are you taking your shirt off?"

Eric chuckled deep in his throat. "Force of habit."

Tessa lowered the phone. "Eric, you're doing it again. Stop deflecting. This isn't a joke!"

"No, I'm serious. This way Dorian will know the picture is legit." Eric pointed at his bare chest. "See?"

Tessa didn't look so pale now. A flush of color spread upward from her collarbone as her eyes came to rest on his well-sculpted pecs. He hadn't followed his daily workout regimen since they ran away, and he'd lost a touch of muscle tone, but he still had some decent definition when he flexed.

"How does that prove anything?" she asked. Her color deepened, and she flicked her eyes back toward her lap. "Pretty sure there are a few million other shirtless photos of you floating around the Internet."

Eric grinned. "Not like this." He lowered his head to view the coating of soft fuzz that grew darker every day. "There's never been a published photo in which I was not fully waxed up top. PR wouldn't allow it."

Her eyes went far away for a moment. Eric knew what she was doing: mentally reviewing the catalog of Eric Thorn pics she'd once kept on her camera roll. "I guess that's true," she said. "It never occurred to me before, but you were always…"

"A life-size plastic action figure?"

"And you think Dorian will notice the difference?"

Eric nodded. "Chest waxing," he explained. "It's the universal curse of the male celebrity."

Tessa looked doubtful, but Eric had his mind made up. Before she could protest, he took the phone and snapped the picture himself. He only paused to add a quick caption before he hit Send.

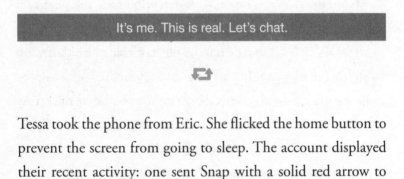

It's me. This is real. Let's chat.

Tessa took the phone from Eric. She flicked the home button to prevent the screen from going to sleep. The account displayed their recent activity: one sent Snap with a solid red arrow to indicate its unopened status.

➤ ShowYouTheDor

"Now what?" Eric asked.

"Now we wait and see if he opens it."

She could sense Eric's nervous energy from the way he drummed his palms against his thighs. Tessa wasn't holding her breath though. She'd never been much of a Snapchatter, but she knew how it worked. Celebrities had filters in place to weed out random fans. God forbid they saw something illegal, like a nude from an underage teenager, and ended up in trouble for viewing child porn. The filters meant that fans were essentially on mute. They could scream and yell and send selfies every day for a year with zero chance that their idol would ever notice them.

There was a time when that reality might have hurt her fangirl heart. Now, Tessa clung to it like a security blanket. *No one would ever see it*, she chanted inside her head. The pic Eric had Snapped would never be opened. *No one. No way. Not ever.*

Not by Dorian.

Not by Eric's record label.

And certainly not by Blair.

At the thought of Blair's name, Tessa felt the automatic spike in her heart rate. She recognized it for what it was. A chemical reaction. Nothing more. Lately, she'd been reading about the body's fight-or-flight response. She could pinpoint the exact sensation when her adrenal glands kicked in and released a dose of hormones into her bloodstream. Epinephrine. Norepinephrine. They were the same kind of chemicals used in EpiPens to treat people with allergy attacks—but to her brain, it felt like fear.

Tessa closed her eyes and focused on her breathing. Her pulse rate had returned to a tolerable level when she felt Eric's hand close around her wrist.

"What happened?" he whispered. "Something changed."

Tessa's eyes sprang open. She blinked at the Snapchat icon on her phone. No more solid red. The little arrow had turned into a hollow outline.

▷ ShowYouTheDor

"What does it mean?" Eric asked. "Did he open it?"

Not only that, Tessa thought. Her jaw went slack as a new icon appeared in the arrow's place.

🗨 ShowYouTheDor

The little blue speech bubble could only mean one thing: an incoming message.

INSECURE

ERIC CLICKED THE Chat window open. He sprawled on his stomach and laid the phone on the mattress in front of him. Tessa peered at the screen over his shoulder.

> **ShowYouTheDor:** Eric! My friend, I had a feeling you were out there somewhere.

My friend? Eric snorted. Dorian had a lot of nerve calling him that after the stunt he'd pulled at the press conference.

> **Snowflake734:** Dude, did you have to call me out like that? Not cool!
> **ShowYouTheDor:** Calm your tits. I didn't say anything the fans weren't already tweeting. You know how they like to cry "death hoax" every time a celebrity snuffs it.

"Wow," Tessa murmured in his ear. "He's so…"

"British?"

She nodded. "Aggressively British. Like, he's going to start talking about bollocks and sticky wickets next."

"I bet he's snickering about how American I sound." Eric laughed softly as he composed another message.

> **Snowflake734:** You're the one who made it trend, bruh. #EricIsAliveToo? WTF?
>
> **ShowYouTheDor:** You're upset. I understand. Believe me, I'm not happy either. We're on the same side. I didn't know how else to get your attention.
>
> **Snowflake734:** What about Tupac and MJ?
>
> **ShowYouTheDor:** Don't be daft, Eric. Wherever they are, they probably don't have Snapchat.

Tessa's voice startled him before Eric could reply. "What does he mean?" she asked. "How are you on the same side?"

Eric had glossed over that part, too focused on the rest of the bizarre conversation. He didn't bother answering her out loud, but he echoed her question back to Dorian.

> **Snowflake734:** What do you mean we're on the same side?

ShowYouTheDor: You saw the news. I'm possibly looking at prison.

Snowflake734: That sucks, man. But what does it have to do with me?

Eric tapped his fingers against his knee as the seconds ticked by. Had he come across too harshly? For a moment, he thought Dorian might not answer, and he vowed to soften his tone. As much as he hated being dragged into someone else's drama, he had to admit that he was curious as hell.

At last, a new text popped up.

ShowYouTheDor: Listen. This is between you and me, right? Can I trust you?

Snowflake734: Sure. I won't leak anything to the media, if that's what you mean.

ShowYouTheDor: Are you on a cell phone right now?

Snowflake734: Yeah.

ShowYouTheDor: Encrypted?

Snowflake734: Ummm no…but it's a new phone. New number. I picked it up in Saltillo on my way down here.

Tessa reared back the moment he hit Send on the message. Eric flinched as he realized what he'd done.

ShowYouTheDor: Saltillo… Where's that, Mexico?

"Crap," Eric muttered. It wasn't much of a secret that he'd fled across the border, but he hadn't intended to confirm it. He felt Tessa's palm press down against his shoulder.

"That's what happened the last time," she whispered. "I messaged you where I lived, and then…"

Eric took her hand and squeezed it. "Overgeneralizing," he reminded her. "Blair isn't eavesdropping on this conversation. And even if he were, we're way outside Saltillo now. Mexico's a big place."

Tessa nodded. He could hear the faint whistle of air as she inhaled through her nose. Her lips moved as she silently mouthed the numbers that made up her breathing exercise. At last she turned her attention back to the phone. "What now?" she asked. "Are you going to answer him?"

Dorian had added another new message.

ShowYouTheDor: Hullo? Eric? Don't tell me you died again…

Snowflake734: Very funny. Haha.

ShowYouTheDor: ;)

Tessa let out a groan. "Is it overgeneralizing or polarizing if I automatically distrust anyone who uses wink emojis?"

Eric shot her a quizzical look. *Emojis bothered her?* That

was news to him. He felt certain that he'd used a wink emoji at some point during their months of DM correspondence. "Pretty sure the wink is the least of our concerns. What should I say about Mexico?"

Tessa didn't answer. She had her eyes closed, with her knees clenched tightly against her chest yet again. Eric stroked her arm to soothe her. With his other hand, he entered a new message.

> **Snowflake734:** Before this conversation goes any further, you're going to have to slow down and fill me in.
>
> **ShowYouTheDor:** What can I tell you that you don't already know?
>
> **Snowflake734:** I don't know anything! I'm totally in the dark here. Like, how is it possible you're not dead?
>
> **ShowYouTheDor:** You know as well as I do. We both needed a way out. People in our position can't exactly walk away and retire in obscurity.
>
> **Snowflake734:** Right. I get that. But how exactly did you pull it off? I mean, it was so convincing. The body…the trial…the girl they convicted for your murder. Who was she?
>
> **ShowYouTheDor:** Don't know exactly. My management took care of all the cloak and dagger.

> **Snowflake734:** Wait, so your label was in on it? They knew?
>
> **ShowYouTheDor:** Of course. Doesn't yours?
>
> **Snowflake734:** Why would your label want to fake your death?
>
> **ShowYouTheDor:** It was the only way to kill the story. You know, about sammo and me. Don't you know? Sorry, I just assumed...

"Oh my God!" Tessa whispered. "Sammo? Does he mean Hugo Samuelson?"

Eric squinted. "His bandmate?"

Tessa clapped her hand across her mouth. "That's real?" she said with a squeak. "Horian Cromuelson is *real*?"

Eric couldn't help but grin. Even he had heard of #HorianCromuelson. He'd seen that hashtag top the trending list time and time again—one of those ridiculous "ship names" the fangirls liked to invent.

> **Snowflake734:** Wait a sec. You and Hugo are actually together?
>
> **ShowYouTheDor:** Since we were 18, off and on. Let's just say all those lovely #Horian fanfics weren't total rubbish after all ;)
>
> **Snowflake734:** Dude, your fans are going to DIE when they hear that!

ShowYouTheDor: That's what I said.
It's publicity! Honestly I don't know why
management had their knickers in such a
twist over it. You see why I had to get out,
don't you?

Snowflake734: OK, I get that. But what
about the girl?

ShowYouTheDor: Which one? I can assure
you that all of my many "girlfriends" were
purely fictional. My publicists have quite the
vivid imagination.

Snowflake734: No, I mean the girl who
supposedly murdered you!

ShowYouTheDor: Oh, right, her. Poor
thing. Locked away like that... I'm told
she's in an excellent facility.

Snowflake734: Who was she though? Was
she really a fangirl?

ShowYouTheDor: A deeply troubled one.
But that's not saying very much, now is it? ;)

"What does that mean?" Tessa asked. Eric could hear the
edge in her voice. Maybe he should have told Dorian that he
had his own former superfan following this whole exchange.

But some instinct warned Eric to keep that information to
himself.

Snowflake734: So...I'm confused. All that psych stuff at the trial? Celebrity stalker syndrome or whatever they diagnosed her with? Was that all made up?

"Celebrity erotomanic delusional disorder," Tessa said. "That was the diagnosis."

ShowYouTheDor: No, no. She really was obsessed. She used to stake out my flat in London and slip love notes under the door. True story. We simply embellished the ending.

Snowflake734: You framed her for murder!

ShowYouTheDor: Come on, Eric. You did the same thing. Look at that Tessa person who supposedly hacked you to bits... The news said her mother kept her locked up in her bedroom. Hadn't seen the light of day in years.

Eric drew in his breath between his teeth. Tessa had fallen silent at his side. He darted a look at her and saw that she'd gone ghostly white. "Are you OK?" he asked, turning toward her.

She nodded, but he could see that she was lying. Her mouth quivered, and she refused to meet his eyes.

"Tessa, it's pure gossip. You know how the media is."

He craned his head to look into her face. Her eyes had gone bright and glossy, ringed with pink. Eric brushed his thumb across her cheek.

She raised her hand to his, and their fingers intertwined. "That's what people are saying about me," she whispered.

"That's what strangers are saying," he corrected, clasping her hand. "That's the thing about fame. Everyone has an opinion, but they don't know you. They have no clue that the real Tessa Hart is brilliant, and kind, and my best friend. And the girl I love."

She cast him a watery smile, but her answer came back so softly he could barely hear the words. "I love you too." She disentangled her fingers. Her eyes flicked toward the phone. "Go ahead. Answer him. You shouldn't leave him hanging."

Eric pressed a kiss against her temple as he picked up the phone again. Dorian had added another message:

> **ShowYouTheDor:** Eric, I have to run, but
> there's something else. Something you
> need to know.
> **Snowflake734:** Go ahead. I'm listening.
> **ShowYouTheDor:** I can't. This is big.
> It goes too high up to tell you over an
> insecure cell network.

Eric felt his heart stop beating for a moment. He didn't know what to make of Dorian's caution. Unencrypted phones? Insecure networks?

Dorian plowed on with another message before Eric could formulate a response.

> **ShowYouTheDor:** Listen. Do you have a car? Could you get yourself to Tijuana?
> **Snowflake734:** I don't know. Why?
> **ShowYouTheDor:** Trust me. Go to Tijuana. There's a gated resort Hugo and I use sometimes. Very discreet. Very secure. It's called the Playa de La Joya Beach Club. Get yourself there, and lay low until I come.

THE INTERROGATION
(FRAGMENT 2)

May 1, 2017, 2:19 p.m.
Case #75932.394.1
OFFICIAL TRANSCRIPTION OF POLICE INTERVIEW

—START PAGE 3—

INVESTIGATOR: Ms. Hart, may I ask your exact whereabouts between January 1 and February 3? You said you were living in a van?

HART: How is that relevant to the case you're investigating?

INVESTIGATOR: This will go a lot faster if you stop asking questions and start answering them.

HART: Whatever. I was in Mexico.

INVESTIGATOR: Were you there with Eric Thorn?

HART: Why?

INVESTIGATOR: Why, indeed. That's what I'd like to ask you. You assisted Mr. Thorn in a fairly elaborate death hoax. Could you tell me the reason why?

HART: I can get you a copy of the official press release if you like. I think it said Eric was suffering from exhaustion. Or maybe mental duress. Something like that.

INVESTIGATOR: Was that the truth? He faked his death because of exhaustion and mental duress?

HART: Sure. I mean, if the media reported it, then it must be true.

INVESTIGATOR: All right, Tessa. Let's start over. Can you please walk us through exactly what transpired during the period of time that you and Eric Thorn went missing last winter?

HART: We were just lying low, keeping our heads down. Eric needed a break, and I was in a position to help him. There's not much more to it than that.

INVESTIGATOR: What led to Eric's decision to return?

HART: Plumbing mostly.

INVESTIGATOR: I'm sorry?

HART: We both needed a shower. You try camping for a month in a VW van and tell me how you smell at the end of it.

INVESTIGATOR: Is that meant to be a joke, Ms. Hart?

HART: Sorry. I'm deflecting. I do that when I'm nervous.

INVESTIGATOR: There's nothing to be nervous about. Just answer the questions. I'd like you to take a look at this photograph, if you don't mind.

HART: Where did you get that?

INVESTIGATOR: Let the record show that Ms. Hart is viewing a photo taken with a cell phone camera in February 2017. Do you recognize this picture?

HART: That was supposed to get deleted. How do you have that?

INVESTIGATOR: Does this picture have anything to do with Eric's reason for returning to the United States?

HART: [unintelligible]

INVESTIGATOR: Ms. Hart, could you speak up?

HART: The picture… Yes. The picture had something to do with it.

INVESTIGATOR: Have you ever seen this photograph before I showed it to you today?

HART: Yes.

INVESTIGATOR: And do you know the identity of the individual who took it?

7

BAGGAGE

February 3, 2017

TESSA ROLLED OVER in bed. She watched the gentle rise and fall of Eric's shoulders as the dawn light filtered through a gap in the dingy curtains.

The Playa de La Joya Beach Club wasn't quite the destination she'd imagined when Dorian suggested it. She and Eric had driven two days straight to get here, and for what? Tessa had expected the five-star celebrity treatment—silk sheets, room service, maybe a discreetly hidden hot tub built for two. Instead, they'd found a loose cluster of run-down bungalows that barely rose above the luxury of the campground they'd left behind. But she supposed the place offered the few amenities that mattered most: a real bed, running water, and privacy.

The man behind the registration desk had rented her the

bungalow at the far end of the beach with no questions asked, and no one had bothered them since.

The thin sliver of light shifted as the sun rose. Tessa watched in silence as it inched across the bed toward Eric's sleeping form. He lay on his side with his back to her, and she resisted the temptation to run a finger along the groove of his spine. Instead, she followed it with her eyes to where it disappeared beneath the blanket, from the broad expanse of his shoulders to his neatly tapered waist.

Tessa turned away, flicking on her cell phone. 6:54 a.m. No use closing her eyes at this point. It was morning—and in any case, she knew sleep wouldn't come. Her insomnia hadn't let up since Eric's Snapchat escapade two days ago. It was as if her peace of mind had gone on vacation the moment their camper van rolled out onto the open road.

Tessa rubbed her eyes, dry and gritty. She wished they hadn't moved. Just when she was beginning to feel at home, Eric had insisted on pulling up stakes and making the trek to Tijuana. He needed to hear Dorian's secret, and Tessa hadn't argued. She could tell he wouldn't rest until he and Dorian talked face-to-face.

Tessa doubted it would happen anytime soon though. Dorian wouldn't come. Not with the eyes of the entire world trained on him. He was too busy fighting to stay out of jail. Was he still in Switzerland, or had he returned to London by now?

Tessa's eyes flickered to the phone. It would be simple enough to find out. Back in her fangirl days, she could track

Eric's location anytime he appeared in public. Wherever he went, someone was guaranteed to spot him and tweet a pic. No doubt Dorian's fandom did the same.

Twitter… She could practically hear that little blue birdie calling her name.

Tessa gripped the phone to stop her hand from shaking. There was nothing inherently dangerous about Twitter. Maybe she should try it. Treat it like a desensitization exercise. Small steps, right?

She clicked the app open and navigated to the profile in question.

Dorian Cromwell ✔ @DorianCromwell

Her eyes landed on his profile pic, and the sight of it made her stomach twist.

Tessa dropped the phone. The mattress bounced as she stood up and crossed the room. She could feel the veil of panic closing in. Her fingernails dug into her palms, and she focused on the painful sensation to keep herself anchored. How was she going to make it through the day?

At least she still had a half-full bottle of Ativan in her bag.

The green canvas duffel sat on a low bureau. Tessa glanced at it, but she hesitated. Those pills were precious now. She couldn't afford to waste them. There wouldn't be any more refills once she used them up.

And then what? Then how would she cope?

The thought filled her with a fresh surge of anxiety. The edges of her vision were going dark. Tessa knew she should do her breathing, but her chest rose and fell in shallow gasps. She needed to get ahold of herself. What would Dr. Regan say if she were here right now?

Don't give in to the anxiety... Think about your other tools...

What else? Tessa cast her eyes about the room until they landed on the duffel bag again. She saw her old, familiar thought journal peeking out of the side pocket, with its dog-eared cover strewn with doodles. She hadn't made an entry since her last therapy session with Dr. Regan, but she'd left a pencil jammed inside the spiral binding.

Tessa picked the journal up. The tension in her shoulders eased slightly as she flipped to a blank page. Sometimes it helped to set her worries down on paper. She obviously had some mental baggage to unpack.

The room was too dark to write, but the morning sun beckoned through the chink in the drapes. Tessa opened them a touch wider. She stood in the narrow rectangle of light, balancing the journal on the windowsill and resting her forehead against the glass. She scribbled down the first words that popped into her head:

> A fangirl...
> A deeply troubled one. But that's not saying very much, now is it? ⌣

She didn't realize what she was quoting until her pencil scratched out the wink emoji at the end. *Dorian.* He'd texted those exact words about the girl locked up in a mental institution for his murder.

Tessa closed her eyes as the insight clicked into place. That was why Dorian's profile pic had triggered her. It wasn't Twitter. It was him. His words. They'd been bothering her ever since that Snapchat conversation.

Tessa's pencil flashed across the page.

> Is that why I haven't been sleeping? Not because we left the campground. Not being followed. Not being watched. Not Twitter. Not Snapchat. Not Blair.
>
> I'm upset about what Dorian did to that girl. How could he do that? I mean, I guess everyone's fighting a battle. Dorian was fighting his management. He felt trapped. They were forcing him to deny his true identity. That must have been horrible. I get that.
>
> But honestly I don't care what battle Dorian was fighting! Just because you're hurting, that doesn't justify hurting someone else.

Tessa stopped writing. She tapped the pencil eraser against her chin. Was that enough to bring on a panic attack? No. She hadn't quite gotten to the root of it. What else had Dorian said?

> That girl had the thing Eric always talks about:

*celebrity erotomanic delusional disorder. She was
obsessed with Dorian. An obsessed fangirl with a
psychiatric history.*

Just like me.

Tessa shivered in spite of the warm sunlight beating down. She realized, clear as day, what Dr. Regan would say if she read this entry:

"You're projecting."

"Of course," Tessa whispered. Projecting…attributing her own thoughts and feelings to someone else. How could she have missed it? She identified with that other fan. That's why it set her off, seeing Dorian dismiss that girl without the slightest trace of regret.

Because that was how the whole world saw Tessa too. She was @TessaHeartsEric, the obsessed fangirl who'd hacked Eric Thorn to bits. Not a human being. An inconvenience that belonged in some facility.

Tessa chewed the pencil eraser thoughtfully, tasting the bitter tang of rubber as she bit down. Her eyes shifted back to the bed where Eric slept. He looked so peaceful, without a care in the world, but her own pulse pounded in her ears. She turned away. Her pencil traced lightly, barely leaving a mark, as she set down her next thought:

*That's not how Eric sees me. Why do I care so
much what the rest of the world thinks?*

Eric's eyes slitted open. He rolled onto his back, expecting to find Tessa's mass of wavy, brown hair strewn across the pillow beside him. Instead, her side of the bed lay empty. Eric stifled a sigh. She couldn't have gotten up too long ago. He could still see the indentation her body had left behind, and he caught a whiff of her lingering fragrance on the pillowcase.

A movement drew his attention from the other side of the room. Tessa stood by the window, stretching her arms and arching her back. Eric lay completely still. He watched the morning light filter around her like a halo.

He silently willed her to turn toward him. Meet his eyes. Tiptoe to the foot of the bed and crawl across it. Slip between the sheets… It wasn't too late. She hadn't gotten dressed yet. She wore nothing but an oversize, white T-shirt that she'd snagged last night from his clean laundry pile. It hung down past the tops of her thighs, with her slender legs completely bare beneath. The thin jersey fabric did little to conceal the rest of her. As she turned, the light from the window caught her from behind, and every curve of her figure stood out in silhouette.

Eric closed his eyes. One corner of his mouth hooked upward as he pictured what would happen next.

Pure fantasy, of course. The smirk on his face slowly faded. He and Tessa had been camped out together for a month now, but he had yet to catch a glimpse of her undressed. She was careful that way, despite the intimacy that came from sleeping side by side. Their physical relationship hadn't progressed beyond long, slow make-out sessions. Delicious while they lasted, but they always left him in the same condition: a sweaty, aching mess of rumpled sheets and unmet need.

Patience, Eric told himself firmly. They weren't in any rush. Tessa required a slow hand, and he'd known that going in. She wasn't the type to strip naked the moment he glanced in her direction—like the fangirls at his concerts who used to throw their bras and panties at his feet at the end of the show.

Wasn't that exactly why he fell for Tessa in the first place? She saw him as more than a piece of meat. She wanted to know what lay beneath the surface—to understand the inner workings of his mind.

That meant long, deep conversations.

Endless talk. Minimal action.

And the reward at the end of all that talk was a girlfriend who truly knew him—probably the only human being he'd ever shown his true self, flaws and all.

Tessa lifted her arms above her head. She pulled her hair into a messy braid, and her T-shirt hitched upward as she moved. Eric couldn't keep still any longer. He sat up in bed and pushed aside the covers. Her cheeks went rosy as she turned and met his eyes.

"How long have you been up?" she asked.

"Not long." Eric averted his gaze. Their cell phone sat on the mattress beside him, and he pretended to look at it. He knew it set her off when she felt like she was being watched.

"What time is it?" she asked.

"Too early. Time for you to come back to bed."

Tessa cast him a shy smile and looked down at the floor. For once, she'd gone without her bunny slippers. She stood in her bare feet, tracing a seam between the tiles with her big toe. She took a halting step in his direction.

Small steps, Eric thought. *Literally.* He made a low noise in the back of his throat. Those small steps of hers would be the death of him. Eric knew he should wait for her to come to him, but sometimes small steps gave way to a total standstill. Maybe she needed him to meet her halfway.

Eric rose from the bed and went to her. He didn't speak. He simply wrapped his arms around her. She laid her hands lightly on his chest as he bent his head to kiss her. He half expected her to pull away, but her mouth lingered against his. She went up on her tiptoes and parted her lips, allowing the kiss to deepen.

His hands started at her waist, but they drifted down her hips. His fingertips played at the hem of her T-shirt, gently grazing the tops of her outer thighs.

Tessa's fingers slid upward, inch by inch, but they stopped their progress at his collarbone. They remained there as a barrier—an unspoken signal between them, telling him to bide his time.

If only she would lift her arms and wrap them around his neck, Eric knew what he would do. He'd scoop one arm beneath her knees and lift her off her feet. Carry her back to bed like the hero in some romance novel...

He was more than ready. He just needed her to give him the

green light. Instead, she ducked her head away and broke the kiss, laying her forehead against his shoulder.

Eric had to grit his teeth to hold back his groan. "I'm sorry," she whispered. "I'm not there yet." Her breath caressed his skin, and the sensation did nothing to dispel the fiery heat that coursed through him.

He needed to cool down.

Eric released her and took a step backward, dropping his arms to his sides. "No problem. I'm going to…" His words trailed off, and he jerked his head in the direction of the bathroom door. "I'll be in the shower for a sec."

He turned, but Tessa caught his arm. "Eric, wait."

"It's OK, Tessa," he said. He reached for the cell phone at the foot of the bed and pressed it into her hand. "Here. Why don't you check the news. I'll be right back."

"Are you upset?"

"No, of course not."

She met his eyes again, and he broke into a sheepish smile. "I'm just a little…backed up. It's no big deal." He lowered his head, letting his forehead clunk lightly against her own.

Tessa nodded, but she didn't seem reassured. If anything, she looked worse. She had that tightness around her mouth—a sure sign of some internal storm brewing beneath the calm surface.

"Tessa, there's no rush," he told her softly. "We're not going anywhere. We've got all the time in the world."

8

TIME'S UP

TESSA INHALED DEEPLY, pulling Eric's scent into her lungs. *He was right*, she thought. He could seriously use a shower. Brushing his teeth wouldn't hurt either. For some reason, the idea made her smile.

She liked that he had flaws. Bad breath. Body odor. It was the only part of him that belonged to her alone. His legions of fans knew his face and the sound of his voice as well as she did, but they couldn't smell him over Twitter.

So why couldn't she relax and enjoy it?

He called her his girlfriend, but it still felt raw and new. It was a complicated feeling when he kissed her. A strange combination of desire and anticipation, mixed with a tinge of panic and a hearty dose of disbelief.

It still didn't feel real. How many times had she succumbed over the years to this daydream? She used to lie in her bedroom for hours on end, staring at her old

#EricThornObsessed pics, imagining how those perfect lips would feel against her own.

Now she knew the answer: volcanic-level heat…mixed with icy tentacles of fear.

She turned away and ambled toward her duffel bag. "Go take your shower," she said over her shoulder. "I need to write a little more." She pulled out her spiral notebook and flipped it open. The bathroom door clicked closed, and relief flooded through her at the sound.

Tessa scowled as she wrote in the journal.

> Why does kissing Eric give me anxiety? What is WRONG with me?

Ever since their first night together, back home in her old bedroom, she and Eric had engaged in this same slow-simmering dance. A few steps forward. A few steps back. Tantalizing kisses that seemed to last for hours…hands roving, threatening to slide beneath the layers of her clothes… But Tessa always stopped it before the wave could overtake her. Each time, she teetered on the brink, closer and closer to the edge—but she couldn't summon the nerve to take the plunge into the unchartered waters below.

She moved to scribble something else, but the tip of her pencil snapped against the page. She knew what she was going to write though. She flipped the pencil over and traced the shape of the word with the eraser. Three letters:

S-E-X

It was way too soon. She and Eric had only been together for a few weeks. In her last relationship, with Scott, they never went past third base—not even after three full years of dating. Three *long* years, marked by Scott's constant pleading and cajoling.

Tessa didn't want to think of Scott, but she couldn't help it. They used to argue on this subject all the time. He didn't understand her hesitation. They both claimed to love each other. Neither of them was particularly religious. It was one thing when they first got together—sophomore year of high school—but by the time he left for college, his patience had worn thin.

Honestly, Scott's whole attitude had always been a massive turnoff. As if he were somehow entitled to sex, simply because they'd been dating forever. Tessa knew that was a load of crap. Plenty of people waited until marriage.

But that wasn't the real reason she'd held back with Scott—or with Eric either. It had nothing to do with virtue. It had *everything* to do with fear.

She'd always had those doubts she couldn't silence, repeating like a drumbeat inside her head. Irrational worries. Distorted thoughts. The seeds of an anxiety disorder in her brain, even before she developed agoraphobia. Tessa knew how those seeds had been planted—and by whom.

The first time she got her period, her mother sat her down and issued a stern warning. Tessa had heard some version of the same lecture every time her boyfriend picked her up for a date. She was a Hart, and the Hart women were cursed. It ran in her blood. Her mother had gotten pregnant the first time she ever had sex.

And then the guy will blame you, Tessa. Don't expect him to stick around. Good luck collecting child support. You'll be the one who has to spend the next eighteen years working your tail off to keep food on the table.

Tessa squeezed her eyes shut to block out the memory of her mother's bitter tone.

Your whole life will be ruined. Trust me. I speak from experience.

Tessa closed her thought journal with a snap. Enough self-therapy for one day. Her mother was pure poison when it came to mental health. If only one positive thing came from the decision to run away with Eric, it was the fact that she'd finally gotten out from under her mother's influence.

She was her own person. She could make her own decisions. She needed to get her mother's voice out of her head.

Tessa heard the tinkle of shower water slowing down. She picked the phone back up, pretending to look busy as she struggled to put her thoughts in order.

Maybe Eric should be her first. So what if it was moving fast? With her ex, she'd dragged her feet because some instinct warned it was wrong. But now the same gut feeling screamed to move forward.

Eric was perfect in so many ways. Physically perfect, but more than that. He was so patient. Understanding. He never pressured her. When they talked, he genuinely cared about every word she had to say. He used to stay up half the night to chat with her over Twitter.

That was the thing, Tessa realized. They'd only been together since January, but they'd talked for months before that. Eric knew her, heart and soul, far better than Scott ever had. That was why she'd run away with Eric. Because he was right for her in all the ways that her former boyfriend had been wrong.

The bathroom door cracked open. Eric reemerged with a threadbare robe around his shoulders, running his fingers through his damp hair. Tessa straightened up, but she remained where she stood.

Not quite facing toward him.

Not quite facing away.

↺

Eric padded out of the bathroom, tightening the belt of the robe at his waist. He'd spent the past ten minutes in the shower planning what to say, but now his carefully crafted words abandoned him. He went for the direct approach.

"Tessa, did I do something wrong? Because if I did, please tell me—"

She took a step in his direction. "It isn't you," she said. "I was journaling about Dorian mostly. Dorian and that girl."

Eric pressed his lips together in a line. *Dorian again…* How was it possible that a man he'd never met kept fouling up his life at every turn? He could feel an epic conversation coming on. Eric sank down on the edge of the bed, shifting his weight backward to find a comfortable position. "Yeah, and you thought *I* was crappy to my fans. Good thing you never started a hashtag called #DorianCromwellObsessed."

Tessa didn't smile back. *Oops.* He probably should have known better than to tease her about that. "Sorry. Too soon?"

She wrapped her arms around herself. "It's not funny. Don't you feel bad for that girl?"

"She was stalking him," Eric said, careful to keep his voice level. "Do you have any idea how freaked out I would be if some fangirl decided to creep around my house and slip notes under the door?"

"You don't know what she might have been going through," Tessa answered. She tapped and swiped at the cell phone screen as she spoke.

Eric crossed the room and peered over her shoulder. He could almost have laughed at what he saw filling the screen.

EVERYONE YOU
MEET IS FIGHTING
A BATTLE YOU KNOW
NOTHING ABOUT.
BE KIND. ALWAYS.

Tessa looked up at him with a question in her eyes, and Eric realized what it was. They weren't really talking about Dorian and that girl. He cupped her shoulders gently. "You know there's a big difference between you and Dorian's stalker fan, right?"

Tessa shook her head.

"Erotomanic delusional disorder." He pronounced the words slowly, enunciating every syllable. "Emphasis on *delusional*. That girl imagined a relationship with Dorian that didn't exist."

Tessa sniffed. "So I'm the nondelusional type?"

"No, you're not a stalker. Period. It's not celebrity erotomanic whateverness if the celebrity in question is *actually* in love with you." He ran his fingers up her neck, cradling her heart-shaped face between his thumbs. "I love you, snowflake," he whispered. "Remember? This is real."

A hint of color blossomed where his fingers brushed her cheeks. At the sight of it, Eric felt something hot and jagged catch in the pit of his stomach. "Come here," he whispered. He dropped his arms and drew her toward him.

She stuck out her tongue at him, but she allowed him to gather her against his chest. "You're annoying."

Thawing, Eric thought. *Definitely thawing*… He broke into a grin and whisper-sang the chorus of the song he'd written for her:

> *Just one snowflake.*
> *She thought that no one cared.*
> *Perfect snowflake.*
> *I'll catch you, don't be scared…*

He watched with satisfaction as the flush of color crept downward from her collarbone and disappeared beneath the vee of her white T-shirt. "I can't believe Eric Thorn turned out to be such a cheesebal—"

But the end of her word was silenced by his kiss.

This time, it was different. Her reluctance melted away. Tessa went up on her tiptoes to meet his lips and wrapped her arms around his neck to pull him closer.

It was Eric who broke the kiss first. He searched her face. Her mouth had gone soft and supple, without a trace of tension. Her lips were swollen from where his mouth had left its mark. "Don't stop," she whispered without opening her eyes. "Keep going."

"Are you sure?"

She nodded. Eric clenched his arms around her waist. He dipped his head to kiss her again. He could see the bed beckoning behind her. He pressed his hips against hers, and she didn't resist as he took a tiny step in that direction.

But Tessa jerked away after a moment.

"What?" Eric asked, with a gasping breath. "No good?"

She didn't answer. Her forehead furrowed as she looked down at the cell phone clutched in her hand.

Eric heard it then—the sound of the phone vibrating. Tessa showed him the screen, and his eyes landed on a new Snapchat notification.

But not from the username he expected.

● RealEricThorn

"What the…" Eric's eyes narrowed. "What is this?"

Tessa clicked the Snap open. Eric bent toward the phone, struggling to make out the image against the glare of sunlight streaming through the window.

He cupped his hand around the screen to shade it, and all the air left his lungs.

He knew what he was looking at: his own face locked with Tessa's, framed between a pair of faded curtains. A caption cut across their chests.

Hey, kids. Nice to see ya. Say cheese!

Eric swiveled on his heels and bounded toward the drapes, but he was too slow. A sudden burst of light filled the room.

A camera flash.

And then another…

And another…

And another…

THE INTERROGATION (FRAGMENT 3)

May 1, 2017, 1:39 p.m.
Case #75932.394.1
OFFICIAL TRANSCRIPTION OF POLICE INTERVIEW

—START PAGE 1—

INVESTIGATOR:	Thank you for sitting down with us, sir. Could you please state your full name and occupation for the record?
GILROY:	The name's Maurice Oliver Gilroy, but you can call me Maury. I'm the founder and CEO of Gilroy Artist Management, LLC.
INVESTIGATOR:	You're a talent manager in the music industry. Is that correct?
GILROY:	Bingo.
INVESTIGATOR:	And who are your major clients?
GILROY:	You want a list? I've been in the biz for thirty years. Cut my teeth with New Kids on the Block back in the eighties. You remember them, right? Then there were Hanson, Boyzone, 98 Degrees, a couple *American Idol* losers until I dropped them—
INVESTIGATOR:	Your current clients will suffice.

GILROY: I've managed Eric Thorn exclusively for the past four years.

INVESTIGATOR: Only Eric Thorn?

GILROY: He's a full-time job. Believe me.

INVESTIGATOR: OK, Mr. Gilroy. We'd like you to take a look at some photographs. From what we can gather, these pictures were taken in the vicinity of Tijuana, Mexico, on or around February 3. Do they look familiar to you?

GILROY: Sure.

INVESTIGATOR: Do you know who took them?

GILROY: I took them myself. Not bad, huh? Might try a second career as a pap if the whole talent management thing doesn't work out. [laughter]

INVESTIGATOR: Can you give us a little more context? How exactly did you come to take these photos?

GILROY: You know how it is. Artists can be a little prickly. Sometimes you need both a carrot and a stick, if you catch my drift.

INVESTIGATOR: This was the stick?

GILROY: Eric had a nice vacation, but he needed to get back to work. I took some pictures to make sure he understood that.

INVESTIGATOR: So you took pictures of him without his knowledge and used them as leverage to force him to resume his public life. Is that your statement?

GILROY: Well, that doesn't sound very good, does it? [laughter] Listen, it was for the kid's own good. He needed to get back to the States before he ended up in real hot water.

INVESTIGATOR: What kind of hot water?

GILROY: Look at Dorian Cromwell. Six months in prison for tax evasion. That's what happens when you don't have Uncle Maury around to clean up after you. It could've gone real ugly for Eric if I hadn't shown up when I did.

INVESTIGATOR: And what can you tell us about the woman in the photos—Tessa Hart?

GILROY: What about her? I think the picture spells it out.

INVESTIGATOR: For the record, Mr. Gilroy is indicating a photograph of Mr. Thorn and Ms. Hart in a state of undress, apparently kissing.

GILROY: Don't worry. I made my presence known before it got too pornographic.

INVESTIGATOR: Were you aware of the romantic nature of their relationship before these photos were taken?

GILROY: Sure. Listen, I know everything that goes on in Eric Thorn's private life. I know it before he does most of the time. That's my job. I'm out there doing damage control before he even realizes he's got a problem.

INVESTIGATOR: So that's why you went to Tijuana in search of Mr. Thorn? Damage control?

GILROY: Exactly.

INVESTIGATOR: And precisely how did you locate him, if I might ask?

GILROY: You don't get to be where I am without acquiring a few friends who owe you favors, if you know what I mean.

INVESTIGATOR: No, I'm afraid I don't.

GILROY: Let's just say the music business is a tight-knit community.

INVESTIGATOR: Someone in the industry tipped you off?

GILROY: I have a guy who works in social media for DBA.

INVESTIGATOR: Dorian Cromwell's record label? Are you saying that an employee of DBA Records leaked the contents of a private conversation between Mr. Cromwell and Mr. Thorn?

GILROY: Private? Trust me, Detective. Nothing in this business is private. Not Twitter. Not Snapchat. Nothing.

INVESTIGATOR: So, for the record, your statement is that you took this series of photos as leverage to coerce Mr. Thorn—

GILROY: Not coerce. Persuade.

INVESTIGATOR: Excuse me. To persuade Mr. Thorn to return to the United States. You then orchestrated the terms of his return with both the federal authorities and his record label.

GILROY: All in a day's work. I'm what you call the cleanup crew. Ninety percent of my job is keeping Eric's fans from catching wind of his latest mess.

INVESTIGATOR: It appears that your cleanup abilities have their limitations.

GILROY: Really? I would respectfully disagree. [laughter] I mean, the kid fakes his death, breaks his contract, sticks up his middle finger at his label, and still comes out smelling like a rose. More than doubled his Twitter following. Record sales went through the stratosphere. All that, and the feds let him off with a fine! We couldn't have staged a better PR stunt if we'd tried.

INVESTIGATOR: That's all well and good, Mr. Gilroy, but it doesn't answer why you're currently being interviewed by a homicide detective.

GILROY: Homicide? Now wait a minute. Hold your horses. What—

INVESTIGATOR: When was the last time you spoke with Mr. Thorn?

GILROY: Who said anything about a murder?

INVESTIGATOR:	And what else can you tell me about Tessa Hart? Her relationship with Mr. Thorn was not made public at the time of his return. Whose decision was that? Yours?
GILROY:	Slow down! Tessa's not dead, is she? I just saw her.
INVESTIGATOR:	Mr. Gilroy, please answer the question. Why was the relationship between Mr. Thorn and Ms. Hart kept secret?
GILROY:	Don't look at me! We could've spun that. It was Tessa who wanted to keep it all hush-hush.
INVESTIGATOR:	Why?
GILROY:	Have you spoken to her? I thought Eric was paranoid, but Tessa takes the cake. Talk about a match made in heaven.
INVESTIGATOR:	What exactly was she paranoid about?
GILROY:	She didn't want to be photographed. Kept going on and on about some shady character who might notice her. Some kind of ex-boyfriend, maybe?
INVESTIGATOR:	Did she mention this individual's name?
GILROY:	I honestly couldn't tell you. How many stalker exes does she have?
INVESTIGATOR:	So Ms. Hart expressed a wish to keep the relationship private, and Mr. Thorn agreed?
GILROY:	He didn't agree. There was much wailing and

gnashing of the teeth until good old Uncle Maury
came up with the perfect solution.

INVESTIGATOR: Which was?

GILROY: I told them the best way to hide her was to leave
                  her in plain sight. Play it like she worked for
                  him—like we hired her from the get-go to orga-
                  nize his little mental-health hiatus.

INVESTIGATOR: A publicist essentially?

GILROY: Right. Social media consultant. I told her to dress
                  in black and walk five feet behind him in all public
                  appearances. That way, if she wound up in a pap
                  photo, they'd crop her out of the shot. Standard
                  operating procedure.

SOCIAL MEDIA CONSULTING

9

March 3, 2017

TESSA PRESSED HER back against the rough concrete wall of the rehearsal space, striving to make herself invisible. Could this day get any worse?

She needed to get out of here. Tessa longed for an empty room. Solitude. Window blinds that shut tight, blocking out the sun.

But she couldn't leave. Not yet. Not until she'd snapped the pic.

Tessa braced her elbow against her side to stop her hand from shaking. "You can do this," she whispered to herself.

She knew the drill. She'd spent the past month since her return from Mexico trailing Eric like a shadow through an endless string of celebrity appearances. Press conferences... meet and greets...photo ops... She couldn't believe the pace he kept. He barely had a moment to himself from the time Maury came to collect him at the crack of dawn each morning to the moment his head hit the pillow at the end of the night.

Tessa's own job? Ever-so-slightly less taxing. In theory, she worked as a member of Eric Thorn's vast PR machine, but she mainly spent her days steering clear of the real publicists… and fending off the panic attacks that threatened whenever she found herself thrust into a crowded room.

A crowded room like this one.

Tessa pulled a deep breath into her lungs and held it for a five-count, waiting for her insides to untwist themselves. Today was proving even more anxiety ridden than usual. Eric was slated to perform live tonight at the YouTube Music Awards. His whole team had flown by private jet from LA to Las Vegas this morning. Now, Eric would spend the day here at the MGM Grand Arena, darting in and out of sound checks and dress rehearsals until he took his turn on the red carpet with the rest of the star-studded lineup. Tonight's performers included every big name on the radio, and that meant Tessa had to contend with the usual pop-star entourage multiplied by what felt like thousands.

She currently found herself in the basement of the MGM Grand, watching from behind her upraised phone as Eric stepped through tonight's dance routine. The room reverberated with the sound of the choreographer counting out the beats and the squeak of rubber soles against the floor.

At least the rehearsal wasn't open to the camera crews. Tessa's main goal for today was to keep her face off live TV. That was key. She couldn't let down her guard. And that wasn't her old phobia talking—it was a perfectly rational fear. Blair Duncan was still out there somewhere, and he knew that Tessa and Eric were together. No doubt he'd be watching every move that Eric made, scouring each photo for some sign of Tessa's face.

The thought of it made Tessa's heart rate leap. She pressed a hand beneath her rib cage to calm the sensation.

He won't show up here, she told herself. Even if he did, he wouldn't see her. Tessa planned to avoid the red carpet at all costs. No way could she contend with the massive throng of people gathering behind the barricades outside. Once she got through this rehearsal, she planned to escape somewhere quiet. Maybe head upstairs to her hotel room and hide out for the rest of the day with the dead bolt securely fastened.

It wasn't like Eric would need anything from her.

Tessa scowled. Maybe it was all a big mistake, this whole plan to pose as Eric's publicist. It had seemed like a good idea back when Maury suggested it—or not exactly a *good* idea, but the best option they had. Eric had been livid at the time, yelling and screaming at Maury to butt out, but Maury had calmly explained to them both that they were in deep trouble. The FBI knew she and Eric had faked the crime. They'd broken several federal laws by staging Eric's death: planting false evidence…possibly fraud…

Thank God for Maury. She understood why Eric found his manager annoying, with his high-handed manner and his endless string of corny jokes, but Tessa had taken an instant liking to Maury. She appreciated the way he took charge of the situation. He had a plan to get them out of the whole mess, and he came in person all the way to Tijuana to rescue them. The only catch was that Eric had to come forward—and Tessa had to pretend that she'd been nothing more than an employee on his payroll the whole time.

A social media consultant, to be precise. What a joke. At least this so-called "job" had forced her to get over her Twitter phobia. It didn't feel so scary, logging in to Eric's account, as long as she could hide behind his celebrity facade. No one could see her after all. None of Eric's Twitter fans would suspect the real identity of the person they were tweeting. Tessa might have enjoyed herself if Eric's management let her interact with her fellow fans for real.

So far, she'd only been allowed to tweet the carefully scripted lines that Maury handed her. She had another one going out later to promote tonight's appearance, and she'd already saved the message to her drafts. She just needed a picture to illustrate the words.

If only Eric would look up. He had his eyes on his feet, his face a mask of concentration. She could see him mouthing song lyrics as he stumbled his way through the steps. If she took the photo now, she wouldn't capture much besides the shape of his latest haircut: short in the back, with a curtain of sweeping bangs to emphasize the squareness of his jaw.

He hadn't made eye contact with her once the whole time

she was in the room. Tessa frowned. She knew he was busy, but he couldn't spare three milliseconds to look up at her and wave? When was the last time he'd smiled in her direction? He was always surrounded by other people. Backup dancers. Hairdressers. Fans swarming him for autographs, buzzing around like flies. Tessa couldn't help but feel like one more annoying pest to him. Not a leech anymore, but not a whole lot higher on the food chain. Maybe more like a mosquito nowadays?

Eric's feet flashed across the floor. He had the hardest combo down, and the fangirl in her glowed with pride as she watched his movements gain confidence.

Tessa bit her lip. She wasn't being fair. He had so much on his plate… And anyway, the whole plan was for him to pretend like she wasn't his girlfriend. She was posing as his employee for her own protection—to keep her out of the spotlight. If anyone caught him flirting with her, it would spell disaster. Her face would end up plastered all over the tabloids, and anyone looking for her would know exactly where to find her.

Eric reached the end of the routine. He paused for a moment to catch his breath, scanning the room. His gaze ran past her as if she wasn't even there. He wiped his face with the towel tucked into the waistband of his jeans. Then he clapped his hands together. "Again!"

This time, his shoulders relaxed as his body flowed through the steps. He looked up. His eyes found her, and Tessa's heart fluttered in her chest. She hit the button to snap the pic before he turned away.

Perfect.

Tessa headed for the door. She'd noticed an empty dressing room across the hall, and she made a beeline for it. She needed to be alone. She could finish composing the tweet from there, safely tucked away from any onlookers.

She sank down to the floor and hugged her knees, ignoring the faint echo of voices from the other room.

"*Five, six, seven, eight…*"

"*Looking good, kid!*"

"*That's a wrap…*"

"*Eric, get your scrawny butt to wardrobe!*"

Tessa fiddled with her phone as footsteps filed past the door. She pulled up the picture of Eric on her camera roll, tracing an idle fingertip across the image of his lips.

It was strange. His face had transformed the second before she snapped, and Tessa recognized the look. Chin down, eyes up—a pair of flaming blue embers directed at the camera lens. She'd seen that expression on his face a million times.

In pictures.

Never in real life.

It wasn't the real him. Tessa's hand rose to her throat as the thought struck her. That seductive stare was all for show. A piece of choreography, no different from the other dance steps he had memorized.

The real Eric… His eyes were softer, his smile lazier somehow…

But Tessa hadn't seen him smile that way in weeks. A month

had passed since they stood together in their beach bungalow, and it felt like a distant memory. How was it possible that everything had changed so fast?

Tessa hung her head. She couldn't count how many days she'd spent exactly like this: studying some image of Eric Thorn on her cell phone screen. At least she'd had him to herself for those few short weeks. That was far more than she'd ever hoped for in her wildest fangirl fantasies. She couldn't really complain.

"Stop moping," she whispered to herself. "Get to work." Tessa swiped the back of her hand across her eyes and clicked on Twitter.

Eric Thorn ✓ @EricThorn

FOLLOWERS
35.7 M

His follower count had stood at 14 million before they ran away together, but it had ballooned in the aftermath of his infamous farewell tweet. Everyone liked a good murder mystery, after all. That tweet was still there now on his profile, with far more retweets than any other message he'd ever posted.

Eric Thorn ✓ @EricThorn
Sleep with a leech, and it just might bleed
you dry.

♻ 1.3M   ♥ 923K

Those words had marked her debut as Eric's social media consultant, although Tessa hadn't realized it at the time. She still remembered how she'd tapped the message into Eric's old cell phone, smeared with bloody fingerprints. Then she'd smashed the phone against the corner of her bedside table to crack the screen and left it on the bedroom floor for the police to find.

Today's tweet might prove slightly less retweetable. Tessa opened the draft message that Maury had dictated to her, tacking on the image from the dance rehearsal.

Eric Thorn ✔ @EricThorn
Hitting the stage tonight! Catch me streaming LIVE at 8 PM EST on @YouTube #YMAs

So dull. So corporate. The fans would know it hadn't really come from Eric. A real flesh-and-blood human being would use an emoji now and then.

"Let's see," she murmured. Tessa pulled up her emoji keyboard and added a few choice characters to the end of the message. Maybe the musical notes…followed by the red salsa dancer…or possibly the Playboy Bunny twins…and then a lipstick kiss…and a big, pink beating heart to round it out.

There. Much better.

A sad smile crept over Tessa's face. She couldn't actually tweet that. She'd probably get fired from her fake position.

Maury had made it abundantly clear that she was "social media consultant" in name only. She was allowed to tweet what he approved and not a single character more.

Tessa tapped Delete and watched the string of emojis disappear. She added a different one in their place to reflect her current mood: the sad little kitty-cat face, with a single tear running down its cheek.

Better delete that too.

Tessa lifted her finger, but she froze. Footsteps rang out in the hall. Were they coming or going? She couldn't tell. She screwed her eyes shut and willed the sound to fade back into silence.

Instead, she heard the dressing room door burst open. A familiar voice boomed in her ears. "Hey, kid! There you are. I've been looking all over for you!"

Maury.

Tessa looked up with a start. Her finger dropped to the cell phone screen, but it didn't hit Delete.

It landed on the Tweet button instead.

Eric stood on his pedestal in front of the three-way mirror. A wardrobe assistant knelt in front of him, and Eric did his best to ignore the proximity of the young woman's fingers to his crotch. The jeans he'd chosen for tonight's performance needed some last-minute alterations. They used to fit like a glove, with the perfect amount of stretch to accommodate his dance moves, but they kept slouching down his hips during rehearsal. Eric hadn't accounted for the amount of muscle mass he'd lost from sitting in a camper van for four weeks.

The wardrobe person had an array of pins clamped between her lips. She took one out, and Eric slid his feet apart a half inch wider, sending up a silent prayer that she wouldn't poke anything but denim.

He couldn't bear to watch. To distract himself, he slipped his cell phone out of his pocket, running his thumb across the smooth metallic case. Amazing, the kind of stuff you got for free when you were famous. His swag bag at check-in had included this limited-edition smartphone in a custom titanium case, with his initials engraved at the bottom. He had to admit, it was pretty slick. A definite upgrade from the hunk of scrap metal he picked up in Mexico.

What was it about firing up a brand-new phone for the first time? It felt like a rebirth. A fresh start. His manager had found some tech guy to give the phone a once-over this morning. The memory had been wiped clean and then loaded up with all his old apps and contacts.

Including Twitter.

Eric's finger landed on its familiar destination. He scrolled through his timeline, barely pausing to read any of the tweets, until one particular hashtag caught his attention.

#FreeDorian

At the sight of it, Eric tensed. A needle of pain pricked the inside of his thigh.

"Dude! Katrina! Watch it!"

The wardrobe assistant let go of his inseam and removed the pins from her mouth, glaring up at him. "Hold still. I *will* poke you if you flex your quads."

He wished one of the newer people could do it. Katrina had been on his crew a long time, but she made him nervous. Why did he have the feeling she derived some kind of sick pleasure from pricking him when he misbehaved?

"Ready?" she mumbled.

Eric nodded, repositioning his legs. He hadn't meant to fidget. That hashtag made every muscle in his body clench involuntarily. It had been trending for a couple weeks, since the news broke that Dorian Cromwell had taken a plea deal. Dorian was serving out his six-month sentence for tax fraud at an undisclosed British penitentiary. Eric couldn't even fathom the fall from grace. Prison? An *actual* jail cell? Sure, Eric liked to complain how he felt handcuffed by his record contract—but Dorian's plight put things in perspective.

Talk about a near miss. Eric couldn't hold it against his manager for forcing him to come back to the States. As much as Maury suffocated him, Eric knew his manager had his back. When push came to shove, Maury had saved his ass, big time.

"Eric! I swear, these pants are going to end up sewn to your gonads if you keep moving."

Eric lifted his chin, relieving the tension in his neck. He needed to relax. Find some less disturbing topic to occupy his mind. But he couldn't shake the memory of those hasty Snapchat messages Dorian had sent.

There's something else…

Something you need to know…

This is big. It goes too high up…

What the hell was that all about? Eric doubted he'd ever find out the answer, and the mystery only fueled the half-baked conspiracy theories running through his head.

He eyed his own reflection in the mirror. He'd always had this tendency toward paranoia. It wasn't healthy. He should really stop reading the news. Eric knew how his brain latched on to certain headlines. Last summer, the Dorian Cromwell murder had occupied his every waking thought. That one turned out to be fake news, but there were plenty of other stories in the papers nowadays.

Like that thing he read last night on NYTimes.com. Eric had only skimmed the article, but he'd gotten the gist. Something about cyberintelligence and the CIA—and hacking into people's home electronics. Laptops, TVs, microwaves…

The thought made Eric's palms sweat. This morning, he'd marched straight over to the mini-microwave in his dressing room and yanked the power cord out of the wall. His bodyguard had looked at him like he'd grown two heads, but Maury had burst out laughing.

"Let me guess, kid. You read the latest story from Wikileaks?"

Eric hadn't been amused. "You saw it, right? If the CIA can do it, the paps aren't far behind. They can hack into stuff and use it to watch you!"

Maury had humored him. He'd waved the unplugged microwave out of the room, and his shoulders had shaken with silent merriment the whole time.

Was it really paranoia? Maybe... Or maybe that was how the gossip blogs kept getting pics of him backstage at all his tour stops. Maybe they'd been using that hacker crap to spy on him for years.

So how could you tell the difference between a valid fear and a fake one?

Tessa would know. He wished he had her here to calm him down. She'd probably rattle off the name of whatever cognitive distortion he'd committed this time. That's all it was, right? This gnawing feeling in his belly that made him distrust everyone around him, from the paps to the record execs to the wardrobe girl at his feet?

Eric glanced at his cell phone again, wrinkling his nose at the Twitter screen. If only he could message Tessa. It used to be so easy. A couple months ago, talking to her was as simple as switching to a fake account. But that whole DM thread was a distant memory now. His old @EricThornSucks account had been frozen by the Texas police, and @TessaHeartsEric was probably deactivated for good. If Tessa went on Twitter at all these days, it was only in her professional capacity, scheduling corporate spam from @EricThorn.

She was probably logged into his account right now. Were they both reading the same Twitter timeline from different phones? If only there were some way to send a direct message to himself…

Eric toggled to his recent tweets. His eyes skimmed over the newest one, tweeted moments earlier.

Eric Thorn ✔ @EricThorn • 32s
Hitting the stage tonight! Catch me streaming LIVE at 8 PM EST on @YouTube #YMAs 🐺

🔁 42   ♥ 396

His eyebrows drew together. That was weird. What the hell was up with that emoji?

10
SAD KITTY CAT

TESSA TRAILED MAURY down the corridor with her eyes pasted to the floor. She'd felt like crying before she sent that tweet. Now all she wanted was to crawl back into bed and hide under the covers for the rest of eternity. Did he really have to ream her out in front of Eric?

Tessa's feet felt leaden. She could barely summon the energy to move forward as the dressing room door approached.

"Tessa!" Maury bellowed. He motioned at her with the two cell phones he held—his own phone and the one he'd confiscated from her. "A little hustle, please!"

She broke into an awkward jog. She was starting to see why Eric found his manager so annoying. Why was Maury making such a big deal out of it? After Tessa hit Tweet by accident, she'd moved to delete the tweet from Eric's feed, but Maury had ripped the phone from her hands.

Tessa still didn't understand what Maury was huffing and

puffing about. *"You can't delete a tweet!"* he kept insisting. He'd spent the whole elevator ride ranting under his breath. Something about screen captures and retweets... *"Once it's out there, you can't pull it back!"*

And now they had to drag Eric into it? Normally she would welcome any excuse to see him, but not like this. What was Eric going to think when he saw the sad face? Maury hadn't inquired why she added that particular emoji, but Eric was sure to wonder. Tessa had no idea how she would explain herself.

Maybe she could play it off as an accident. Her finger slipped. *Right*, Tessa thought. *A typo.* Nothing to do with the fact that her boyfriend barely made eye contact with her anymore.

Tessa drew up her shoulders as she passed through the dressing room door.

Eric stood on a raised platform in front of a full-length mirror. He had his back to the door, with his head down and his hands unfastening his belt. Tessa's jaw dropped open as Eric unzipped his fly and began peeling off his skintight jeans. A young woman with heavy eye makeup and a lip piercing rested on her knees in front of him, staring intently at Eric's crotch.

"Go slow," she said in a hushed voice, smoothing her hands against one of his thighs. "That's it. Gently..."

Eric wiggled his butt. The woman's hand darted to his waistband and helped him ease the jeans past his hips.

Tessa clapped her palm over her mouth. Eric must have heard her gasp. He glanced up and met her eyes in the mirror, and a guilty flush of color suffused his cheeks.

She felt the bile rise in her throat. She'd seen that same wardrobe person before, sniffing around Eric. She was one of the few people on his team that he ever addressed by name. Katrina. Tessa first encountered her at the press conference Eric had held after he returned from Mexico. He'd been wearing a T-shirt, and Katrina had practically torn it off him with minutes to go before airtime, muttering something about how he needed a smaller size.

Katrina definitely wasn't shy, but this... Tessa shook her head. It wasn't what it looked like. *That* couldn't be part of the pre-performance warm-up ritual... Could it?

Eric finished kicking off his pants and stepped down off his pedestal. His white T-shirt flapped around his hips, concealing most of his boxer briefs. Katrina draped the jeans over her arm and scurried toward the door. "I'll have these alterations back in twenty," she said as she passed.

Alterations.

Tessa blinked. She needed to get a grip. It was all perfectly professional. No reason to get upset...just because some seamstress had a more intimate relationship with Eric's anatomy than Tessa did.

"Hurry it up," Maury replied. "I'm going to need this kiddo fully clothed for social media."

Eric groaned. "Now what?" He held up his phone and flashed the screen in Maury's direction. "What's up with this tweet anyway?"

"We have a situation." Maury pushed the dressing room door closed and clicked the lock. When Tessa met his eyes, she hardly recognized him. None of the usual Maury Gilroy laughter. His face was deadly serious.

Tessa braced. This day kept getting worse. Why did she get the feeling that Maury was about to fire her? Eric wouldn't let him do that, would he? Or would Eric even care? *Stupid, idiotic kitty-cat face*, she thought. Was that really a fireable offense?

Eric watched in silence as his manager shut the door behind Katrina. The moment Maury locked it, Eric tossed his phone onto the makeup counter and crossed the room to Tessa in two long strides.

He'd been holding his breath from the moment he caught sight of her in the doorway. It took a huge force of will not to break into a grin. Every time he laid eyes on her, his heart beat a little faster, and the corners of his mouth quirked upward with a mind of their own.

But he couldn't let his feelings show in front of other staff. For Tessa's own protection, they'd agreed that he would treat her like any other publicist on his PR team. If anyone else in his entourage caught wind of their relationship, the story would leak to the media in three seconds flat, and her picture would end up all over the tabloids.

The stakes were too high to risk a smile in her direction or even a lingering look. He found the safest strategy was to avoid looking at her at all. When others were in the room, he forced his attention elsewhere. Another person…a camera lens…even his own reflection in the mirror…

Just now, his gaze had only rested on Tessa for a second, but he hadn't missed the expression on her face. Not happy. Close to tears.

Again.

Eric had noticed the strain on her face more and more lately. He knew the past month was taking its toll. Tessa wasn't used to being around so many people. It was hard for her, especially combined with the breakneck pace of his day-to-day life. Hell, *he* wasn't used to the speed he'd been going either. Since his return from Mexico, his label kept him more overscheduled than ever. They used to allow him the occasional day off, but he'd been in a full-speed sprint for thirty days straight now.

His to-do list ran from the crack of dawn to the late-night hours with barely enough downtime for minor details like eating or sleeping…or DM'ing with his girlfriend. It wasn't just his newfound respect for cybersecurity that kept him from texting her. Lately, his eyes closed the moment his head hit the pillow out of sheer physical exhaustion.

Eric knew what the record label was doing. Throwing their weight around. Showing him who was boss. He had tried to escape their grasp, and he had to face the consequences. They were letting him off easy compared to what they could have done.

Maury had reassured him that the current pace would only continue for a couple months. It wasn't in the record label's interest to drive Eric into an early grave. They would ease up on the schedule by summertime. He'd have the energy to sneak into Tessa's hotel room late at night. He might even get days off. Soon. Very soon. He just needed her to hang in there a little longer.

Right now, he saw the edges of her mouth quivering, and his arms ached to reach out. He couldn't lose her. It was bad enough that he was back here, trapped in this pop-star life that he despised. Seeing Tessa's face, however briefly, was the only ray of sunshine in his long and grueling days. If she left him, he'd be utterly alone again—back to that dark, lonely place where he had spent his days and nights before she wandered onto his Twitter feed last year.

"Eric," she whispered as he came closer. "It was a typo. I swear. I am so, *so* sorry…"

She looked like she was near her breaking point. All this angst over a stray character? Really? Eric bent his head to search her face. "Tessa, it's OK. It's no big deal."

Maury cleared his throat. "It's a moderate-sized deal."

"Her finger slipped," Eric said, turning back toward his manager. "So? What's with the guilt trip?"

Maury tilted back his head and stared up at the ceiling. A vein throbbed in his neck. Eric couldn't remember the last time he'd seen his manager so close to losing his composure. No wonder Tessa looked like she wanted to shrivel up into a ball at Eric's feet. "Do you kids have *any* idea what I do for you? Do you have any idea how many strings I had to pull to save your image after the mess this girl made—"

"Maury, chill! It's one emoji!"

Maury held up Tessa's cell phone, dangling it between his thumb and forefinger like a piece of dirty laundry. "Don't you see how this looks?"

"Um, like he's sad?" Tessa offered. She reached for her phone, but Maury pocketed it.

"Exactly," Maury said. "Not happy to be here. Not rested and refreshed after a brief hiatus. No, Tessa. You made him look *sad* to be performing at the YMAs."

"Maury," Eric said. "It's just Twitter."

Maury turned on him. "I'm not going to sugarcoat it, Eric. Twitter is her job. What if Katrina over there"—Maury waved a vague hand in the direction of the three-way mirror—"decided to improvise and alter your jeans into a pair of assless chaps?"

Eric shrugged, trying not to laugh. "It would probably get me some retweets."

"Not the kind of retweets we're going for, kid."

"I still don't understand why we can't delete it," Tessa said.

Maury shook his head. "No way. Not so soon after the death hoax. Then it looks like he's trying to cover something up."

"But—"

"Goddammit, Tessa. Be quiet and let me think!"

Tessa looked down at the floor, and Eric glared in his manager's direction. Maury didn't have to snap at her that way. She was new to all of this. Couldn't Maury laugh it off like usual?

"Tessa," Eric said, slipping his arm around her shoulders. "Are you OK?"

She didn't answer. Somehow his question must have been the final straw. Her expression crumpled, and she turned to bury her face in Eric's chest. His arms squeezed tight around her, and he dipped his head to hear her words, muffled against his shirt. "Why am I here, Eric? I'm just getting in the way."

"You're here because I need you."

"Do you?"

"Of course I do!"

She looked up at him, her eyes ringed with smudged mascara. "You barely even look at me," she whispered.

Eric smoothed a loose strand of hair from where it clung to her damp cheek. "Tessa, we agreed. I can't show you any special attention when we're not alone."

"I know." Her face sank against his chest again. "But we're *never* alone."

Eric sighed. He dipped his head and inhaled the scent of her hair. It felt so good to hold her again. He hadn't realized how much he missed it.

"Shhh." He hushed her softly, his mouth brushing against her ear. "We'll make time. Just you and me. Tonight. Come find me after the show."

She nodded, but Maury interrupted before she could answer. He'd turned his attention to his phone during their whispered conversation, but now his voice dripped with impatience. "I hate to break this up, but the Twitter situation needs to be addressed. Promptly."

"So delete the damned thing!" Eric exclaimed. He released his hold on Tessa and held out his hand for the phone.

"Too late. There's already a meme circulating." Maury showed him the screen once again. This time it bore a tweet from a fan account, and Eric did a double take when he saw the username.

> **MET** @MrsEricThorn • 2s
>
> Awwwww, what's the matter baby??? Don't you love us anymore? 😭 #WeLoveYouEric

Eric couldn't help but marvel at MET's speed. Only a few minutes had passed since the initial tweet. Somehow, MET had already captured the photo from his dance rehearsal and embellished it with a cartoonish trail of tears flowing down his cheeks.

And it had already racked up fifty retweets.

"MET," Tessa said with a sniff. "She's always first. Every time!"

Maury nodded grimly. "We can't backpedal now. The only thing to do is bury it."

"Bury it how?" Tessa asked.

"Tweet blast." Maury switched back to Tessa's cell phone. He spoke without looking up, and his finger flashed across the screen with lightning speed. "Here we go," he muttered. "That's a start."

Eric craned over Maury's shoulder to get a better look. "Wait a sec. Did I just retweet Ariana Grande?"

Maury didn't answer. He turned the cell phone's camera lens toward Eric and took a step backward to frame the shot. "Go ahead. Blow her a kiss."

"Maury, no! I can't tweet that at Ari. They'll say we're dating!"

"Nah," Maury answered with a cackle. "They'll say you're hitting on her. That's how we'll spin it. We'll say you have a thing for her, and she's playing hard to get—and that's why Eric Thorn was crying backstage at the YMAs."

Eric's eyes darted to Tessa. It wasn't the worst plan. He knew how the fans always shipped him with Ariana. Tessa herself used to speculate that the two of them were an item, back in her #EricThornObsessed days. The fandom would explode if @EricThorn tweeted a kissy-face at @ArianaGrande.

Tessa met his eyes with a reassuring smile, but something about it looked forced. "It's OK, Eric," she said. "Go ahead."

"It's for Twitter," he told her. "It doesn't mean anything. You know that, right?"

She nodded. "Of course. I trust you."

"Eric, sometime today?"

Eric tore his eyes away from Tessa and back toward the camera. He blinked twice, and then his face contorted—a caricature of his usual selfie look, with puckered lips and smoldering come-hither eyes. He blew a few kisses with his hands.

"Got it," Maury said. He tapped a few more times to compose a message, and Eric read it over his manager's shoulder.

Eric Thorn ✔ @EricThorn
Just one snowflake. It melted and I cried...
@ArianaGrande #YMAs

"No," Eric said. "Wait—"

But Maury ignored him. He added the sad cat emoji and hit Tweet.

Eric winced as the message appeared at the top of his feed. He didn't dare look at Tessa. Of all the things that Maury could have tweeted... Did he have to quote the lyrics from "Snowflake"?

"Are we done now?" Tessa asked.

Maury tossed Tessa's phone into her hands. "That's a start," he said. "Now I need another selfie going out every half hour for the rest of the afternoon—"

Eric's eyebrows rose. "How is Tessa supposed to—"

"Forget Tessa." Maury pointed to Eric and snapped his fingers. "It's all you, kid. Try to tweet at least a couple from the red carpet."

"A couple selfies?"

"Sure." Maury crossed the room to pick up Eric's phone. He handed it to Eric and then turned to straighten his tie in the dressing room mirror. "Go make fish faces with Taylor Swift or something. Make it a love triangle."

"Isn't Taylor Swift with—" Eric broke off as he met his manager's eyes in the glass. "Who is she with again?"

Tessa answered. "I heard on TMZ yesterday that she might be dating her hairstylist."

Eric snorted. "Yeah, and you'll hear on TMZ tomorrow that I might be dating Ariana Grande."

Maury turned back toward him, bracing his weight against the counter with his elbows. "So go give Zayn Malik the finger. Start a Twitter feud. I don't care. Try to show an ounce of creativity!"

"No," Tessa said. "Eric's right. It'll seem fake. You're basically asking him to act out the plot of an entire fanfic in the space of one award show."

Maury cocked his head at her, his eyes narrowing in thought. "Tessa, that's not half bad. You used to write that garbage, didn't you? If you can get a fanfic up on Wattpad in the next two hours, that's even better. Then Eric can notice it somehow. The fan girls will go bananas. And then… Oh wait, I have it." Maury snapped his fingers, as another idea came to him. "Even better. You saw the hashtag going around. #WeLoveYouEric?"

"Right," Eric said slowly. "So?"

"So," Maury continued, "we need something to kick off your new Snapchat account. Tessa, I want you to Snap a story. Something to tell all the fans how much Eric loves them back. We'll plant you in the crowd tonight, as close to the stage as you can get. Try to get a shot of Eric making googly eyes at some fan while he performs. You got it?"

"Me?"

Tessa let out a gasp, and Eric rushed to her defense. "Maury, Tessa can't! The TV cameras are going to be all over the place tonight."

"So?"

"She can't get her face on TV!"

Maury waved away Eric's words. "No one's going to be looking at the crowd shots."

Eric flashed a glance at Tessa. It was a terrible idea. A concert? A packed performance hall? He knew it was her worst
nightmare come to pass.

"Can't one of the other publicists do it?" she asked in a
small voice.

"Everyone's got their hands full as it is." Maury opened the
dressing room door and shot his final instructions over his
shoulder as he made his way out. "Look, Tessa. I feel for you.
I really do. But you're going to have to suck it up tonight. Be
a team player."

"But, Maury—" Eric called after him.

"It's her job, Eric!" Maury disappeared behind a rolling
wardrobe cart, but Eric could still hear his manager sounding
off all the way down the hall. "Don't blame me. She's the one
who made this mess. If you want to point the finger at someone, look at her!"

THE INTERROGATION
(FRAGMENT 4)

May 1, 2017, 2:19 p.m.
Case #75932.394.1
OFFICIAL TRANSCRIPTION OF POLICE INTERVIEW

—START PAGE 4—

INVESTIGATOR: Tessa, I'm going to ask you again. Please describe the nature of your relationship with Eric Thorn.

HART: I already told you.

INVESTIGATOR: You told me that you worked for him as a social media consultant. We both know that was not the full extent of your relationship.

HART: OK! Fine. That wasn't the full extent.

INVESTIGATOR: Please answer my question. What was the nature of your relationship with Mr. Thorn over the last ten months?

HART: I honestly don't even know sometimes.

INVESTIGATOR: Was your relationship romantic in nature?

HART: Yes.

INVESTIGATOR: When did it become romantic?

HART: I don't know. Last fall sometime. Before we

went to Mexico. We met over Twitter, and then it became…romantic. And he came to Texas to meet me, and we ran away together. That's the whole story, I swear.

INVESTIGATOR: Were you boyfriend and girlfriend?

HART: In Mexico? Yes.

INVESTIGATOR: And after your return from Mexico? Did you still consider yourselves boyfriend and girlfriend?

HART: Yes and no. I mean, technically yes, but we were trying to keep it under wraps.

INVESTIGATOR: No one else knew of the relationship other than yourself and Eric?

HART: Just Maury. He was helping us keep it secret. The whole social-media-consultant thing was Maury's idea. That way Eric and I could still see each other, but we were hardly ever alone together.

INVESTIGATOR: I have to confess, I find that very odd.

HART: Well, it was an odd situation. I found it pretty odd myself.

INVESTIGATOR: No, I mean I find it odd because of the pictures that surfaced in the course of our investigation. Are you the unidentified female with Eric Thorn in these photos?

HART: No. I can't… I can't look at those.

INVESTIGATOR:	Please let the record show that we're looking at a series of six photos depicting Eric Thorn and Tessa Hart engaged in a variety of intimate activities. Is that a fair description, Tessa?
HART:	[unintelligible]
INVESTIGATOR:	Tessa? Could you speak up?
HART:	Could I possibly get a ginger ale?
INVESTIGATOR:	This isn't a restaurant, Ms. Hart.
HART:	I'm sorry. It's the only thing that helps.
INVESTIGATOR:	Andy, can you grab the wastebasket over there?
HART:	[unintelligible]
INVESTIGATOR:	Are you all right?
HART:	No, I need to go home. I really need to lie down.
INVESTIGATOR:	There's a washroom down the hall. Why don't you take a moment and—
HART:	Can we please just finish? What else do you need to ask?
INVESTIGATOR:	Where were we? [pause] Right. The photos. I take it these pictures were taken without your knowledge?
HART:	Yes.

INVESTIGATOR: When were they taken? Do you know?

HART: A couple months ago in March. The night of the YouTube Music Awards.

INVESTIGATOR: You're certain of that timing?

HART: Yes. I-I'm sure. Eight weeks and three days ago.

INVESTIGATOR: You calculated that off the top of your head?

HART: I'm smarter than I look.

INVESTIGATOR: You look plenty smart to me. Do you have any idea who took these photos?

HART: Probably.

INVESTIGATOR: Would you care to enlighten us?

HART: I don't have any proof. It's my word against his.

INVESTIGATOR: Your word against whose?

HART: It had to be him though. There's no other rational explanation.

INVESTIGATOR: Ms. Hart, for the record, could you please state the name of the individual you're discussing?

HART: He's been stalking me off and on for almost a year. His name… [pause] His name is Blair.

11

THE SHOW

BLAIR PULLED HIS hoodie over his head and leaned against the wall behind him, blending as best he could into the shadows. He hadn't expected it to be so crowded. People wandered past him in packs, and Blair tensed every time someone cast a glance in his direction.

He didn't know why that guy insisted on conducting the transaction in person—let alone in such a public place. It seemed shady. Some kind of setup? Maybe he should leave. Be more patient. Bide his time…

Blair shook his head. He couldn't bail. It might be a long time before he got a better chance, and he'd been patient enough already. A full month had passed since Eric Thorn's miraculous resurrection, and not one single picture of Tessa's face had surfaced on the Internet in all that time. Where the hell was she hiding?

Blair knew she hadn't gone back to Texas. He'd dropped by

Midland two weeks ago to make sure. No sign of her at her house. Blair had even checked up on that therapist of hers, Dr. Regan. He'd wasted a solid week trailing that clueless shrink around, hoping she might lead him straight to Tessa.

But after all that trouble, he'd come up empty.

Tessa wasn't making it easy on him. She'd *better* appreciate his effort in the long run. She would, he vowed. He'd make sure of it. Someday, Tessa would thank him for his steadfast refusal to give up on her, in spite of all the obstacles she threw in his way.

For now, Blair's first step was to confirm her whereabouts. Was she still with that ass-clown? Was she trailing around after him like a pathetic lost puppy dog? If so, it wouldn't be easy for Blair to catch a glimpse of her. Not with all the bodyguards and security everywhere Eric Thorn went.

But Blair might have found a way—assuming this guy from the DNM showed up to complete the transaction. It was mind-blowing what you could score online, if you knew where to look. Most people lacked the creativity to venture beyond eBay and Amazon Prime. But then again, most people had no idea what a dark net market was.

There were risks, obviously. If the seller didn't deliver, you couldn't exactly call up customer service to complain. And you *definitely* couldn't go to the police. The biggest risk was getting scammed. But Blair had gone back and forth over the details a hundred times, and the guy seemed legit. Probably some wannabe paparazzi freelancer who didn't have the stomach for the job.

His loss. Blair's gain…or make that *Tessa's* gain.

Blair bit the inside of his cheek to keep from smiling.

Soon, he thought. Soon he would have answers. Then he would have *her*.

Tessa followed in the wake of the security guard as he cleared a path through the swarming fans. She kept her eyes fixed on his back, reaching out to brush it with her fingertips whenever the crowd threatened to separate them. His black suit jacket strained across his massive shoulders as he pressed his way through the crush of people toward the roped VIP section in front of the stage.

She forced herself to focus on the center seam of the guard's jacket, rippling and puckering with every step he took. Better to think about poor tailoring, if it kept her mind off the crowd surrounding her. She watched the stitching between his shoulder blades tense and relax, tense and relax, tense and relax… and each repetition echoed the sensations inside her own clenched throat.

At least she had a security detail. She didn't have to do this alone. Eric couldn't get her out of this nightmare publicity assignment, but he'd ordered his personal bodyguard, Clint, to stick by her side through the whole ordeal. The former NFL linebacker normally doubled as Eric's limo driver, or the man who carried Eric's umbrella on rainy days, but today he served the role of human shield. People got out of the way in a hurry when they caught sight of his towering bulk. Clint had to be close to seven feet tall and three hundred pounds—double the size of most concertgoers in this auditorium. No wonder he had trouble finding a blazer that fit properly.

"You still back there?" Clint peered down over his shoulder.

Tessa squinted up at him, nodding, but she couldn't tell if he said anything else. The overhead TV lights blinded her, turning his face into a featureless blob. Tessa had to cup her hands around her mouth to be heard over the shrieks of the fans. "Can you get me closer? I need to be right up against the stage!"

"You got it, boss."

He gave her a thumbs-up and resumed his slow progress forward. Tessa did her best to ignore the dirty looks of the people they displaced. She pulled the brim of her black baseball cap down until it nearly touched her nose. She couldn't allow herself to think about how many people might be looking at her. How many sets of eyes...

Anyone could be watching. *He* could be here in this room, watching from a thousand different vantage points.

Tessa gritted her teeth, swallowing against the sour taste in her mouth. "That's a distorted thought," she said out loud, although she couldn't hear her own voice over the crowd noise. Blair wasn't here. He couldn't be. Tickets weren't available to the general public. Everyone in the audience had entered a lottery last fall, and resales were strictly prohibited. Tessa had spent the past twenty minutes scouring eBay and StubHub to reassure herself that no last-minute auctions were taking place.

There was zero chance that Blair had a ticket. *Zero.* It was impossible. Illogical. Irrational…

So she only had to worry about the millions of people streaming tonight's broadcast from the comfort of their homes.

Don't think about that, she commanded herself. She willed herself to ignore the cameras that swooped and glided overhead, suspended above the crowd on giant cranes. She wouldn't allow them to capture an image of her face. Between the baseball cap over her eyes and Clint's formidable presence in front of her, she couldn't possibly end up in a crowd shot.

Tessa ducked her head and kept her eyes on Clint's heels. *Think about something else. Good thoughts. Happy thoughts.*

Like, maybe, the fact that she was living out a dream come true.

How many times had she imagined this scenario? Only a few months had passed since she lay on her bed, staring up at her Eric Thorn concert poster and picturing herself pressed against the stage at one of his shows.

Tonight it was happening for real. She would watch Eric perform live for the first time. She knew that he'd be searching for her face in the sea of fans. He'd probably make eye contact and cast a secret smile in her direction.

And his performance onstage was only the beginning. A pulse of electricity coursed through her as she remembered Eric's promise.

We'll make time. Just you and me. Tonight. Come find me after the show…

Finally, she thought. Tessa pushed away her fears. She wouldn't give in to the anxiety. Tonight, she would enjoy herself. Even if it killed her.

Clint stopped. Tessa nearly crashed into his back, but he shuffled sideways. She found herself at her destination, pressed up against the railing at the edge of the round center stage.

Eric would perform his five-minute set from here. If Tessa dared look up, she might catch his last-minute preparations in the rafters overhead. She knew what to expect from the dress rehearsal this afternoon. Eric would descend on a hydraulic platform as he sang the opening verse of "Snowflake" in a thick down parka. Then, once he hit the chorus, he'd whip off his winter coat to reveal his shirtless torso beneath. He'd break into his breathless dance choreography while lip-synching his way through a montage of older songs.

Tessa felt in her pocket for her phone. She pulled up Snapchat and tested her camera angle. Clint had positioned her well. Her plan was to record Eric interacting with a fan between the second and third song change. She knew the exact moment when the choreography called for him to drop to his knees at the edge of the stage.

Tessa used the phone to block her face, as she swept it back and forth. *Which fan would Eric pick? Maybe that one? She was cute. Or no…her.* A face came into view. A Kim Kardashian look-alike in a pink tube top, screaming and waving toward the TV cameras. Tessa frowned. Was she a true Eric Thorn fan? She looked more like a model. Maybe she was… Maybe Maury planted her there on purpose.

Or maybe Eric found himself surrounded by drop-dead gorgeous superfans every time he looked out into a crowd.

The girl caught sight of Tessa's phone aimed in her direction, and Tessa quickly swung it away. Just then, the lighting shifted. A hum of excitement washed over the audience as the telecast came back from commercial break. The whole stage and VIP section went dark. The concert lights skimmed across the faces in the risers farther back as the opening piano chords of "Snowflake" sounded.

Tessa didn't look upward to watch Eric's descent. She kept her eyes trained forward, but a shy smile sprang to her lips as she hummed along with the lyrics.

> *I watch the snowflakes falling.*
> *Too many for me to see.*
> *Each one just like the others.*
> *Not special or unique.*
>
> *Then I opened up my window.*
> *One snowflake fell inside.*
> *I saw that it was beautiful…*

He was almost to the stage, but the brim of Tessa's cap blocked her view. She longed to lift her head, to see the look on his face as he sang. She had a feeling she would see him looking back.

Would he be disappointed if she didn't meet his eyes? Tessa gathered her nerve. The TV cameras wouldn't be showing crowd shots right now. They'd all be directed at Eric, up there in his spotlight.

With a deep breath, Tessa slowly lifted her head toward the place where Eric floated.

But her eyes didn't land on Eric. The lighting shifted again, and for one brief moment, Tessa caught sight of something in the crowd behind his platform.

Or not something.

Some*one*.

Tessa gasped. She'd only seen it for an instant, but she knew that face. She would have recognized it anywhere. That hoodie sweatshirt. Those hollow eyes and sunken cheeks that still haunted her in her sleep.

It couldn't be…

Her ears filled with the sound of a thousand screams as Eric hit the stage. Was one of those voices her own? Tessa couldn't tell. Her eyes remained fixed on that spot in the crowd, now cast in total darkness. But even if the lights came up, she wouldn't have seen Blair's face. She couldn't see a thing. The tunnel vision had taken over, and the world was lost in shadow. She couldn't see. She couldn't hear. She couldn't breathe.

Tessa turned and thrust her phone toward Clint as her knees

gave way beneath her. Only the railing and the press of the
crowd kept her from sinking to the floor.

Eric pushed his way backstage, scanning the dim hallway
for any sign of Tessa. He hadn't seen her in the audience.
Between the blazing lights and the manic choreography, it
was hard to get a clear look. She must have been there with
Clint. He'd noticed his bodyguard at the front of the crowd,
holding up a cell phone. A figure stood beside him in a baseball cap, leaning over the railing with her head in her arms.
Was that Tessa?

Eric pulled on a clean T-shirt to cover his bare torso. He had
a bad feeling. She should have been the one holding the camera
phone, not Clint. And both of them should have been back
here to meet him after his set. Instead, Eric caught sight of his
manager shuffling over.

"Maury, have you seen her?"

"Who?" Maury asked with a wink. "Ariana Grande? She
goes on next."

Eric glared. "You know who," he said, dropping his voice.
"Where is she?"

His manager's grin transformed into a tight scowl. "I dunno,
Eric. I'm not her babysitter."

"Can you get hold of Clint?"

With a sigh, Maury pulled out his phone, pressing his

Bluetooth into his ear. Eric bounced on the balls of his feet, his eyes searching. He had too much nervous energy to keep still.

Maury clapped him on the shoulder. "No worries, kid. The big guy took her back to her room."

"Is she OK though?"

"She's fine. Clint says she took a pill and went to sleep."

Eric nodded. He turned in the direction of the elevators, but Maury's voice rang out behind him before he could take a step.

"Where do you think you're going?"

Eric stopped short. He knew what Maury was going to say. He hadn't finished his performance for the night. Eric had to do press now, followed by an appearance at the after-party. For the next two hours, he was contractually obligated to look like he was having the time of his life—all within eyeshot of the paparazzi.

Eric rounded on his manager, eyes blazing. "Maury, I can't! Make up an excuse. Tell them…tell them I had a medical emergency."

"You can't go to her room, Eric."

"To hell with my contract! Let the record label fine me. I don't care!"

His manager gestured for him to lower his volume. Maury's own voice fell to a near-whisper. "Listen to me. You can't go up there if you want to keep this thing with Tessa quiet. The whole hotel is crawling with paps."

Eric looked down at the floor. His manager had a point. He didn't know what was worse—exposing Tessa to the prying eyes of those hyenas or abandoning her in the middle of a panic attack.

"Let her rest," Maury said, patting his arm. "She's asleep. You'll see her on the plane in the morning. You want me to go check on her?"

Eric ground the heels of his hands into his eye sockets. He had a monster headache coming on. What would Tessa want? Not Maury. If she was having a panic attack, she probably wanted to be alone. Better to leave her in peace. Get through his obligations. Then find a way to check on Tessa himself before he went to bed. "Forget it," he said to Maury. "I'm sure she's fine."

With that, Eric stalked off. He couldn't keep the gossip reporters waiting. They needed to shoot their mug shots and interrogate him about his make-believe love life. A stylist pulled him aside before he reached the podium. Eric faced her silently, chafing with impatience as she swabbed his face with a towel and blotted him with powder. She reached for a compact of bronzer, but Eric pushed her hand away.

"Enough," he muttered. He stepped past her through the curtains and braced against the onslaught of flashing bulbs.

"*Eric!*"

"*Eric! Over here!*"

"*Hey, Eric! Eric! Can you tell us what's up with you and Ariana?*"

INDIRECT MESSAGES

ERIC STAGGERED INTO the darkened hotel suite and collapsed onto the couch. His body cried out for sleep, but he fought the feeling. He couldn't give in to the urge until he'd checked in with Tessa.

Could he sneak over to her room without anyone noticing? Not likely. The hotel was sealed tight with security to keep the creepy stalker-fans away, but members of the media were allowed. There were bound to be paps skulking around the hotel corridors, keeping an eye out for any late-night celebrity trysts.

He couldn't risk it.

He didn't dare call or text her either. Not over an insecure cell network. Ever since that exchange with Dorian Cromwell, he'd been extra cautious. Could cell phone transmissions be monitored? Intercepted? Would his number be recognized and linked back to him? Or was that pure sci-fi paranoia? Eric didn't know, but he and Tessa had agreed to keep their communication face-to-face.

That rule might have to bend tonight. Surely, a text message would be safer than going to her room.

Eric slipped his phone out of his pocket, thumbing through his contact list. He'd filed her under *S* for social media.

Wait a minute, Eric thought. *Social media...*

Had she posted the concert video? That might give him some clue whether she was OK. Eric closed his contacts and flicked open Snapchat instead.

A crease formed between his eyebrows as he took in the minimal display. A white ghost floated above the only two options on the screen.

LOG IN
SIGN UP

Eric scratched his nose. No auto-login? He'd forgotten this was a new phone. He had his Twitter password memorized, but not Snapchat. At least, he didn't know the password for his official account: RealEricThorn.

Eric paused as he realized that he had another option. "Of course," he said under his breath. *Even better.*

Snowflake734

Tessa had set up this account, but Eric could guess the

password. "Totally unhackable," he said under his breath, as his thumbs picked out the sequence of letters and numbers that only the two of them would know: the license plate number from their van.

TEXASjf97bv

Eric hit Enter. He sucked in a shaky breath as the account sprang to life on his screen. Why did he feel like such a cyberstalker? He wasn't doing anything wrong. This account belonged to him as much as Tessa. No reason not to use it... even if he was using it to spy on his girlfriend.

Eric shook the thought out of his head. He needed to check on her, and this was the safest option he had.

The app logged him in, and Eric stared blankly at the screen. He had no idea how to use this thing. Had they purposely designed Snapchat to baffle anyone over the age of thirteen? There were practically no words anywhere.

Search...

Chat...

Stories...

He swiped at random. First up. Then down...

There, he thought, as a new set of options appeared. *Add friends.* That sounded promising.

RealEricThorn   (+ Add)

"Now what?" Eric muttered, growing more impatient by the second. There had to be some way to see what RealEricThorn was up to. What was it Maury told Tessa to do? Post a… What was it called? A story?

At last he found the option he needed.

⋮ Stories

Eric tapped and let out a grunt of satisfaction as his own name slid into view.

RealEricThorn
🌀 5m ago

"There we go!" He rocked forward on the hotel couch, resting his elbows on his knees. His clock showed a quarter past two in the morning, but someone was awake and active. Tessa? Or someone else on his team?

Eric opened the story and studied the video clip that played. It showed him midway through his set, sliding across the stage on his knees. He wound up in front of a screaming teenager and reached out to grasp her fingertips, singing earnestly into the mic. The clip ended, and a still shot popped up in its place—a close-up, cropped to look like a selfie, with a caption that contained a bald-faced lie:

To my snowflakes, I love you all. Great to be back onstage!

But it was mainly the time stamp at the top of the screen that captured his attention:

Yesterday from Camera Roll

Had Clint saved this footage to her phone? Tessa was supposed to stream the story live during the show. Instead, she must have woken from her medication-induced sleep five minutes ago and threw it up on Snapchat. Better late than never, right?

Which meant that Tessa could still be online right now. She might be watching the responses pour in from fans around the globe.

The story ended, and Eric hit Replay. This time, his gaze landed on the option at the bottom of the screen:

⌃
CHAT

Eric hesitated. Should he do it? If he sent RealEricThorn a message from this account, he would blend in with all the other fans—but maybe Tessa would recognize the handle. Maybe if he messaged something that only she would understand...

For a moment, his mind drifted back to the first words he ever tweeted her, when she was @TessaHeartsEric and he was @EricThornSucks. *Perfect.* He broke into a crooked smile as he composed his message, complete with Twitter-esque @'s and #'s.

@EricThorn What a narcissistic pretty-
boy douche nozzle. Get over yourself
#EricThornSucks

He hit Send and settled back against the couch cushions to wait. She might not see it. The messages must be coming at her by the thousands. And here he was among them—one snow-flake in a blizzard. He should probably Chat again…

Eric couldn't deny the sense of irony as he tapped another message into his phone. This must be how his fans felt all those years, trying to get his attention over Twitter. Message after desperate message with no hint of a reply. Why would anyone subject themselves to the soul-crushing futility?

He should probably give up and go to bed, he thought. Instead, he entered messages, as fast as he could tap them into his phone.

> **Snowflake734:** Hey, Eric, personality quiz.
> If you were an animal, what kind of animal
> would you be?
> **Snowflake734:** You know what kind of
> animal Eric Thorn would see, if he ever
> noticed you existed?
> **Snowflake734:** Hint: five letters, rhymes
> with peach.
> **Snowflake734:** And then he would flick you
> off with his fingernail and go about his day…

Snowflake734: You know there's a word for this. It's called projecting. You should look it up.

He was just finishing that last one, when something interrupted him. A reply had popped up at the bottom of the screen.

RealEricThorn: Who is this?

"Yes!" Eric pumped his fist. He stood and paced across the spacious hotel suite as he considered his next move. Was that Tessa running the Eric Thorn account? He couldn't be sure. Probably, right?

He started composing a reply, but he was interrupted by another new message.

RealEricThorn: Identify yourself.

What did she want, his social security number? He chuckled as he messaged back:

Snowflake734: It's me!
RealEricThorn: OK, that's not vague at all…
Snowflake734: I'm trying to be safe here. You know who this is. You really want me to spell it out?
RealEricThorn: No. Don't.

> **Snowflake734:** Thank you. And who am I
> speaking to right now?
> **RealEricThorn:** This is Eric Thorn.

Eric rolled his eyes. Either he'd completely lost his grip on reality, or someone was messing with him. Could it be Maury? It sounded like his manager, cracking one-liners. Maury was probably cackling at his phone somewhere—probably found this whole exchange hilariously funny.

Or maybe not. It could be Tessa, acting paranoid. How was he supposed to tell the difference?

> Ummm, pretty sure that isn't true... Tessa,
> is that you?

Eric typed the message into his phone, but he stopped himself before he hit Send. Better not to use any names. There was a chance it could be some other publicist, someone who didn't know that he and Tessa were together. There had to be some way to ask her indirectly.

A grin flashed across his face as the answer came to him. He deleted her name and input a different message instead.

> **Snowflake734:** Foot selfie. Right now. Go.
> **RealEricThorn:** Huh?

Eric frowned. Definitely not Tessa, then. She would know

what he meant. There was no way she could have forgotten the only selfie she'd ever sent him: a picture of her feet in a pair of pink bunny slippers.

He was about to flick the phone back off when a new icon popped up.

RealEricThorn
Tap to view

A Snap? Eric clicked it open.

The image was hopelessly blurry. It looked like she'd zoomed in as far as the camera lens would go. To anyone else, it would look like a mistake—but Eric recognized the shade of pink, and the fuzzy oblong outline of a rabbit's ear.

It was Tessa. It had to be! And when he recognized the image, she would know that it had to be him.

Eric messaged again.

> **Snowflake734:** Could you bring those slippers over here please? I think you know the room number.
>
> **RealEricThorn:** Are you joking?
>
> **Snowflake734:** No. I need to see you. Face-to-face. I'd go to you, but there might be paps…
>
> **RealEricThorn:** I can't!
>
> **Snowflake734:** It's safer if you come to me. No one will bother following you. They're looking for celebrities.

RealEricThorn: You don't understand. I
can't leave my room.

"Crap," Eric muttered. Was she back to full-blown agoraphobia? She'd been doing so well with her iTherapy and her
relaxation techniques. Not that she didn't have anxiety twenty-
four seven, but she'd been able to function.

Was all that progress out the window?

Eric didn't know what to say. He raised his eyes and looked
across the room at the blank wall opposite him, fighting the
urge to go bang his head against it. He could only imagine how
frustrated Tessa must feel. With a sigh, he returned his attention to the phone. She'd added another message.

RealEricThorn: He's here!
Snowflake734: What? Who?
RealEricThorn: I saw him! He was in the
crowd earlier!
Snowflake734: Wait…Him???
RealEricThorn: HIM!
Snowflake734: Ughhh. Are you sure?
RealEricThorn: No. Not completely. I only saw
him for a sec. There were so many people…

No wonder she'd panicked. Eric could feel his own heart
rate pick up at the thought of Blair Duncan. Here. In the same
city. Sharing the same airspace…

Snowflake734: When exactly? During my set?

RealEricThorn: Yeah. I spotted him in the risers behind you, but I lost sight of him when the lighting changed.

Snowflake734: Did you get a picture of him?

RealEricThorn: No. It was only for a second. OMG I freaked. I haven't had an attack that bad in months...

Snowflake734: OK, stay calm. Deep breaths.

RealEricThorn: I'm trying. I took my meds.

Snowflake734: Is it possible your eyes were playing tricks on you?

RealEricThorn: I don't know. I don't think so.

Snowflake734: It would be totally understandable. You were in a big crowd of people. That's one of your triggers.

RealEricThorn: But what if it was real? I don't know what to do.

Snowflake734: Why didn't you tell me???

RealEricThorn: I didn't know how! After Clint left, I just locked the door and hid under the covers.

Snowflake734: OK, to hell with the paps. Sit tight. I'm coming.

RealEricThorn: NO!!!

Snowflake734: YES. You can't be alone right now.

RealEricThorn: But what if he's watching?

Snowflake734: There's no way he's in the hotel. No way.

RealEricThorn: You don't know that!

Eric wiped his palms against the rough fabric of his jeans. He needed to think clearly. Keep his head on straight…

Snowflake734: Security wouldn't let him in without some serious press credentials. The crowd at the concert, maybe…but not the hotel. It's impossible.

RealEricThorn: Are you sure?

Snowflake734: There's a friggin' police blockade outside. This hotel is probably the safest place you could be.

RealEricThorn: I guess. OK…that makes sense.

Snowflake734: Tell me your room number. I'm coming.

RealEricThorn: Wait! No. That's stupid.

Snowflake734: You have to!

RealEricThorn: No, I'm OK. You're right. It's probably all in my head. There's a psych term for that. It's called "priming."

Snowflake734: I don't know that one.

RealEricThorn: It means you're more likely

to perceive something if you're exposed to some other stimulus that you associate with it. The mind perceives what it expects to find, even if it's not really there...

Snowflake734: Example, please?

RealEricThorn: I associate being in a crowded room with HIM. That's where I first encountered him. In a crowd. So when I was back in that environment again, my brain was primed to think I saw him.

Snowflake734: But you didn't really see him?

RealEricThorn: Probably not. Probably someone else who looked like him.

Snowflake734: Right! That's what I was saying. Your eyes were playing tricks on you.

RealEricThorn: It was totally just priming!

Snowflake734: Whatever fancy word you like. Does that make you feel better?

RealEricThorn: Yeah. A little bit. I'm laughing at myself :P

Snowflake734: OK, good. I'm still coming over.

RealEricThorn: No, wait. I'll come to you.

13
LOSING IT

TESSA CREPT DOWN the hotel corridor, careful not to trip. She could only see a tiny sliver of space directly in front of her face. Her peripheral vision was obscured by the thick hotel bedspread wrapped around her body and up over her head.

So far she'd been lucky. She hadn't encountered anyone who looked like a photographer. She'd come face-to-face with hotel security when she stepped off the elevator on the VIP floor, but the guards let her through after she lowered her blanket and flashed her ID badge.

Now she was safely inside the secure perimeter. Tessa took a deep breath to steady her nerves. No one could follow her here. This stretch of corridor was probably the safest place on the planet, just like Eric had said.

Not that she'd faced any kind of danger at the concert earlier. Eric was right about that too. The apparition she had seen for a split second—tall and lean, with a hoodie sweatshirt over his head—wasn't real. Her brain had simply reacted to a stimulus with the psychologically predictable response.

When it came right down to it, she only had one enemy that no bodyguard could keep away. Not Blair Duncan. Her own mind held the power to take away her freedom—to shut her in a room and lock the door.

But only if she allowed her anxious thoughts to gang up on her.

Tessa frowned. That concert should have been a happy memory. She'd had a front-row view, pressed against the railing, perfectly positioned to win a smile from the boy up on the stage. Tonight should have been everything a fangirl could ever wish for her first live show. She'd lost her Eric-Thorn-concert virginity, and she hadn't even enjoyed herself.

What was the matter with her?

Tessa gave her head an angry shake. She let go of the comforter clutched around her shoulders and let it drop to the floor. She didn't need some security blanket. She needed to get her head on straight. Forget the concert. Forget Blair. Focus on what really mattered.

Eric.

All alone with Eric Thorn, in his pop-star VIP hotel suite.

Tessa hastily ran her fingers through her hair to smooth out the tangles. She grew painfully aware of her appearance as she came to a stop at Eric's door. Her baggy flannel pajamas engulfed her legs and pooled at her ankles, swallowing up the bunny slippers on her feet.

Why hadn't she slipped into something a little more... appropriate? Tessa wrinkled her nose. She couldn't help recalling Ariana Grande with her crop top and micro-miniskirt. Even that wardrobe assistant Katrina had worn something cuter than the atrocity Tessa had on.

It was too late now though. She was here. Tessa undid the top button of her pajama top and knocked softly.

The door cracked open, but only a few inches. Tessa moistened her lips with the tip of her tongue, waiting for him to speak. Did he expect her to say something? Some signal? Tessa opened her mouth to whisper his name, but she thought better of it. Instead, she kicked off one of her pink slippers and stuffed it through the narrow gap.

She heard his soft laughter from the other side. The door opened with a creak, and Eric stood motionless before her.

"Hey," he whispered.

He looked exhausted. Dark shadows smudged his eyes, half concealed behind the curtain of his bangs. He was still wearing the skintight jeans from tonight's performance, with a clean white V-neck T-shirt thrown on above them.

Tessa's heart clutched at the sight of him. He looked so tired. Why was he still dressed? He should be the one in pajamas, as much as she appreciated the way the thin denim stretched across the muscles of his thighs. He should be tucked in bed, fast asleep. He only had a few hours before his morning wake-up call, and then his personal trainer would grab him for his daily three-hour workout.

"You look like hell," he murmured, his eyes tracing up and down.

"Thanks. So do you."

He broke into a crooked grin and reached for her elbow, pulling her across the threshold. Tessa heard the door click closed behind her. She tried to step past him into the darkened room, but he blocked her. The rigid door pressed against her shoulder blades as he took a half step closer. She looked up at him, and her pulse rate climbed as the gap between them shrank.

"Are you OK?" he whispered. He dipped his head to look into her face. "Did you see anything suspicious out there?"

Tessa shook her head. "All clear. Super-tight security, like you said." Her throat had gone dry as sandpaper. Eric lifted a lazy arm and rested it against the door beside her, trapping her in place.

"You look scared," he said.

"Nervous," she corrected.

He studied her in silence for a moment. "Nervous about Blair?"

"No."

"Really?" His eyes bored into her like lasers.

Tessa felt her cheeks heat up beneath his scrutiny, and she gave a tiny shrug. "He isn't here," she said. "I have to stop letting him control my life."

Eric nodded. "I agree." He shifted another inch closer. "I kind of wish he were here though."

That surprised her. Tessa looked up into his face.

"I swear to God," he said, his voice dropping an octave lower. "If that parasite ever shows his face again, I'll kill him. I will crush him like a bug with my own bare hands." His palm was pressed flat against the door, but he balled it into a fist. Tessa rested a hand on his forearm, rigid with flexed muscles and popping veins.

"No," she whispered. "Then you'd go to jail."

"Maybe." He leaned in all the way and rested his forehead against hers. "Maybe I don't care."

"Well, I care." She slid her hand up his arm until it rested at the crook of his elbow. "Then what? Are you and Dorian Cromwell going to share a cell?"

"Pretty sure his jail cell's in England."

Tessa shot him a tart look. "Maybe you two can start a jail-house band together," she said. "You'd make a good-looking duo."

Eric laughed, and she felt his soft breath tickle her cheek. "Maury would probably love that."

"You can pitch it to Maury in the morning." Tessa let go of Eric's elbow and pushed lightly against his chest. "It's late. I'm fine, Eric. Really. Thank you for checking up on me. You should go to bed."

He rocked backward a fraction of an inch. "What are you nervous about, if not Blair? You didn't answer me."

Tessa's hand lingered on the white fabric of his T-shirt. She kept her eyes glued to the vee of his collar. "I don't know," she said. "Maybe because I'm alone in a hotel suite with the hottest guy at the YMAs?"

Her eyes flitted to his face, and she saw the corner of his mouth hitch upward. "Who? Harry Styles?"

"No, not Harry Styles."

"Justin Bieber?"

"Eric, don't be dense."

His face hung before her, his blue eyes blazing in the darkness. "Some girls like Justin Bieber," he said softly.

"Some girls like Eric Thorn," she whispered back.

Eric didn't answer. Not with words. His arm swept around her waist and pulled her toward him, and his lips came down on hers. His mouth moved slowly, teasing, and Tessa let her own lips drift apart. She heard a low rumble from somewhere in the back of his throat. The sound of it sent a shock wave of heat rippling through her.

Forget the concert, Tessa thought, as she laced one arm around his shoulders. That wasn't the real fangirl dream-come-true. This. Now. Alone with Eric…tasting his breath…sweeping the hair from his eyes with her fingertips…

This was the fantasy. This time, nothing would distract her.

With her free hand, Tessa groped behind her, searching blindly for the dead bolt. Eric's head tilted to deepen the kiss. His arm tightened, locking her against him.

Tessa dropped her hand. *To hell with the dead bolt.* This was where she felt safe. Here in Eric's arms. As if to underline the point, he bent down and scooped her up. She didn't question what he was doing as he carried her into the next room.

He laid her gently on the bed and eased himself above her.

For a moment, he hovered there, and Tessa met his eyes—two points of electric blue, glowing in the light from a bedside lamp.

"Is this OK?" he whispered.

She dragged his mouth back toward her. "Yes," she said against his lips. "Don't stop."

Tessa's mind flashed back to that final morning in Tijuana. She'd felt the same way then—standing on the threshold, about to take the leap. They'd been interrupted, but nothing could distract her tonight. This time, she needed to block out all other thoughts, shut down all other senses but the feeling of Eric's lips and his body pressing down on top of her.

Tessa closed her eyes. She heard nothing but his whispered words as they peeled off each other's clothes.

"Tessa, I love you... I can't keep pretending... I need to be with you so bad..."

"Wait." She didn't know why she said that.

The word slipped out, and Eric froze. He rolled onto his back. "What's wrong?"

Tessa pulled the top sheet and slipped beneath it, gripping it across her chest. "Do you have a condom?"

"Of course."

He groped in the dark for a moment. Tessa watched in silence as he found his discarded jeans and fished for his wallet in the back pocket. She heard the crinkle of foil, and she swallowed hard.

"I came prepared," Eric said. A tiny smirk tugged at his mouth, and it sparked a vicious flair of heat in the pit of her stomach.

Tessa squeezed her eyes closed. "OK," she said. "Good. Go ahead."

Eric stopped. When she reopened her eyes, his face had grown serious. "Tessa, I love you, but this doesn't have to happen today. Not if—"

"No," she said firmly. "I want to."

"Are you sure?" He held up the black foil packet. "Should I open this or not?"

Tessa nodded, letting the sheet around her chest relax. She knew why she kept holding back. She still had her mother's warning, permanently etched into her psyche.

Listen to me, sweetheart. It only takes one time. I got in trouble the first time I ever fooled around…

She couldn't give in to it. She couldn't let her mother ruin this for her. "I'm ready," she told Eric. "I'm just… I need to look something up." Tessa reached off the edge of the bed to retrieve her phone.

"Seriously?" Eric murmured in her ear.

Tessa held up a finger to shush him. "Information," she explained. "*Clinical* information. You know how it's the only thing that relaxes me sometimes."

Eric leaned back against the pillows. A look of comprehension flashed across his face. He'd seen her do this a thousand times. She'd spent countless hours in Mexico reading article after article full of psych jargon. The world seemed far less terrifying when she armed herself with facts.

Now, she simply needed to research a slightly different

topic. Eric watched over her shoulder as she entered a Google search:

Condom effectiveness

A Wikipedia page popped up on the screen, and Tessa read the title out loud. "Comparison of birth control methods, in order of effectiveness."

Contraceptive implant ranked at the top, followed closely by *vasectomy.*

Eric drummed his fingers against the mattress. "Thanks, Wikipedia. Way to set the mood."

Tessa ignored him, scrolling down.

IUD...

Cervical cap with spermicide...

Oral contraceptive pill...

Finally, she reached the row she was seeking: *male latex condom.*

"See?" Tessa said, looking up from the screen.

"What? It says ninety-eight percent effective."

"Ninety-eight percent with *perfect* use," she corrected. "Eighty-two percent with typical use."

Eric let out a tiny sigh. "What exactly is typical use?"

Tessa flicked the phone back off and glanced again at the condom packet in his hand. "You know how to use it, right?"

"I took sex ed, Tessa."

"Just try not to be typical, OK?"

He grinned in response, and another pulse of heat flashed through her. Tessa looked down, suddenly breathless, as she pressed a hand beneath her rib cage. "Tessa, look at me," he said. He tipped her chin up, and his eyes drilled into hers. "I'm Eric Thorn," he whispered. "There's nothing typical about me."

In another mood, she might have laughed. But not tonight. Not with the way he looked at her—like he might devour her whole. All the air went out of the room. Tessa twined her fingers through his hair and pulled his lips down to her again.

At last her senses focused, like a radio dial tuning in to the right station. She shut out all the noise and listened only to the music. The constant chorus of anxious thoughts faded from her mind. She no longer heard the faint shouts of the people partying in the lobby, or the whir of the elevator as it rose and fell. She lost herself to everything but the feel of Eric's kisses…the elegant movements of his body…the scorching fire in his eyes.

And so she didn't hear it—the faint sounds that her ears would have registered on any other day:

Low voices in the corridor.

The scrape of a turning doorknob.

The swish of creeping footfalls across the hotel carpeting.

The barely audible *click, click, click* of a camera shutter outside the bedroom door.

THE INTERROGATION (FRAGMENT 5)

May 1, 2017, 1:39 p.m.
Case #75932.394.1
OFFICIAL TRANSCRIPTION OF POLICE INTERVIEW

—START PAGE 3—

INVESTIGATOR: Mr. Gilroy, going back to these photographs you took in Mexico—

GILROY: Are we almost done? I don't mean to cut you off, but my phone's been vibrating for half an hour straight.

INVESTIGATOR: I'll try to keep it brief. As I mentioned, these pictures were turned over to us in the course of our investigation by a freelance photographer. The same individual recently sold a different photo to the *Daily Mail*, depicting Eric Thorn and an unidentified woman engaged in an intimate act. Are you familiar with this image?

GILROY: Pretty sure the whole world is familiar with that image.

INVESTIGATOR: For the record, can you confirm that the man in this picture is Eric Thorn?

GILROY: Yes. Confirmed. That's my client's naked left butt cheek that trended number one on Twitter last week.

INVESTIGATOR: The girl has her face turned away from the camera. Can you identify her?

GILROY: Let's not beat around the bush, Detective. You and I both know that's Tessa Hart.

INVESTIGATOR: But this wasn't one of the photos you took in Mexico. Is that correct?

GILROY: Of course not. I'm not some kind of perv.

INVESTIGATOR: Any idea who took it, or how the *Daily Mail* gained access?

GILROY: Yes and no. I did some digging. Eric had a fit when he saw it. He asked me to get to the bottom of it.

INVESTIGATOR: And what did you discover?

GILROY: Best I could tell, the photos leaked from a fan-run Twitter account. One of the oldest and biggest. Goes by the name of MET.

INVESTIGATOR: This one here?

GILROY: You already know about it? Nice work, Detective. Color me impressed.

INVESTIGATOR: Let the record show that we're looking at a Twitter account with username @MrsEricThorn, or MET for short.

GILROY: You ever consider moonlighting in private security? Because I could use a sharp guy like you.

INVESTIGATOR: Mr. Gilroy, please—

GILROY: I'd make it worth your while, if you catch my meaning. And you can call me Maury, by the way.

INVESTIGATOR: Mr. Gilroy, if I may continue?

GILROY: Please.

INVESTIGATOR: When exactly did you inform Eric Thorn that the MET Twitter account was the source of the photo?

GILROY: A couple days after the story popped up in the *Mail*.

INVESTIGATOR: Would you say that conversation took place before or after the evening of April 26?

GILROY: Four days ago? Why? What happened on April 26?

INVESTIGATOR: Please answer to the best of your recollection, Mr. Gilroy.

GILROY: Let me check my calendar… [pause] Probably told him on the 26th. Sometime that day.

INVESTIGATOR: And who else knew that this Twitter account was involved?

GILROY: As far as I know, just Eric and me. And maybe whoever bought the photos at the *Mail*.

INVESTIGATOR: What about Tessa Hart. Was she aware?

GILROY: I didn't discuss it with her.

INVESTIGATOR: Could Eric have told her?

GILROY: I wouldn't know.

INVESTIGATOR: But Tessa Hart does have access to the Twitter
                  account with username @EricThorn. Correct?

GILROY: Eric's official account? Sure. She helps run it.
                  We've been over this.

INVESTIGATOR: Who else had access to that account, other than
                  Mr. Thorn and Ms. Hart?

GILROY: Just the two of them.

INVESTIGATOR: You didn't have access yourself?

GILROY: Nah, Eric doesn't trust anyone with that. He was
                  always paranoid about people tweeting for him,
                  putting words in his mouth. I try to respect his
                  boundaries.

INVESTIGATOR: He didn't trust you with his Twitter account, but
                  he trusted Tessa Hart?

GILROY: Yeah, well, what can I say? True love.

INVESTIGATOR: Mr. Gilroy, is it true that Eric Thorn came to Los
                  Angeles this past week to shoot a music video?

GILROY: Yes, that's true.

INVESTIGATOR: And were you aware of Mr. Thorn or anyone on
                  his team recruiting fans to serve as extras in the
                  video?

GILROY:	Fans? No, we use a casting agency for extras. Never fans. That's a security nightmare waiting to happen.
INVESTIGATOR:	So you had no knowledge of the direct messages that passed on April 26 between Eric Thorn's Twitter account and the account with username @MrsEricThorn?
GILROY:	Oh no. Don't tell me. What did Tessa do now?
INVESTIGATOR:	Why don't I show you the thread? Let the record show that Mr. Gilroy is looking at a transcript of a DM conversation time stamped April 26, 2017, at 11:16 p.m. I'm going to read the first message into the record. The message states, and I quote: "Hi, my name is Tessa Hart. I'm a publicist on Eric's team. Eric will be shooting a music video on May 2, and we need some lucky fans to act as extras in the video. Congratulations on being selected!"
GILROY:	Goddammit.
INVESTIGATOR:	Mr. Gilroy?
GILROY:	I swear, it's like babysitting a bunch of toddlers sometimes. I should quit the music business and open up a day care center.
INVESTIGATOR:	I take it you were not aware of this message thread until now?
GILROY:	No, I don't know what to tell you. This is the first I'm seeing it.
INVESTIGATOR:	It's your opinion that the messages were sent by Tessa Hart?

GILROY: That's what it says, isn't it?

INVESTIGATOR: And the only other person who might have had access
                   to send it was Eric Thorn himself. Is that correct?

GILROY: I don't want you talking to Eric without a lawyer
                   present. Is that understood? I'm not joking around
                   now. I don't know what kind of mess Tessa just
                   stepped in, but—

INVESTIGATOR: Sir, no one's under arrest. Our investigation is still
                   in preliminary stages.

GILROY: Where is Eric, anyway? Is he here?

INVESTIGATOR: Mr. Gilroy, please take your seat.

GILROY: Shit. Shit. Double shit.

INVESTIGATOR: Mr. Gilroy—

GILROY: Am I free to go?

INVESTIGATOR: Of course. But we may need to ask you more
                   questions at a later date.

GILROY: If you want to ask me more questions, Detective,
                   then you're gonna have to answer a few of mine.

INVESTIGATOR: Such as?

GILROY: Let's start at the beginning. Why don't you tell me
                   who's dead?

PISTOLS AT DAWN

14

April 30, 2017

BLAIR SWIPED THE back of his hand across his forehead. The sweat kept running into his eyes, distracting his attention from his task. That was one thing he missed about the coffee shop back home in New Orleans. Air-conditioning. How was he supposed to concentrate in this heat?

He turned toward the narrow casement window and contemplated raising the sash. A little cross breeze would surely help cool down the stifling atmosphere. But Blair didn't move to open it. He had the blinds shut tight, and he didn't dare adjust them. That was the whole reason he'd left his coffee-shop days behind.

Privacy.

He couldn't afford any prying eyes. All he needed was for some passerby to catch a glimpse through the window at one of the images on his laptop screen…

He couldn't risk it. Not now, with the object so close at hand.

Another rivulet ran down his temple. Blair lifted the hem of his dank T-shirt and used it to mop his brow.

Soon, he thought. Eric Thorn had finally returned to LA to shoot some new music video. *Hooray for Hollywood.* Blair let out a coarse laugh. Not that he'd ever been a huge fan of moving pictures, but he did have his own personal video project in the works.

All his patience and dedication would pay off. Where Eric went, Tessa followed. He knew that she was close. He could sense it. He could taste it, like the tang of his own sweat… And she had *basically* invited him to join her. That was the best part.

Not that he was surprised. He knew how girls like Tessa operated. Always playing games. Playing hard to get. Going ghost and popping up again when you least expected. But it only meant they wanted to be chased.

And Blair? He'd always enjoyed a friendly game of hide-and-seek. He was more than happy to oblige.

⇄

"Cut! Wardrobe, can somebody deal with Eric's cravat situation, please?"

Eric glanced across the studio backlot at the video director. Cravat? What the hell was a cravat? His head wardrobe assistant popped up beside him and reached for the silk neck scarf tied in a knot at his throat. Eric lifted his head to give her better access, squinting against the glare of the hazy LA sunshine.

It was a new experience for him, shooting a music video fully dressed. He normally spent his entire time on set shirtless. Pant-less half the time as well. Eric chafed under the stiff layers of silk brocade that encased his shoulders and strained against his thighs. He'd never shot a period piece before. He'd thought Katrina was pranking him this morning when he saw his costume laid out: top coat, waistcoat, and knee breeches, all in matching pale-blue silk. And tights? Did they really expect him to wear tights?

"Trust me," Katrina had reassured him. "Your calves are gonna look amazing in those things. Haven't you seen *Hamilton*?"

Eric wasn't so sure. Would the fangirls really go for this look? He wondered what Tessa would say when she saw him all decked out. She should have been here by now. He'd left her hiding out in his private trailer, but she'd promised him that she would come and watch the shoot this afternoon. Where was she?

"C'mon, people. We're losing daylight. Let's move!"

Katrina tightened the tie at his throat with a jerk, and Eric let out a choked noise. He lifted a hand to loosen the knot, but she swatted it away. "It needs to be tight," she told him, as she carefully arranged the frills of white fabric on his chest.

"I can't breathe," Eric muttered hoarsely.

"You'll get used to it. Hold out your arms."

Eric forced himself to swallow, his Adam's apple bobbing up and down. Why did he have this unshakable sense that Katrina *might* accidentally strangle him with his own necktie? It was probably the lip piercing, he thought. It gave off a hard edge—and a subtle hint of sadism.

At least she wasn't waving scissors around his junk this time.

Eric extended his arms, and she took a step back to admire her handiwork. Another girl went over his thighs with a lint roller. A third one showed up and placed an object in his outstretched hand. Eric's fingers closed over the cold, hard metal body of a gun.

They were shooting the climactic action sequence today. "Pistols at Dawn" was the title of the song. He'd scribbled out the lyrics on the plane ride home from Las Vegas last month. Everyone loved it…except Tessa. She was the only person alive that understood who those lyrics were about, and he could tell she wasn't a fan.

> *You're going down.*
> *Let's get it on.*
> *I'll lay you out.*
> *Pistols at dawnnnnnnnnnnnn.*
> *Bang! Bang! You're gone!*

Oh well. They couldn't all be love songs. The label wanted a harder sound, and the music video was a no-brainer: a duel to the death to preserve a fair maiden's honor. He'd besmirch her honor tomorrow when they shot the love scene. After all, he couldn't spend the *entire* video fully dressed…

A heavy palm clapped him on the rear end, and Eric spun around. Katrina stood behind him holding out her hand. "Cell phone," she said.

"Seriously?"

She gestured toward the back pocket of his breeches. "You can see the outline," she explained. "It's throwing off the silhouette." She wiggled her fingers impatiently. "Give it here. I'll leave it on your makeup chair."

Eric fished the phone out of his pocket. He would have protested, but the director was already breathing down his neck…and frankly, Katrina made his balls shrivel with the way she looked at him sometimes. He handed his cell phone over, glancing at the lock screen one last time.

4:15 p.m.

No new notifications.

Would Tessa come? She'd been awfully quiet when she read over the video treatment. But then again, Tessa had been awfully quiet in general lately. Alternately antsy and withdrawn. She was like a little turtle, the way she hid herself away inside that hard, external shell. He couldn't seem to draw her out, no matter how he tried. She'd been that way for a week now. Ever since the story ran in the *Daily Mail*.

Eric's grip tightened around the handle of the pistol. Just a prop, of course. This gun only shot blanks, and it was a lucky thing for the person responsible for those pictures. The real duel to the death would come later, and Eric wouldn't hesitate to use his own bare hands.

It had to be Blair. He and Tessa both knew it the moment they saw the photos, even though neither one of them had breathed her stalker's name aloud. They both recognized the scene: a suite at the MGM Grand. Normally, all the hotel rooms ran together in his head, but that particular night in that particular room…that one he would always remember.

That should have been a perfect memory. A *private* memory. Not splashed across the tabloids for all his fans to see.

Enough was enough. Eric knew what he needed to do. It was easy, with Maury's media connections, to identify the source of the photos. Eric had been thrown for a moment when his manager showed him the account.

MET @MrsEricThorn

FOLLOWING   FOLLOWERS
78   **1.1M**

Eric still didn't know what to make of it. Was it possible that Blair had been behind the MET account all along? Seemed hard to believe. Whoever ran that account had been fangirling over him for years. She might be stalkerish as hell, but she was an Eric Thorn stalker, not a Tessa Hart stalker. No, Blair was either working with MET, or he'd somehow hacked the account. That was the only explanation that made sense.

It didn't matter. He didn't particularly care who MET was, as long as she could lead him to Blair.

Tessa had been sleeping over the other night when Eric hatched his plan. That was one good thing about the *Daily Mail* story, he supposed. No need for the two of them to skulk around anymore. The secret was out. Tessa's face was obscured in the photo, but everyone on his crew could clearly recognize her. The two of them could spend every night together now, and no one would blink an eye.

Not that he and Tessa were having much fun lately. She was a ball of nerves, and Eric didn't blame her. He'd worried after the photo leaked that she would go into hiding, run back home to her mother's house in Texas.

The thought of losing her made Eric's throat constrict. He needed to act. As long as Blair Duncan existed, it was only a matter of time before Tessa ran away. If not to her mother, then she'd find somewhere else to hide. Somewhere Blair couldn't find her, and Eric might not be able to find her either. He couldn't imagine the loneliness of this hollow pop-star existence without Tessa in his life.

The same worries had been turning over and over inside his head the other night, with Tessa snoring softly at his side. She'd finally fallen asleep after a week of relentless insomnia—and an inexplicable refusal to take her anxiety medication for relief. She had her phone beside her on the pillow, flashing with incoming notifications, and Eric had pocketed it so it wouldn't wake her.

"Places, everyone! Let's move!"

Eric trotted across the asphalt to his mark. He waited for his cue, with his pistol lowered at his side. His forearm quivered inside its silken sleeve as he gripped the gun. Soon, it would be time for action.

But the sun shifted behind a cloud. The video director issued a muffled curse at the change in light. Eric's arm relaxed as his shadow on the pavement disappeared.

He tapped the pistol rhythmically against his outer thigh, and his mind went back to the other night. He'd tiptoed into the bathroom with Tessa's phone and opened one of the notifications. It brought up Twitter, logged in to his account. Mrs. Eric Thorn was the one causing all the commotion that night. She'd been online and tweeting. Eric must have sat there for half an hour, staring at the screen as MET posted tweet after tweet. And all the while, he kept coming back to the words beside her username.

> MET (@MrsEricThorn) FOLLOWS YOU

And then the DM button…

Eric knew what he had to do. It hadn't been hard once the idea came to him. If Blair was running that account, it would be easy enough to tempt him out of the shadows. Eric had squared his jaw as he typed out his first DM:

> **Eric:** Hi, my name is Tessa Hart. I'm
> a publicist on Eric's team. Eric will be

shooting a music video on May 1, and we
need some lucky fans to act as extras in the
video. Congratulations on being selected!

MET: ARE U SERIOUS?

Eric: If you would like to participate, you will
need to arrive on set before dawn on the
morning of May 1. We suggest that you stay
overnight in the LA area on April 30. If you
do not live in the area, a hotel room will be
booked on your behalf at the Beverly Hilton.

MET: TESSA?

Eric: Yes, this is Tessa Hart.

MET: OMGGGG! I THOUGHT that was you
in the pic!

Eric: Like I said, I'm a publicist on Eric's
team. I will personally be coordinating the
extras for this video shoot. Would you like
to participate?

MET: Wait. Waitwaitwait. I can get to LA,
but will you be there? Tessa?

Eric remembered how the mirthless grin had split his face
when MET asked that question. *Bingo*, he'd thought to himself. *It had to be Blair. Had to be!* Blair must have hacked the
account. Why would some fangirl care about seeing Tessa?

The next message confirmed it.

MET: Because there's something I want to
talk to you about. But not on Twitter. Better
in person.

Obviously, Blair had taken the bait. He thought this was his
big chance to get Tessa alone. Eric had played along.

Eric: Talk about what?
MET: There's something you should
know… It's important. Is there any way we
could meet? Somewhere private?
Eric: I could come to your hotel room the
night before. Is that good?
MET: Good. But don't bring anyone else.
Not anyone, OK? Just you, Tessa.
Eric: I'll be there. Beverly Hilton, April 30.
Let's say 9 p.m.?
MET: Awesome. It's a date ;)

Eric had deleted the DM thread afterward. Destroyed
the evidence. Tessa had access to his Twitter account, and
he didn't want her to know anything about this particular
conversation.

There was no way she could have seen it though. He might
have left his own phone in the bedroom, but Tessa wouldn't
have looked at it. She was asleep the whole time. And even
when she logged on to Twitter these days, Eric knew she never

ventured near the message tab. The mere sight of a DM sent her spiraling into panic mode.

Eric tensed his pistol arm again. The light reemerged from its hiding place, warming his skin. The director called instructions through his bullhorn.

"Clear the set. And...action!"

Eric looked across the back lot toward the actor playing his nemesis. The sun hung low in the sky, glaring into Eric's eyes. They only had time for a few more takes before calling it a wrap. Then Eric would head back to his trailer. Change into his regular clothes. Kiss Tessa on the cheek, and make up some excuse to head out again. Some errand to run—an errand that led him in the direction of the Beverly Hilton.

Tessa didn't need to know the details. It was better if he kept her in the dark. He'd tell her later, of course. Tomorrow, after it was over. After his "errand" was complete.

"OK, Eric," the director's voice called. "I need you to raise your gun slowly. Squint a little bit, like you're aiming. That's it."

Eric did as he was told even as his mind raced forward.

Tonight.

It would all go down tonight.

"Good, Eric. Hold that pose... That's it. Now pull the trigger."

THE INTERROGATION (FRAGMENT 6)

May 1, 2017, 3:24 p.m.
Case #75932.394.1
OFFICIAL TRANSCRIPTION OF POLICE INTERVIEW

—START PAGE 1—

INVESTIGATOR: Thank you for sitting down with us, Mr. Thorn. My name is Detective Tyrone Stevens. This is my partner, Detective Andrew Morales. Today is May 1, 2017, at 3:24 p.m. This interview is being recorded.

THORN: Yeah, I know the drill.

INVESTIGATOR: I need your full name and occupation for the record.

THORN: Eric Taylor Thorn.

INVESTIGATOR: Occupation?

THORN: Like I said, Eric Taylor Thorn. It's a full-time occupation.

INVESTIGATOR: Can we go with professional entertainer, perhaps?

THORN: Sure. Sounds good.

INVESTIGATOR: OK, Eric. Are you aware of the direct messages exchanged several days ago between your

Twitter account and the account with username @MrsEricThorn?

THORN: How... I thought I deleted that. I don't understand.

INVESTIGATOR: The thread was found on the victim's cell phone. Let the record show that we are looking at a message thread, dated April 26, 2017 —

THORN: That was me. OK? I sent those messages myself.

INVESTIGATOR: You sent this message here? The one that states, and I quote: "Yes, this is Tessa Hart."

THORN: I used her name. It was all me. She didn't know about it. I was...I was trying to trap him.

INVESTIGATOR: Him?

THORN: Blair Duncan. He's been stalking Tessa for almost a year. I thought he might have gained access to the MET account. That's his MO. He hacks things and takes creepy photos of her. There's a whole record of it from last winter in Texas. He was arrested and everything, but the charges were dropped.

INVESTIGATOR: I see. And you're saying that Ms. Hart had no knowledge of your plans to entrap Blair Duncan?

THORN: No way. Are you kidding me? She would've freaked.

INVESTIGATOR: So essentially, you were using Ms. Hart as bait without her knowledge. Is that your statement?

THORN: No, you're twisting everything. I wasn't using her
                   as bait. I was trying to protect her.

INVESTIGATOR: Without her knowledge?

THORN: She's been having a rough time lately. Insomnia.
                   Panic attacks. I can't convince her to take her
                   meds. It's all because of Blair…because of the
                   picture.

INVESTIGATOR: Her meds?

THORN: She has an anxiety disorder.

INVESTIGATOR: Do you recall the name of the medication she takes?

THORN: I don't know. It's one of those drug names. Some
                   antianxiety thing.

INVESTIGATOR: This medication was prescribed to Ms. Hart by a
                   psychiatrist?

THORN: I guess she's a psychiatrist. Tessa used to do ther-
                   apy with her back in Texas. Dr. Regan.

INVESTIGATOR: Are you aware of any other medications that Tessa
                   may have been prescribed?

THORN: Why?

INVESTIGATOR: Please answer the question, Eric.

THORN: No, I'm not aware of any other drugs. I'm telling
                   you, Tessa had nothing to do with this. She wasn't
                   even around last night.

INVESTIGATOR: Can you walk us through what happened yesterday evening? Did you go to the Beverly Hilton?

THORN: Yes. Listen, I tried to help. Really. I called 911
and everything. You have to understand… I have
to worry about the media, how it would look. I
couldn't… It was too late to do anything anyway.

INVESTIGATOR: The victim was already deceased by the time you
arrived?

THORN: I think so. Someone else got there before me. The
door was cracked open.

INVESTIGATOR: Did you speak to anyone else at the hotel?

THORN: No.

INVESTIGATOR: Can you think of anyone else who knew of your
intention to meet someone at the Beverly Hilton
that night?

THORN: No.

INVESTIGATOR: Could anyone else have seen the messages you
exchanged with MET to set up the meeting?

THORN: No. I don't see how.

INVESTIGATOR: You're sure?

THORN: Yes, I'm sure! How many times are you going to
ask me the same question?

INVESTIGATOR: My apologies. I'm simply trying to establish who else could have known about your meeting in that hotel. The only two people with access to the @EricThorn account were yourself and Tessa Hart. Correct?

THORN: Yes. But maybe the MET account was hacked. Maybe Blair…

INVESTIGATOR: Again with Blair Duncan.

THORN: He hacked one of my other accounts once. I wouldn't put it past him.

INVESTIGATOR: OK, Eric. Let's go back to the direct messages exchanged on the night of April 26, arranging the meeting. You're still sticking to the story that you sent these messages yourself?

THORN: Yes! It's not a story. I'm telling you, I sent them.

INVESTIGATOR: From the time stamps, it looks like the messages started at 11:16 p.m.—

THORN: We've already been over this!

INVESTIGATOR: Do you happen to recall where Ms. Hart was at the time when you were exchanging these DMs with @MrsEricThorn?

THORN: Tessa was asleep.

INVESTIGATOR: Was she with you at the time?

THORN: Yes.

INVESTIGATOR: In the same room?

THORN:	I was in the bathroom. She was asleep in bed.
INVESTIGATOR:	The message exchange began at 11:16 p.m. and continued until 11:42 p.m. You then deleted the thread from your account. Did you delete it immediately after the conversation ended?
THORN:	Yeah. I didn't want Tessa to see it.
INVESTIGATOR:	To the best of your recollection, did you leave the bathroom at any time between 11:16 p.m. and 11:42 p.m.?
THORN:	Probably not. No.
INVESTIGATOR:	That's a period of twenty-six minutes when that message thread would have been visible to anyone logged in to the @EricThorn Twitter account. Isn't it possible that Tessa could have woken up and seen those messages at some point during those twenty-six minutes?
THORN:	No. She was asleep.
INVESTIGATOR:	You're certain of that.
THORN:	Yes! For the millionth time, Tessa had nothing to do with this!
INVESTIGATOR:	You said Tessa was unwilling to take her anxiety medication?
THORN:	What? Why…why do you keep asking about her medication?

INVESTIGATOR: Answer the question, Eric.

THORN: I don't know. She said she was running low. She didn't want to waste the last few pills in case she couldn't get a refill.

INVESTIGATOR: Do you know if Tessa requested a refill from her former treating physician in Texas?

THORN: Oh my God! Seriously? What does that have to do with anything?

INVESTIGATOR: Calm down, son. We just have a few more questions.

THORN: Your questions make no sense. You're not listening to me!

INVESTIGATOR: About what? Blair Duncan?

THORN: Yes!

INVESTIGATOR: Let me make sure I have this right. You went to the Beverly Hilton yesterday evening, expecting to find Blair Duncan in the room.

THORN: Right.

INVESTIGATOR: But the person you found in the room, already deceased, was not Blair Duncan.

THORN: Obviously not.

INVESTIGATOR: You'd previously met Blair Duncan in person?

THORN: Yes. In December. New Year's Eve. I-I helped the
                    police capture him.

INVESTIGATOR: In Midland, Texas?

THORN: Yes.

INVESTIGATOR: So you're certain that the victim in the hotel was
                    not—

THORN: Seriously, how dense are you? It wasn't Blair!
                    OK? Blair Duncan is a guy. The person I found in
                    the hotel room was definitely female.

15

FEMALE PROBLEMS

TESSA SAT IN *a corner seat with her eyes down on her lap. She pulled out her braid and let her hair swing loose to hide her face. The waiting room was fuller than she'd expected. Most of the other girls had boyfriends or husbands seated beside them…and bellies the size of bowling balls. Everyone but her.*

"Hart. Tessa Hart?"

She stood and followed the nurse through a swinging door. How big was this clinic anyway? The corridor looked endless. Door after door after door… One of them stood open, and Tessa peered inside as she passed. A girl about her own age lay on an operating table, feet in stirrups.

They made eye contact for a fleeting moment. Then the girl grasped her swollen stomach, and her face contorted in pain.

Tessa looked away. She didn't like this place. She wished she hadn't come. She'd forgotten to control her breathing. Now the air rushed in and out in shallow gasps.

At last, the nurse stopped at a door. The room was empty, aside from an exam chair with a black medical bag beside it.

That bag... She'd seen it before...

"You're here for a test?"

Tessa nodded, but her throat was too parched to produce a sound.

"Last menstrual period?"

She thought back, counting the weeks on her fingers. Sometime after they returned from Mexico. February? It didn't really matter. She knew the exact date when the damage was done. The night of the YouTube Music Awards: March 3.

The nurse made a note. "Sit tight. The phlebotomist will be in shortly to take a blood sample."

Blood sample? Tessa gulped. She'd been expecting to pee in a cup.

Her eyes roved around the windowless room and across the stark white tile floor. The black bag sat beside her within arm's reach, and Tessa couldn't take her eyes off it. She knew with a sudden certainty where she'd seen that bag before—and what it contained.

Needles.

Tubing.

Packets of sterile gauze.

A tourniquet in case of heavy bleeding...

Tessa nudged the bag open with her elbow. Just a peek. She saw the label beneath the clasp. Black marker on white tape, in handwriting Tessa knew almost as well as her own.

PROPERTY OF CARLA HART

3 Sycamore Lane

Midland, TX

Mom?

A knock sounded. Once. Twice. The doorknob slowly turned. A cold tremor sliced through her, and Tessa slammed her eyes shut. She heard the door creak open. And she recognized the voice that greeted her, dripping with I-told-you-so contempt.

"You knew what would happen, Tessa. How many times did I warn you?" Tessa heard the snap of latex gloves against her mother's skin. "You're a Hart. It's in your blood. You know, I got knocked up the first time your daddy ever looked at me sideways…"

🔁

Tessa jolted awake. Her hair stuck to the sides of her face, drenched with sweat, despite the blasting AC. She lay on her side with her legs curled to her chest on the unfamiliar motel bed. Black spots danced in front of her eyes as she sat up. Too quickly. The gorge rose in her throat, and she barely made it to the bathroom in time.

Long moments ticked by as she kneeled in front of the toilet, struggling for breath.

This was why she couldn't be at Eric's video shoot right now. The nausea was getting too intense—and too hard to explain.

Tessa stood and washed her mouth out with water cupped in her hands. *It was a dream,* she told herself. *It didn't mean anything.*

But Tessa knew it was more than a bad dream. She'd known for weeks. She had to face the truth. It was all playing out the way her mother had predicted.

And Eric was starting to suspect.

She wasn't showing yet, but she knew she was acting funny. The morning sickness was hard to conceal. Not to mention the mood swings. Bloating. Tenderness. She'd googled *early pregnancy signs* the other day, and she ticked off nearly every check box on the list.

So far, she'd blamed it all on anxiety, and Eric seemed to buy it. Why wouldn't he? It was true in a way. Anxiety had always made her pukey. And Tessa had plenty to be anxious about, since that picture surfaced in the *Mail*.

But Tessa knew she couldn't use that excuse forever. At some point, she had to tell him the truth, and the thought of that conversation filled her with dread. She'd awakened before the second half of her mother's favorite lecture, but Tessa could recite the rest by heart.

He'll blame you…

Good luck collecting child support…

Your whole life will be ruined. Trust me, I speak from experience…

Another wave of nausea swept through her, and Tessa leaned over the sink. What if her mother was right? Eric wouldn't take the news well. He wasn't ready to have a kid. He might even want her to get rid of it.

Tessa's hand rose to her throat. *Eric one…Eric two…Eric three…*

She could never do that. It wasn't an option. She supported abortion access, but only as a choice for other people. Not for herself. Not when she had been the product of an unwanted pregnancy. She would never have existed if her mother had made that choice.

So that meant this baby was coming, and Eric had to be told. Maybe he'd be happy. Excited. Tessa wanted to believe that, but she knew she was kidding herself. Why would Eric let himself get saddled with a baby and a baby mama when he had plenty of more attractive options?

Like that wardrobe person…Katrina. The thought of her made Tessa grind her teeth. Every time she walked into some backstage dressing room, she found that girl with her hands all over Eric's body.

Tessa couldn't help nursing a low-key hatred for Katrina Cortez—with her smoky eyeshadow and bad-girl piercings. She was one of those girls who snarled more often than she smiled. The type who only listened to hard-core punk bands and turned up her nose at anyone who fangirled over the kind of music Eric made.

But that didn't stop her from wanting Eric's body. She was constantly touching him. Could she be any more obvious?

Tessa rolled her eyes. She should probably do a journal entry. These were distorted thoughts. She knew better than to make assumptions about people based on how they looked. And Katrina worked in wardrobe. It was her job to fuss with Eric's clothes.

So why couldn't Tessa shake this secret wish for Katrina Cortez to drop dead?

Tessa hated to admit it, but she'd found herself missing her old therapy sessions lately. What would Dr. Regan say to all this? She closed her eyes and inhaled deeply, summoning up the inner therapist's voice inside her head.

I hear you saying that you feel judged by your mother. Could you tell me more about that?

Tessa groaned.

She left the bathroom and flopped down heavily on the lumpy motel bed. Why had that particular therapy session sprung to mind? Because of the dream, obviously. That dream had nothing to do with Eric or Katrina—and everything to do with her nonexistent relationship with her mother.

Tessa remembered Dr. Regan asking that same question over and over. They always came back to it, and Tessa always answered the same way. *As far as my mom's concerned, I'm the worst thing that ever happened to her. I ruined her life from the moment I was conceived.*

Now history was repeating itself. Her mother would probably crow with laughter when she heard. She'd probably consider it some kind of cosmic justice. Tessa covered her face with her hands as the dark thoughts welled up inside.

She needed more than therapy. She needed her meds.

But she didn't dare touch them. Not if she was pregnant. Tessa intended to keep this baby and take the best care of it she possibly could. That was the most important thing. She might have repeated her mother's mistake by getting pregnant, but she wouldn't repeat the rest. She would never let this child feel like it wasn't wanted.

Never, Tessa vowed. She'd tell her baby that it was a treasure. The *best* thing that ever happened. And she'd repeat that story over and over and over until her child could recite it by heart.

Tessa rolled onto her side. Her phone rested on the pillow beside her head, and she picked it up. Eric's video director had probably called it a wrap by now. Eric must have returned to his trailer and discovered her absence. Did he wonder where she went? Did he even care?

She swiped past her lock screen. Her eyes went to the Snapchat icon, but there were no new notifications. He hadn't messaged her.

Tessa looked away, directing her eyes upward to the motel ceiling. She knew deep down that she was the one who needed to message him. She needed to come clean. The longer she kept this pregnancy to herself, the more the secret would fester—until it ate them both alive.

But not tonight.

She wasn't ready. She'd spent the past few nights sleeping over at Eric's house in the Hollywood Hills, but she couldn't think clearly there. She needed a night on her own to plan what she would say to him...and where she would go if he didn't react well.

She didn't have a lot of options. If Eric washed his hands of her, there was only one place Tessa could turn. For a moment, she closed her eyes and sucked in a deep breath.

Eric one…Eric two…Eric three…Eric Thorn…Eric five…

Then she swiped away from Snapchat and input a text message instead.

Mom? Are you there? It's me.

⇄

Eric trotted across the pavement of the studio back lot, shielding his eyes against the bright-orange glare of the setting sun. The director had called a wrap to the day's video shoot after filming a half-dozen takes of Eric's death scene. At the end of the duel, Eric's shot went wide, and his rival's bullet found its mark. Eric died of a gunshot wound to the chest.

Now, he still wore the remnants of his elaborate costume with the entire left side of his coat in tatters, stained with fake movie blood. He wondered what Tessa would say when she caught sight of him. He'd grown accustomed to the heavy costume, and the bullet hole definitely added to the look. He might keep it and use it for Halloween in a couple months. Tessa could get some eighteenth-century ball gown to match.

Not that she would be up for Halloween parties. Eric knew better than that. She'd never materialized to watch him shoot the duel, and he did his best to ignore the sinking feeling beneath his ribs. He couldn't take it personally. Some days she needed solitude. She probably always would…

He rapped briskly on the trailer door and swung it open.

Empty.

Where was she? Eric frowned. Back on set after all? Had he missed her somehow?

He slipped out his phone, relieved to have it back in his possession. He'd felt naked without it before. He wasn't used to walking around without Snapchat burning a hole in his back pocket. Strange, he thought, how he'd never used that app before this year, and now it was his go-to form of communication. It was like an inside joke with Tessa. The mutual double catfish. He was Snowflake734. She was RealEricThorn.

With a dry chuckle, Eric flicked on his phone and saw that she'd beaten him to it. He had a chat message, time stamped five minutes ago.

RealEricThorn: Did you see this?
http://www.dailymail.co.uk/tvshowbiz/
article-3264609

The *Daily Mail*? Not again… They must have leaked more photos. He clicked the link, bracing for the worst. Goddamn Blair. How bad was the damage this time? Full-frontal nudity? He prayed they didn't have a picture of Tessa's face.

The article came up on Eric's screen, but it wasn't Tessa in the photo. Another girl, standing in front of a large stone building. Eric recognized her face. He'd seen her in countless pictures, although he hadn't laid eyes on her for almost a year.

He knew the face in the second photo too. It looked like an old PR headshot. Eric's forehead furrowed as he studied the side-by-side images: Dorian Cromwell next to his ex-murderer.

Why was Tessa sending this to him?

The article was dated over a week ago. Eric's eyes skimmed over the headline:

Exonerated! Fourth Dimension Fan Released. Dorian Facing Additional Charges for Conspiracy.

Eric didn't read the rest. He knew how Tessa felt about Dorian Cromwell. Someday, those two would end up in a Twitter war. Eric wouldn't want to be in Dorian's shoes when Tessa opened fire.

He tapped out a message, and she responded right away:

> **Snowflake734:** Hey, where are you?
>
> **RealEricThorn:** Did you see the link?
>
> **Snowflake734:** More jail for Dorian. That sucks…
>
> **RealEricThorn:** Did you read the part about the girl?
>
> **Snowflake734:** No, just the headline. What did it say?
>
> **RealEricThorn:** It took them this long to release her because they had to wean her off the meds. They had her locked in a

hospital, doped up on so many drugs she
could barely speak.

Snowflake734: That's horrible.

RealEricThorn: And all Dorian can do is
issue some canned statement from his
publicist. "Sorry if we caused you any
trouble, dear. Here are some free tickets
to my next concert. Blah, blah, blah."
Are you kidding me? He ruined this girl's
LIFE!!!!!!

Eric cringed. He knew how Tessa identified with that girl.
He wished they were having this conversation in person instead
of by text. He could barely keep up with her. How did she
manage to compose whole paragraphs in the time it took him
to write a single sentence?

Snowflake734: I mean, Dorian's shady. I'm
with you on that. At least he cleared the
girl's name.

RealEricThorn: It's just so…
UGHHHHHHHHHHH. I hope she hunts
him down and murders him for real. He
SO deserves it…

Snowflake734: Where are you?

RealEricThorn: Like don't you get it, Eric?
Don't you see?

Snowflake734: Tell me where you are, and
I'll come meet you.

He glanced out of the narrow trailer window, scanning for
any sign of her. The sun had sunk below the horizon, but the
crew still buzzed about outside, preparing the set for tomorrow's
bedroom scene.

RealEricThorn: She didn't kill anyone. She
was framed. And me... Well, I was framed
too. Except I'm the one who framed myself.
Nobody's coming forward to exonerate me.
I DID IT TO MYSELF.
Snowflake734: But, Tessa, everyone
already knows you didn't murder me.
RealEricThorn: They still think there's
something wrong with me!
Snowflake734: What? Who thinks that?
RealEricThorn: EVERYONE

Eric glanced at the clock at the top of his screen, tapping
his foot. It was getting late. He wanted to talk to Tessa, but he
also needed to be in Beverly Hills by nine. He hadn't forgotten
about his plans for the rest of the evening.

Snowflake734: Why? Seriously, Tessa, tell
me where you are. I don't have a ton of

time. I have to be somewhere at 9. We need
to talk.
RealEricThorn: No kidding, we need to talk.
Snowflake734: OK...
RealEricThorn: I'm sorry. It's not you. I'm
really upset right now.
Snowflake734: Where is this coming from?
RealEricThorn: Nowhere. I texted my mom.

Eric's eyebrows shot up. Now they were getting somewhere.
Contact with his parents always had a way of ruining his mood
too. His relationship with his mom and dad had grown more
strained since his return from Mexico—but Tessa and her
mother were beyond distant. The last he'd heard, Tessa had no
intention of ever speaking to her mom again.

Snowflake734: Did she answer?
RealEricThorn: Yeah. I think I preferred
noncommunication.
Snowflake734: What did she say?
RealEricThorn: Oh I don't know... That
I ruined her life. She had to move out of
her house. The reporters wouldn't leave
her alone. So even if I did go back, she
wouldn't let me crash there.
Snowflake734: Go back? Tessa, where are
you???

RealEricThorn: Look at this. She actually sent me this. Unbelievable.

The message contained another link. Eric squinted in confusion at the website it brought up.

CHALET SANTÉ

Hit Refresh…on your life.

"What the hell?" he muttered. From the pictures, it looked like some luxury spa resort, but the words in smaller print gave it away.

Voluntary inpatient treatment in a secluded, technology-free setting.

"Shit," Eric swore under his breath. This conversation was starting to make more sense.

RealEricThorn: She said she'll only help me if I agree to check myself in for treatment. Did you read it? Ninety-day voluntary lock-in.
Snowflake734: WHAT? Treatment for what???
RealEricThorn: For being an obsessed stalker murderer, duh.

Eric cocked his head sideways, trying to make sense of her words. Could her mother really be that clueless? Tessa had to be exaggerating. But then again, his own mom had greeted his return from the grave by sending him a care package of store-bought cookies and a list of bills that went unpaid during his absence.

So much for parental support.

> **Snowflake734:** Forget your mother. She doesn't know what she's talking about. WHERE ARE YOU?
>
> **RealEricThorn:** I'm out.
>
> **Snowflake734:** Could you be a little more specific?
>
> **RealEricThorn:** I left. I went to a hotel. I'm sorry.

"What does *that* mean?" Eric whispered. His shirt collar suddenly felt too tight around his neck. He tugged at the knotted silk to relieve the tension in his throat. *She left? Like, she left the trailer? Or...*

> **Snowflake734:** Tessa, we need to talk about this! You can't leave. What hotel?
>
> **RealEricThorn:** I need to be by myself tonight.
>
> **Snowflake734:** Are you OK?
>
> **RealEricThorn:** No...but I will be.

Snowflake734: We should talk.

RealEricThorn: I know. There's something I really need to tell you.

Snowflake734: Is it urgent, or can it wait?

RealEricThorn: It's fine. Go do whatever you have to do at 9. I'll tell you tomorrow.

Eric glanced at the time again. It was dark outside the trailer. He needed to get a move on.

Some instinct told him to forget Blair. Go find Tessa. She obviously needed him right now. Only her mother could get her this riled up.

But Blair…

He couldn't bail on the meeting. As much as he wanted to be with Tessa, Blair had to be dealt with first. It was a matter of priorities. If he could get Blair Duncan out of the picture once and for all, that would do more for Tessa's state of mind than any other comfort he could give her.

"Priorities," Eric muttered, as he sent off one more text.

Snowflake734: OK. I love you. I'll message you when I'm done.

THE INTERROGATION
(FRAGMENT 7)

May 1, 2017, 2:19 p.m.
Case #75932.394.1
OFFICIAL TRANSCRIPTION OF POLICE INTERVIEW

═══

—START PAGE 5—

INVESTIGATOR: Ms. Hart, I need to ask you your whereabouts on the afternoon and evening of April 30.

HART: Yesterday? I don't know. I spent most of the day hiding out in Eric's trailer at the video shoot.

INVESTIGATOR: Did you leave the trailer at any point?

HART: I left before he got back.

INVESTIGATOR: Where did you go?

HART: A hotel. Eric's driver took me.

INVESTIGATOR: Which hotel?

HART: Some motel in West Hollywood. I forget what it was called. Something Spanish. Del Mar? Del Vista?

INVESTIGATOR: West Hollywood? Not far from Beverly Hills?

HART: If you say so. I don't know my way around LA that well.

INVESTIGATOR: What's the name of the driver who took you?

HART: Clint. He's Eric's bodyguard. He can probably tell you what motel if you ask him.

INVESTIGATOR: But you yourself can't tell us the name of the establishment where you spent last night?

HART: I don't remember.

INVESTIGATOR: And you arrived at this motel around what time?

HART: Maybe four in the afternoon. I'm not sure.

INVESTIGATOR: Did you leave your room at any other point that evening?

HART: No.

INVESTIGATOR: Did you talk to anyone while you were there?

HART: I texted my mom, and I Snapchatted with Eric for a little bit.

INVESTIGATOR: Did you speak to anyone in person?

HART: No.

INVESTIGATOR: You didn't order yourself a pizza or anything like that?

HART: No. Nothing. I wasn't very hungry.

INVESTIGATOR: Tessa, can you think of anyone who might be able to corroborate your whereabouts last night?

HART: Just Clint. And Eric.

INVESTIGATOR: Eric saw you that evening?

HART: No, but we chatted. I told him I was staying at a
                   hotel for the night.

INVESTIGATOR: But you didn't tell him any more specifics?

HART: No. I was kind of upset.

INVESTIGATOR: You didn't tell him the name of the motel?

HART: No.

INVESTIGATOR: A motel in West Hollywood with a Spanish-
                   sounding name.

HART: Right. I think so.

INVESTIGATOR: You're not certain?

HART: I don't know. Like I said, I was kind of upset.
                   I wasn't really thinking about the name of the
                   motel.

INVESTIGATOR: You were upset about somewhere Eric was going
                   that evening. Is that correct?

HART: What? No, I don't think… What do you mean?

INVESTIGATOR: Were you aware of Eric's plans last night?

HART: No. Not really. He just said he had to do some-
                   thing at nine.

INVESTIGATOR: You didn't ask him what?

HART: We don't usually make a habit of interrogating each other.

INVESTIGATOR: OK, Tessa. Let me ask you this. At what point yesterday evening did you go to the Beverly Hilton?

HART: What? I didn't.

INVESTIGATOR: Did you go there before or after you Snapchatted with Eric?

HART: I didn't. I never went to the Beverly Hilton!

INVESTIGATOR: Are you sure?

HART: I told you, I didn't leave my room all night. I didn't go anywhere.

INVESTIGATOR: Tessa, are you aware that a woman was found dead in her room at the Beverly Hilton Hotel last night at approximately 9:00 p.m.?

HART: No. I don't know anything about that! I was nowhere near—

INVESTIGATOR: Eric didn't tell you?

HART: Eric? Wh-why would Eric...

INVESTIGATOR: Eric was the one who found the body.

HART: Wait, what?

INVESTIGATOR: But you weren't aware that Eric had plans to meet a woman in her hotel room yesterday. Correct? [pause] Tessa, is that your statement?

HART: I don't…I don't know anything about it.

INVESTIGATOR: You didn't intercept any Twitter direct messages setting up a rendezvous between Eric and a woman?

HART: No, of course not.

INVESTIGATOR: However, you do have access to the Twitter account with username @EricThorn. Yes?

HART: Yes, but I never look at the DMs. Not after…after what happened.

INVESTIGATOR: Tessa, have you and Eric talked since yesterday?

HART: No. He's busy shooting his video. We were supposed to talk later.

INVESTIGATOR: I see. Let's go over your movements one more time. You say you checked into a motel room yesterday at 4:00 p.m. and did not leave again at any point that evening. You are unable to provide the name of the motel or anyone who could corroborate your story. Is that correct?

HART: Whatever. It doesn't matter. You obviously don't believe me anyway.

INVESTIGATOR: Tessa, what exactly did you do at the motel all evening?

HART:	I took a nap. I texted my mom. I surfed the Internet. I chatted with Eric. Then I went to sleep again.
INVESTIGATOR:	What time did you go to sleep?
HART:	I have no idea!
INVESTIGATOR:	Did you take any medication to help you sleep?
HART:	No.
INVESTIGATOR:	Have you ever taken any medication to help you relax?
HART:	Sometimes. But not…not lately.
INVESTIGATOR:	What kind of medication?
HART:	Ativan. It was prescribed to me. I have an anxiety disorder.
INVESTIGATOR:	Are you currently under psychiatric care?
HART:	No. Not since last winter.
INVESTIGATOR:	Who was treating you last winter?
HART:	My psychotherapist in Texas.
INVESTIGATOR:	Dr. Laura Regan?
HART:	Yes. How did you—
INVESTIGATOR:	And what other drugs did Dr. Regan prescribe for you besides Ativan?

HART:	Nothing else. Just some behavioral psychotherapy.
INVESTIGATOR:	So if we were to call up Dr. Regan right now, she would confirm that you were never prescribed anything other than Ativan?
HART:	No, she'll probably tell you to talk to her malpractice attorney. That's what she told the police in Midland.
INVESTIGATOR:	Tessa, did Dr. Regan or any other physician ever prescribe you a drug called phenobarbital?
HART:	No, that's a barbiturate. That's like a hard-core sedative.
INVESTIGATOR:	How do you know that?
HART:	I don't know, I read about stuff. It relaxes me. I'm thinking about majoring in psych if I go to college.
INVESTIGATOR:	Were you ever given phenobarbital?
HART:	No! Why do you keep asking about phenobarbital?
INVESTIGATOR:	As you said, it's a sedative. It wouldn't be out of the ordinary for such a drug to be prescribed to a patient experiencing an acute emotional disturbance.
HART:	I was never given phenobarbital, OK? Just Ativan.
INVESTIGATOR:	Do you have any idea why our victim might have had phenobarbital in her system at the time of death?

HART:	I told you, I don't know anything about that! Maybe she was a junkie. I don't know!
INVESTIGATOR:	OK, Tessa. Calm down. Let's go back over your statement. You say you spent the afternoon in Eric Thorn's private trailer. You then got a ride from a limo driver with no last name who took you to an unknown motel in the vicinity of—
HART:	Am I under arrest?
INVESTIGATOR:	Not at this time.
HART:	Am I free to go?
INVESTIGATOR:	We just have a few more questions. Please bear with me if you don't mind.
HART:	No. I think I'm done now.
INVESTIGATOR:	That's fine, Ms. Hart. You're free to go. If I were you, I wouldn't make any plans to leave town.

16

UNRELIABLE WITNESS

May 1, 2017

BLAIR STRETCHED. HIS back ached from too many hours hunched in front of his laptop. He needed to shut down for a while. Go outside. Get some sunlight. Work the kinks out of his legs.

He looked toward the door, shut tight with the chain lock fastened. But he didn't move. He couldn't bring himself to rise from his desk chair. Not now. He didn't want to miss her…

He needed to see Tessa's face. He needed to hear her voice. He couldn't go too long without the craving coming back. She was like a drug, and he was an addict. He started breaking down if he went too long without a fix.

Blair slammed the laptop closed and pushed it aside. Useless. He'd have a better chance of seeing Tessa and her idiotic boy toy on the pages of *Us Weekly*. He already had the pictures from the *Daily Mail* tacked to the wall, blown up three times their original size. But those grainy images would never be enough to satisfy him. Not by a long shot.

He knew he'd allowed his hopes to rise too high yesterday. He'd spent all afternoon unable to keep still, thrumming with anticipation—counting down the minutes until he would catch a glimpse of Tessa's face.

But in the end, she hadn't appeared. It was only Eric. Alone.

Blair made a fist and smacked it against his palm. His patience had worn thin. Just look at his cell phone screen. Barely usable. Cracked from being chucked too hard onto the surface of his desk. It was Tessa's fault. She *made* him do that. Why couldn't she cooperate? It drove him to the brink of violence every time. Now she was on the loose, and Blair had no idea when she might turn up.

Tonight? Next month? Next year? Or maybe not. Maybe never...

The thought sent a tremor through his shoulders. For all he knew, she'd left LA. Slipped between his fingers once again.

Blair stood and paced the narrow room. He couldn't allow himself to think that way. She could still appear at any moment. He needed to be patient. Enjoy the chase.

But the sweet flavor of anticipation had given way to bitter fear. He didn't know how much longer he could hold out. He'd grown tired of this game. Cat and mouse...

Or maybe more like cat*fish* and mouse...

Blair's lips twisted. His screen was cracked but not beyond

redemption. He picked up the phone and balanced it gently in his palm. Was she dumb enough to fall for the same trick twice? Did she realize he had access to that fake account with its asinine username?

Blair turned the cell phone on, but he hesitated. He didn't want to spook her. There was no telling how she might react to a DM.

"No," he said aloud. It was an unnecessary risk. He should wait. Bide his time. She'd wander back between his crosshairs soon enough. He set the phone back down and returned to his perch before the laptop.

He didn't need to mess around with Twitter.

Not anymore.

Not when he had a connection…

Tessa hesitated on the concrete steps in front of the Los Angeles police station, unsure which way to turn. The bright afternoon sunshine warmed her face, but it did nothing to dispel the fogginess in her head. How was it still daylight? She felt like she'd spent hours in that stuffy interrogation room, answering question after question. She'd thought it would be well after dark by the time she stepped outside.

Now what?

She needed to sit down. Her knees felt weak. She couldn't get the sound of that policeman's final words out of her head:

If I were you, I wouldn't make any plans to leave town.

Tessa understood what that meant. She wasn't under arrest, but she probably would be soon. She knew how she must look to the police. All those leading questions—those hints and innuendoes. Now it all made sense.

What was the nature of your relationship…?

No one else knew…?

If we were to call up Dr. Regan right now…?

I have to confess, I find that very odd…

"Very odd," Tessa muttered, remembering the way the detective had looked at her as he said it. An assessing look, with his chin tilted up and his eyes narrowed, viewing her down the bridge of his nose. A look that dripped with skepticism. "Very odd, indeed."

Tessa knew where the interrogation was heading, and the thought made her heart judder and skip inside her chest. She'd seen this story before, played out across the headlines. Look what had happened to Dorian's alleged killer. It didn't matter what that girl had to say in her own defense. Tessa could only imagine the horror the girl must have faced as she sat there in the witness box, testifying on her own behalf and seeing that same look of skepticism on every face in the courtroom. That girl had sworn under oath that she was nowhere near Dorian's hotel the day he died. She'd told the same story again and again. She was home alone that morning, fast asleep in bed. But no one had believed her.

Tessa gave her head an angry shake. Unreliable,

unstable—and quite possibly a danger to everyone around her. That was how a good portion of the world still viewed mental illness. Didn't matter if it was anxiety or depression or schizophrenia. Sure, they might pay lip service to the notion that a mental disorder was a health condition, not a reason to judge. But plenty of people didn't believe that. Not deep down. Even her own mother thought she was out of control. The memory of that messed-up conversation made Tessa feel like vomiting all over again…

Or maybe that was the pregnancy hormones racing through her veins.

Tessa sucked at the inside of her cheek. She wished she'd told Eric last night. She should have gone back to his house and talked to him face-to-face. It would have given her an alibi if nothing else.

Unless, of course…

Tessa pressed a palm against her collarbone. What if Eric believed the same thing as the police? What if *he* thought she was guilty? That would explain why he hadn't contacted her since their chat last night—those rushed messages, just before he went to meet another girl at a hotel…

Honestly, Tessa didn't know what was worse: the idea that might have Eric cheated on her or the idea that he considered her capable of murder. The thought left her light-headed, and she reached out for the handrail to steady herself. She eased herself down slowly to sit on the bottom step, burying her face in her hands.

She should have trusted her instincts about Katrina, the way that girl always manhandled Eric and his clothes. Obviously, Eric and his wardrobe assistant were up to more than "alterations." How long had he been seeing her? Maybe they'd been in a secret relationship the whole time. Sneaking around, DM'ing each other from secret Twitter accounts to arrange their secret meet-ups...

Of course, Tessa thought, her back stiffening. Why was she surprised? She knew exactly how Eric operated. She knew firsthand.

Maybe Katrina was the murder victim. The police hadn't said... But if so, Tessa could only imagine what Eric must have been thinking.

She could forget telling him about the baby, obviously. Would he back up her statement that the two of them were in a relationship? Why did she have this horrible feeling—like everything her mother had ever warned her about was coming true?

Tessa slipped her phone out of her pocket and flicked it on. No new Snapchat notifications. The sight of her empty lock screen filled her with a fresh jolt of despair.

No one knew where she was right now.

And no one cared.

Still, a voice whispered in the back of her head that these might be distorted thoughts. Catastrophizing? Leaping to conclusions? The list of cognitive distortions suddenly seemed endless.

Tessa forced herself to breathe. She couldn't write off Eric as a liar and a cheat. She didn't know his side of the story. She'd be as bad as the police if she presumed Eric guilty without giving him a chance to defend himself. Maybe there was some other reason he hadn't messaged her. Maybe…maybe the police had confiscated his phone?

It seemed awfully hard to believe.

Tessa shook her head. Something didn't add up. The police said he'd set up his booty call over Twitter. Direct messages…

The very thought made her stomach heave. Tessa pressed the back of her hand to her mouth to keep from retching while she waited for the bout of morning sickness to pass. She needed to get over this DM aversion. It wasn't rational anyway. If she wanted to know the truth about Eric, all she had to do was look.

Small steps, Tessa thought. That's what Dr. Regan would have told her. She would just look for a minute. If she felt her panic level rising, all she had to do was close the app.

With a resolute nod, Tessa flicked on to Twitter, already logged in to the usual account: @EricThorn.

And there it was.

For a moment, she closed her eyes. Was that real? Was she hallucinating? She blinked rapidly, and her vision blurred with sudden tears.

Of course Eric still loved her. How could she have doubted? There was all the evidence she needed. Her eyes weren't playing tricks on her. That message was real. A new DM from an account she didn't know she followed.

Snowflake734: Sit tight. Don't be scared.
Everything's OK.

Tessa let out a tiny sob. "Oh thank God," she whispered. He hadn't abandoned her. She wasn't alone. Her finger shook as she messaged back:

EricThorn: I'm so confused. What's going on?
Snowflake734: Shhhhh...not over Twitter.
I'll tell you face-to-face. Get in the car.

The car?

Sure enough, a black SUV with tinted windows appeared at the end of the block. Tessa could just make out the silhouette of a shadowy figure sitting in the driver's seat.

She put away her phone and stood to meet it at the curb.

THE INTERROGATION
(FRAGMENT 8)

May 1, 2017, 3:24 p.m.
Case #75932.394.1
OFFICIAL TRANSCRIPTION OF POLICE INTERVIEW

—START PAGE 3—

INVESTIGATOR: Eric, are you aware of the victim's identity?

THORN: The one at the hotel? No. It was a woman. I never saw her before in my life.

INVESTIGATOR: You didn't meet her in Midland, Texas, when you were there?

THORN: No. Why? Who was it? It wasn't...it wasn't Tessa's mom, was it?

INVESTIGATOR: No, Eric. The woman found dead at the Beverly Hilton was Tessa Hart's former psychotherapist.

THORN: Wait. Dr. Regan?

INVESTIGATOR: Do you have any idea why Laura Regan would be in LA?

THORN: No. That's totally random.

INVESTIGATOR: She was pronounced dead at the scene, and her cell phone was taken into evidence. We found this.

THORN:	W-wait a sec. Let me see that.
INVESTIGATOR:	Let the record show that Mr. Thorn is looking at the home screen of the Twitter account with username @MrsEricThorn. The account was found open on the victim's cell phone.
THORN:	Seriously? Are you telling me that MET was being run by Dr. Regan?
INVESTIGATOR:	You tell me, Eric. Does that scenario sound plausible to you?
THORN:	No. That's completely bizarre.
INVESTIGATOR:	I agree. It seems more likely that the person running the MET account is our murderer. He or she may have logged the victim's phone into Twitter in an attempt to throw off our investigation.
THORN:	It must've been Blair. He's behind it somehow, I'm telling you.
INVESTIGATOR:	Do you have any reason to suspect that Blair Duncan was in communication with Dr. Regan?
THORN:	I don't know. Dr. Regan was with Tessa when Blair went to Midland last December. Maybe the two of them were working together somehow.
INVESTIGATOR:	Blair and Tessa were working together?
THORN:	No! Blair and Dr. Regan.
INVESTIGATOR:	That seems like a stretch, don't you think?

THORN: I don't know. None of this makes sense.

INVESTIGATOR: We have no evidence of any involvement in this case from Blair Duncan.

THORN: I know but—

INVESTIGATOR: Eric, is there any chance that the MET Twitter account could have been run by Tessa?

THORN: No, of course not! That's ridiculous.

INVESTIGATOR: Is it? When you first came into contact with Ms. Hart last year, you met her on Twitter. She was running an Eric Thorn fan account with username @TessaHeartsEric. Isn't that true?

THORN: Exactly. She had a different username. She wasn't running MET.

INVESTIGATOR: It wouldn't be unusual for someone to run more than one account.

THORN: No. Detective, listen to me! You've got it all twisted.

INVESTIGATOR: I know this isn't what you want to hear, Eric. At this point in the investigation, our best guess is that Tessa Hart may have planned the murder and used your rendezvous with MET to frame you for the crime.

THORN: You obviously don't know Tessa. Where is she right now? Did you talk to her?

INVESTIGATOR:	We tried. She left here shortly before we sat down with you. She refused to answer further questions.
THORN:	Good!
INVESTIGATOR:	The fact remains that someone else beat you to the Beverly Hilton last night. Who else other than Tessa could have seen the messages setting up your meeting?
THORN:	I don't know. Maybe…maybe I killed Dr. Regan myself. Did you ever think of that?
INVESTIGATOR:	Is that a confession?
THORN:	No, but it wasn't Tessa, OK? I'm telling you for a fact. I know her.
INVESTIGATOR:	OK, Eric. Let's pull up your Twitter account one more time. I want you to look through and point me to anything here—any tweet or direct message—that could have been sent by someone other than yourself or Tessa Hart. Can you show me a single one?
THORN:	I don't know! Probably not, but that doesn't mean… [pause]
INVESTIGATOR:	Eric?
THORN:	Wait. What is this?
INVESTIGATOR:	What?
THORN:	This message. The top thread.

INVESTIGATOR: Let the record show that Mr. Thorn is indicating a direct message sent today at—

THORN: What time is it right now?

INVESTIGATOR: —from a Twitter account with username @Snowflake734—

THORN: Did you guys send this DM? Who sent this?

INVESTIGATOR: Eric, please take your seat.

THORN: This was twenty minutes ago!

INVESTIGATOR: Let me read the message into the record, please.

THORN: F*** the record! Don't you see? That's me! I'm @Snowflake734! That's my other handle!

INVESTIGATOR: The message states, and I quote—

THORN: You said she left half an hour ago? Did she get into a car with someone?

INVESTIGATOR: Andy, can you go see if anyone out there has a visual on Tessa Hart leaving the station?

THORN: Holy shit! Will you listen to me now? I told you! I told you she was being stalked!

INVESTIGATOR: Eric, we're going to get to the bottom of this. Please calm down.

THORN: You know I didn't send that message. You know! I was sitting here talking to you!

INVESTIGATOR: Who else had access to the account with user-
                  name @Snowflake734?

THORN: No one! I never even sent a tweet from that handle.
                  It's just an empty second account on my phone
                  that I never bothered deleting. Blair must have—

INVESTIGATOR: Hold on, Eric... [unintelligible] Go ahead,
                  Detective. I read you. Copy that. Did they get the
                  plates?

THORN: What? What is he saying?

INVESTIGATOR: Ms. Hart was seen entering an unmarked black
                  Cadillac Escalade outside Los Angeles Police
                  headquarters this afternoon at approximately 3:15
                  p.m. The car proceeded northwest in the direction
                  of the 101 Freeway. A license plate number was
                  not obtained.

17

RADIO SILENCE

TESSA GAZED OUT the rear passenger window as the Escalade weaved in and out of traffic. She wished they would slow down. It was enough to make anyone motion sick, the way they kept switching lanes.

She'd expected to find Eric in the back seat of the car. Her shoulders had slumped with disappointment when she popped the door open and found it empty—except for Clint, waving a friendly salute from the driver's seat.

"Hop in," the driver had said by way of greeting. "We don't have much time."

"Where's Eric?" She'd clicked the door closed behind her as Clint maneuvered the SUV away from the curb. He'd held up one finger, signaling her to wait. Tessa had slipped her phone out of her pocket, but Clint had reached back a hand from the front seat, snapping his fingers to get her attention.

"No phones. We're in damage control mode. Give it to me."

He'd snapped again, and Tessa had handed the phone over. Some instinct warned her not to question. Clint wasn't just a limo driver after all. He was security. Eric's most trusted bodyguard. And Tessa could tell from his clipped tone that he meant business.

She twisted her hands in her lap. She wished Clint would give her some clue what was going on. Where was Eric? Was Clint taking her to him? She looked into the front seat and met the driver's eyes in the rearview mirror. His hands gripped the steering wheel, and his massive biceps flexed inside the sleeves of his black blazer. She could see the seams straining, threatening to burst under the pressure every time he turned the wheel.

She opened her mouth to speak, but Clint cut her off with an infinitesimal shake of his head. He raised one finger to his lips. *Not here*, the gesture said. *No talking. Radio silence.*

Tessa nodded, pressing her lips together. She needed to clear her head and do her relaxation exercises. She turned her attention back to the passing traffic as she counted the breaths inside her head.

The car switched lanes again, and a freeway exit sign flashed overhead:

Exit 29

Mulholland Drive

Tessa let the tension out of her lungs, visualizing it leave her body like a puff of steaming air. She knew that road sign. She'd been this way before. Her suspicions were confirmed as the car wound its way through the twists and turns of the Hollywood Hills, and they pulled into a gated driveway.

Eric's house.

Eric must have DM'ed her from here and sent Clint to fetch her.

Clint pulled the car into the covered carport. He got out and motioned for her to follow. Tessa scampered in his wake up the front walkway. The bodyguard stood inside the door, waiting for her to catch up. "This way," he said in a low voice. "Don't be nervous. Everything's under control."

Tessa crept into the house and let the door swing shut behind her. She heard a muffled voice coming from upstairs somewhere. Was that Eric? He must be up there in the master suite—unless there were other rooms upstairs besides his bedroom. Tessa didn't have the layout of the place committed to memory. She'd only spent a couple nights here this past week.

She stood still for a moment and listened, but his voice was too faint to hear what he was saying.

Was that really Eric? Was he talking to someone, or was he on the phone? His voice sounded funny.

"Go ahead," Clint said, pointing up the staircase.

Tessa nodded. She could feel her adrenal glands kicking in—eliciting their predictable response. Her brain was practically screaming at her: *Danger! Danger! Danger!*

But it wasn't real, Tessa told herself. It wasn't rational. It was a chemical in her brain. She pushed the feeling away.

Eric had DM'ed. He was up there waiting for her. Everything

would be OK once she was with him, once they had a chance to talk. With her boyfriend's arms locked tight around her, the tide of panic would recede as swiftly as it had come.

Upstairs.

He was waiting.

"Right," Tessa whispered to herself. She reached for the bannister and took the steps two at a time.

THE INTERROGATION (FRAGMENT 9)

May 1, 2017, 3:24 p.m.
Case #75932.394.1
OFFICIAL TRANSCRIPTION OF POLICE INTERVIEW

―START PAGE 5―

THORN:	What do you mean a license plate was not obtained? Where did they go? Where did he take her?
INVESTIGATOR:	Eric, I need you to take your seat.
THORN:	No! I'm out of here. I'm going to find Tessa.
INVESTIGATOR:	Our dispatcher has sent out an all-points bulletin. We have two police choppers in the area―
THORN:	Looking for a black Escalade? Do you know how many cars in LA fit that description?
INVESTIGATOR:	Sit down, Eric. The best way to help us find her is by answering my questions.
THORN:	What questions? It's Blair. Blair Duncan! What else can I tell you?
INVESTIGATOR:	If Blair Duncan was behind this as you believe, do you have any idea where he may have taken her?

THORN:	No. I don't know. I can't believe this is happening again. Why would she get in a car with him?
INVESTIGATOR:	Is it possible that she got in the car with someone else?
THORN:	Who else? Who else would pretend to be me? I'm telling you, that's what he did the last time! Blair hacked my second account, and she thought it was me.
INVESTIGATOR:	Hold on… [pause] Roger that. Eric, I'm getting word that a vehicle has been sighted at a private residence in Hollywood. They have reason to believe it's the same car.
THORN:	Well, go get them!
INVESTIGATOR:	Our units are trying to gain access. I'll update you as I hear further information. Eric, please sit down.
THORN:	I'm going. I want to be there!
INVESTIGATOR:	Please, try to remain calm. Let's go over what we know.
THORN:	I'm telling you—
INVESTIGATOR:	We know Laura Regan is dead. We know she arrived in LA yesterday on a flight from Midland International Airport. We can only presume that she thought she was going to that hotel to meet Tessa.
THORN:	I don't think you should assume… Wait. Wait, wait, wait. I just thought of something else.

INVESTIGATOR:	Go ahead.
THORN:	There was a DM. That means my @EricThorn account must have followed @Snowflake734 on Twitter!
INVESTIGATOR:	I'm not sure how that's—
THORN:	Look! Right here. It's the most recent account I followed. Don't you see what that means?
INVESTIGATOR:	Tessa must have been logged in and followed the @Snowflake734 account herself.
THORN:	No way. She would've Snapchatted me. Not Twitter. Blair must've hacked @EricThorn too...
INVESTIGATOR:	Slow down, Eric.
THORN:	Listen, you wanted evidence of someone other than Tessa and me with access to my Twitter. Well, here it is!
INVESTIGATOR:	You think Blair Duncan hacked three different Twitter accounts now?
THORN:	What's the third one?
INVESTIGATOR:	@MrsEricThorn.
THORN:	Oh, right.
INVESTIGATOR:	Eric, let's talk about the MET account.
THORN:	Now? Why? Just focus on Tessa!

INVESTIGATOR: Hear me out. Who else could have been using the MET account to leak material?

THORN: I don't know! I'm sorry, but I honestly don't care right now about leaked photos. Tessa is out there somewhere with some total—

INVESTIGATOR: I understand, but it seems to me the MET account is the key to this whole case, including Tessa's whereabouts right now.

THORN: How do you figure that?

INVESTIGATOR: Whoever runs that account killed Dr. Regan and is attempting to frame Tessa Hart for the crime. It might have worked if you hadn't noticed those direct messages.

THORN: Wait. So you think whoever runs MET just kidnapped Tessa?

INVESTIGATOR: That seems more likely than any other theory. Who else had behind-the-scenes access to you? Maybe someone on your support staff?

THORN: There's a ton of turnover. I don't even know a lot of their names... [pause] Oh, wait a sec. Katrina!

INVESTIGATOR: Go on.

THORN: She's head of wardrobe. She comes to all my gigs. And... [pause]

INVESTIGATOR: Eric?

THORN: She had my phone! Yesterday. I totally spaced.
                    My phone was messing up my costume, so she
                    took it.

INVESTIGATOR: How long did she have your phone in her
                    possession?

THORN: I don't know. She said she'd leave it on my
                    makeup chair. It was there when I finished shoot-
                    ing. I knew that was a bad idea!

INVESTIGATOR: All right, Eric. Do you know where this Katrina…

THORN: Katrina Cortez.

INVESTIGATOR: Any idea where she might be right now? Is she
                    supposed to be on set at your video shoot?

THORN: No, she's off today. Just makeup artists on set. We
                    were scheduled to shoot the nude scene.

INVESTIGATOR: I'll have our officers see if they can locate her.

THORN: Wow. Katrina. She always seemed a little bit…
                    intense.

INVESTIGATOR: Hold that thought. I'm getting word… [pause]

THORN: About Tessa? Did they find her in that car?

INVESTIGATOR: Right. I read you. Copy that. OK, thanks, Nancy.

THORN: What's happening?

INVESTIGATOR: I'm sorry, Eric.

THORN: What do you mean? What did they say?

INVESTIGATOR: They searched the car and the premises. They
                    didn't find anything suspicious.

THORN: But what about Tessa? Was she there?

INVESTIGATOR: No, they had the wrong car. They're fanning out
                    now to cover a wider search area.

THORN: You mean you know nothing. You guys have
                    absolutely no idea who she's with or where she is.

18

FALSE EVIDENCE

TESSA ROUNDED THE corner into Eric's bedroom, and she froze. It wasn't Eric's face that greeted her.

"OK, gotta go… I'll see you tomorrow."

The words were spoken into a cell phone held by a pair of hands clad in blue latex gloves. They were the same kind her mother had used for the blood draw in Tessa's dream yesterday. Maybe that was why she felt like she'd stepped into a nightmare. She'd already been hovering on the brink of panic, and the sight of those gloves sent her heart rate skyrocketing.

The questions whirled through her mind in time with her rushing pulse. *Why gloves? Why now? Why here?*

"You?" she asked. "What are you doing here?" Her voice sounded far away, like it hadn't come from her own throat. Try as she might, Tessa couldn't tear her eyes away from those gloves. The latex stretched and gathered as they moved. "Where's Eric?"

"You don't know?"

"I thought he was here. He DM'ed me."

"No he didn't."

"Well, somebody DM'ed me from—"

The left glove gestured abruptly, cutting her off in midsentence.

"That wasn't Eric?" Tessa stammered. "That was you? B-but how do you even know about that username?"

"Trust me, I know."

Tessa's eyes dropped to the floor, and her forehead crinkled. *What were those?* Her mom hadn't worn those in her dream, although Tessa had seen them once or twice at the hospital where her mother worked. The surgical nurses wore them in the operating rooms—those light-blue, puffy booties that went over their shoes. *What were those doing here?*

The booties whooshed across the bedroom carpeting, nearly silent. Tessa followed in their wake.

"You two really floor me sometimes. How do I know? I see everything, Tessa. I've been watching from the beginning. Every single word."

Tessa stutter-stepped. She wrapped her arms around herself as a tremor swept through her frame. She didn't like this conversation. She should leave. She needed to find Eric...or at least find Clint. Had he left? Or was he still downstairs?

Tessa didn't dare attempt the staircase. The curtain of panic enveloped her, and she didn't trust herself to navigate the house. She was moving through a thick, black fog, blind to her surroundings—and through it all, the only things she could see were those pale-blue hands and feet.

The feet swished to the far side of the room. The hands picked up a remote control that rested on the bedside table. The dark fog swirled and eddied around her as the window blinds shuddered closed, casting the bedroom deeper into shadow.

"Hit the light switch, would you?"

Tessa didn't move. Were those gloves really there, or was she hallucinating? "Why are you wearing those?" she asked.

"Fingerprints." The remote control thudded back down onto the nightstand. "Listen, sweet pea. I'd love to stand around and chat, but we don't have time. Are you gonna help me out here or not?"

Sweet pea? Did she hear that right? Eric hadn't called her by that nickname in ages. He'd mainly used it over DM, before she knew he was Eric Thorn... Back when the mystery boy on the other end of the messages was named Taylor, with the handle @EricThornSucks.

No one else knew about that name. Not unless...

"Sweet pea," the voice repeated, laughing through the words. "Bunny slippers...rabbit's feet... You two crack me up sometimes. Don't look so surprised, Tessa! You know there's no such thing as cybersecurity."

"Oh my God," she whispered.

"Relax. I'm here to help." A rubber-covered index finger pointed again toward the light switch. This time Tessa obeyed. She turned and flicked the switch, half listening to the voice that spoke behind her. "We need to get a few things cleaned up before the cops search the place. Which side of the bed do you sleep on when you're here?"

Tessa ducked her chin. She stared at the feet, and then back up at the rubber gloves. The hands were close enough to touch her. Blue latex rested on her shoulder, and Tessa registered surprise at the heaviness of the hand inside.

Tessa closed her eyes. The room was spinning. She needed to breathe, but she'd forgotten how to make her lungs operate. "Should I have gloves on too?"

"Nah, everybody knows about you and Eric. The police will expect to find your fingerprints all over the place."

The booties padded across the bedroom carpeting again, back toward the center of the room.

Fingerprints, Tessa thought. *Why were they cleaning up fingerprints?* None of it made sense.

Tessa inhaled as deeply as she could, grateful for the influx of oxygen. She knew she was having a panic episode. That was why her senses weren't working properly, why her thoughts came slow and distorted, like they'd been filtered through molasses. Molasses up to her neck, too deep to escape, even with all her breathing tricks and mindfulness techniques.

She needed to take her meds.

But she couldn't…for some reason. Some reason she couldn't quite remember…

"This side?" A bedside drawer slid open, empty inside. "You don't keep anything here? Toiletries or anything?"

Tessa shook her head.

The feet moved again, padding through a doorway to the over-size master bath. "What about in here? Toothbrush? Makeup?"

Tessa followed. It was brighter in the bathroom. She could see a little more. She stood on the bath mat in the middle of the room and looked up, meeting that familiar pair of eyes in the mirror above the sink. Narrowed eyes. Grim mouth. Then the reflection disappeared as the mirrored door of the medicine cabinet swung open.

I do keep something here, Tessa thought. She could have cried with relief. Her last few precious doses of Ativan. They were there. In that cabinet. In the little pill bottle she'd left behind the last time she was here. *Thank God.*

Tessa opened her mouth to speak, but she was interrupted before she could get a word out. She turned her head at the sound of footsteps creeping up the stairs behind her.

⇄

Eric stood in the windowless police interrogation room, pacing back and forth beneath the flickering fluorescent lights. The lead detective sat on the other side of the table, but Eric had long since abandoned his own molded plastic chair. He couldn't sit still. Not now. Not while Tessa was still out there somewhere.

With Blair?

Or with Katrina?

Eric glanced toward the policeman, hunched over the interrogation table. Detective Tyrone Stevens spoke in low tones into a beige multiline phone that looked at least thirty years out of date. He had his face lowered, and Eric stared at the top of his clean-shaven head, glistening in the harsh light. At least he seemed to know what he was doing. The middle-aged black man projected an air of calm authority in his crisp, white dress shirt and blue tie.

The other one, his partner, had left the room earlier and hadn't returned.

Had they found something? Eric wished the detective would put the phone on speaker mode. Eric needed to know…something. Anything. He couldn't take the tension that made his fists clench and unclench. A part of him wanted to bolt for the door and head out on his own, but he fought the impulse. He'd be useless to Tessa out there. He didn't have the slightest clue where Katrina would have taken her—or why.

And if Blair was the one who'd taken her, then it might already be too late…

Eric's knees gave way. He clattered back down into his chair, resting his head against his fists. His cell phone lay facedown on the interrogation table in its sleek metal case, and Eric picked it up.

It seemed better than doing nothing. If Tessa had her phone, maybe she would try to get word to him. He opened Twitter, but his face fell. No little blue flag. No new DMs. Not even an outgoing tweet from his account in the past twenty-four hours.

Eric drummed his fingers on the table. His mind kept darting from one thought to the next. He was still reeling from the theory that he and Detective Stevens had worked out.

Katrina? Running the MET account? Catfishing him and everybody in his fandom, all this time... It made sense in a weird way. He always had the feeling that Katrina got off on torturing him. Maybe when she grew tired of needling him with sewing implements, she turned to tweets and leaked images instead.

Could that be true?

Eric pulled up the account on his screen.

MET @MrsEricThorn

FOLLOWING	FOLLOWERS
78	**1.1M**

His eyes skimmed down the recent activity. MET tweeted all day long, every single day. How could Katrina keep up that pace? She'd have to be on her phone constantly. Not to mention the tone. If this wasn't the work of a teenage fangirl, then it was a pitch-perfect imitation. Look at the last thing she'd tweeted yesterday.

MET @MrsEricThorn • 1d

Not to be overdramatic but if Eric doesn't leak us something from the #pistolvideo, I

may commit a felony #justkidding #notreally
#ericthornobsessed

She'd illustrated it with one of her disturbing Photoshop
edits. Eric vaguely recognized the image from an underwear
campaign he did a couple years back—shirtless, with the
waistband of his tighty-whities peeking out from his low-rider
jeans. But MET had embellished it slightly. She'd added a giant
target, tattooed on his back.

Eric shuddered. He swept his finger upward, and the tweets
whizzed by in a blur, like the spinning dial of a slot machine.
They came to a stop at random, and he drew in his breath
between his teeth.

MET @MrsEricThorn • 3/03/17

Awwwww, what's the matter baby??? Don't
you love us anymore? 😭 #WeLoveYouEric

pic.twitter.com/r59Edy2k

He'd seen that tweet before.

Eric's thumb made contact with the picture, but he already
knew what he would see: a candid shot, going over choreography with his backup dancers…with two hastily sketched trails
of tears running down his cheeks.

He'd been in his dressing room at the YouTube Awards, face-
to-face with Tessa. Eric closed his eyes as he pictured it. Maury

had shut the door and locked it…seconds after Katrina hurried out. She'd been altering his pants. Jutting pins within millimeters of his crotch.

Could she have lurked outside in the corridor? Eavesdropped on their whole conversation?

She'd only been gone a moment before Maury had interrupted Eric and held up this tweet.

"*There's already a meme circulating.*"

Eric's face darkened. Katrina must've heard them talking. She must've composed that tweet herself, right under their noses. Did she think it was funny, seeing him squirm? The sheer betrayal made his hands shake. Eric dropped the phone, and the metal case clanged against the tabletop.

The detective looked up.

"What's going on?" Eric demanded, raking his fingers through his hair. He needed information. Now. "Did they find the right car this time? Did they find Tessa?"

"Not yet. They're still searching."

Eric's chest tightened as he tried to read the policeman's face. It wasn't good. He could tell that much.

Detective Stevens hit a button and replaced the phone receiver in its cradle. "Eric, can we resume our interview? There are a few more details I need you to go over."

"What?" Eric asked. "What else?"

"You told me that Tessa used to take a medication for anxiety."

"What about it?"

"Eric, I need you to remember the name of the medication. For the record. It's important."

Eric tipped his head back and looked up at the ceiling, trying to picture the little orange bottle. He'd noticed it this morning when he was brushing his teeth. Tessa must have left it in his medicine cabinet. He'd taken that as a good sign. A sign that she wasn't leaving him. A sign that she was coming back...

"Eric?" the detective prompted.

"I don't know," he said. "I think it might have started with an *A*."

"Ativan?"

"Maybe." Eric nodded. "I think so. That sounds right."

The detective jotted a note. "Did you ever see any other prescription medication in Tessa Hart's possession other than Ativan?"

With her heart thudding, Tessa turned. She saw Clint, clad in a matching set of gloves and surgical booties, with his arms folded at his chest. His hulking frame filled the bathroom door behind her.

Tessa shook the tension out of her arms. She'd forgotten about the bodyguard downstairs. *See? No reason to be scared.* If Clint was here, it had to be all right. Eric trusted Clint with his life... And Eric didn't bestow his trust easily.

The bodyguard looked past her to the figure at the sink. "Picking up some cross talk on the police scanner."

"And?"

"They're searching the area. Sounds like they're focused on another vehicle over on Mulholland at the moment."

"Good. You pulled into the carport?"

"Done. It's out of sight."

Tessa's eyes narrowed slightly as she struggled to make sense of their conversation. A vehicle? Why were the police looking for a vehicle?

"You ready for me in here yet?" Clint took a step forward into the bathroom, cracking his knuckles inside his surgical gloves. Tessa inched sideways, suddenly claustrophobic. All the air had gone out of the room as Clint filled up the space.

"Almost ready. Give me another minute."

"Almost ready for what?" Tessa asked. "What's going on?" Her voice sounded small, and she wrapped her arms around herself. The room had started reeling side to side. She could feel her legs go numb, and she prayed she wouldn't fall as her thoughts careened around her in helpless disarray.

Evidence... The police... The police were coming to search this house... Eric's house...

Tessa tasted blood inside her mouth. She must have bit her tongue, but she didn't feel the pain—only a stabbing sensation beneath her rib cage as the realization hit her.

Eric.

Eric hadn't sent her that DM. Where was he? Why wasn't he here?

Tessa swayed slightly as a sick feeling washed through her.

She looked down at the bathroom's cold, hard marble floor. She needed her meds. Now. Before she blacked out and cracked her skull open.

"Is that my bottle?" Tessa reached toward the figure at the medicine cabinet. "Are those my pills?"

"These?"

A gloved hand materialized in the center of her field of vision. It held an orange prescription pill bottle. Tessa took it, turning it between her fingers to read the label.

Rx# 4109568

HART, TESSA
**TAKE 1–2 TABLET(S) BY MOUTH AS
NECESSARY**
ATIVAN
Dr. Regan, Laura L.

Relief coursed through her. Tessa twisted the cap and slipped two pills beneath her tongue, waiting for them to dissolve. *Strange*, she thought. *They tasted different somehow…*

But then again, she hadn't taken a dose in weeks. Her bare index finger grazed against the rubber of the gloves as she handed the bottle back.

"Eric, this is important. I need you to think back. Did you ever see Tessa with a drug called phenobarbital?"

Eric stared. The detective spoke resolutely, in spite of the tense situation. How could he be so calm? And why did he keep asking about Tessa's medication of all things? Ativan…phenobarbital…

Who cared?

"How should I know?" Eric snapped. "Honestly, what difference does it make? She's out there! She's in trouble! Stop talking about her meds and go find her!"

Detective Stevens raised his palm. "I understand your frustration. Our officers are chasing down multiple leads."

"What leads? Will you please tell me what's going on?"

"Tell me what you know about Tessa and her therapist, Dr. Regan."

Eric's fingers twitched. He lowered his hands to his chair and wedged them beneath his thighs, fighting the urge to reach out and shake the detective by his shirt collar.

"Eric? To your knowledge, have they been in communication recently?"

"No. Not since Tessa left Texas."

"And you yourself never had any contact with Dr. Regan before you found her in the hotel room?"

Eric shook his head. "I only heard about her from Tessa."

Detective Stevens raised an eyebrow. "You didn't meet Dr. Regan when you were in Midland last December?"

"That's what I just said!"

Eric couldn't sit still any longer. The chair legs screeched against the floor as he pushed himself away from the table. He stood and resumed pacing back and forth across the room. He barely registered the detective's next question, addressed to his turned back.

"Who else was with you last December in Midland, Texas? Katrina Cortez?"

Tessa could already feel the medicine taking effect, like a blanket wrapping itself around her shoulders. Warm and safe.

Something was different though. She couldn't quite put her finger on it. The blanket felt…heavier somehow…

Tessa sighed. She needed to lie down. Her meds always made her sleepy, but it didn't usually hit her quite this fast.

"Wait a minute," she said slowly. "Can I see that again?"

The pills rattled inside the orange plastic cylinder shoved in her direction. Tessa's mouth scrunched to the side as she gripped the little bottle between her fingers. She felt like she was moving in slow motion, but at least her thoughts had slowed their chaotic swirling.

She could focus.

She could see.

She could think.

Her eyes fell once again to the medication label, but something was off. She'd misread it in her panic. *There was a word for that*, she thought. *Priming*. Her brain had filled in the drug name she expected to find on a pill bottle—not the one she saw clearly now, spelled out in bold black lettering.

Rx# 4109569

HART, TESSA
**TAKE 1–2 TABLET(S) BY MOUTH AS
NECESSARY**
PHENOBARBITAL
Dr. Regan, Laura L.

Tessa's mouth gaped open. Her knees wobbled, threatening to give way. She met eyes once more with the face in the mirror, laughing as he stripped the pill bottle from her hand.

"You don't look so good, kiddo. Maybe you should rest."

He pointed through the doorway toward Eric's big four-poster bed. Before Tessa could utter a sound, she felt Clint's arm go around her shoulders and his heavy palm clamp over her mouth.

THE INTERROGATION
(FRAGMENT 10)

May 1, 2017, 3:24 p.m.
Case #75932.394.1
OFFICIAL TRANSCRIPTION OF POLICE INTERVIEW

—START PAGE 7—

INVESTIGATOR: Who else was with you last December in Midland, Texas? Katrina Cortez?

THORN: No, only Maury and I went to Midland. Everyone else went straight to the next tour stop in Santa Fe.

INVESTIGATOR: Maury Gilroy?

THORN: Sure. He's my manager. He goes everywhere I go. I can't even take a crap without Maury knowing about it.

INVESTIGATOR: But he didn't know your whereabouts during your time in Mexico. Correct?

THORN: No, but he tracked me down.

INVESTIGATOR: How much access does Mr. Gilroy have to your private hotel rooms?

THORN: I mean, we don't share bunk beds or anything. It's not like that.

INVESTIGATOR: Does he have copies of your hotel key cards?

THORN:	My bodyguard keeps those. But I guess Maury's walked in on me before when I overslept…
INVESTIGATOR:	Your bodyguard let him into the room?
THORN:	I suppose… Wait. Your phone is blinking.
INVESTIGATOR:	Hold on.
THORN:	Please concentrate on finding her.
INVESTIGATOR:	I see. Can you repeat that, please? Copy that. Which border point? Tijuana?
THORN:	What? What are they saying?
INVESTIGATOR:	Just a moment, Eric. Sorry, Nancy, come again?
THORN:	What's going on? [pause] What? Tell me!
INVESTIGATOR:	As I said, we have officers following up on multiple leads.
THORN:	Who's in Tijuana? Katrina?
INVESTIGATOR:	Officers successfully located Ms. Cortez at her residence in Oakwood. They're questioning her now.
THORN:	So she's not with Tessa? But… No! That means it's Blair!
INVESTIGATOR:	Try to stay calm. I know it's hard. One of our choppers spotted a different black Escalade proceeding

toward the Mexican border at high speed. We're having the car stopped and searched by immigration. We should get word in a few minutes if it's the vehicle we're looking for.

THORN: Blair's taking her to Mexico?

INVESTIGATOR: Eric, what can you tell me about Tessa's relationship with Mr. Gilroy?

THORN: With Maury? Why?

INVESTIGATOR: It's important. I need you to bear with me.

THORN: I mean, Maury is her boss. They butt heads sometimes. Like, this one time she was supposed to tweet something, and she added the wrong emoji. Maury flipped out.

INVESTIGATOR: Because of an emoji?

THORN: Yeah, and then MET spread it before Tessa had time to delete it. I just had that tweet on my phone. Here. This one.

INVESTIGATOR: You and Tessa were together when this was tweeted?

THORN: Right. We were talking. I was hugging her. So there's no way she could be MET. See! She didn't even have her phone when this was tweeted. Maury took it.

INVESTIGATOR: Maury was with you as well?

THORN: Right. Tessa and I were talking, and Maury was
                  in the room. He was doing something on his...
                  [pause]

INVESTIGATOR: Go on, Eric.

THORN: No.

INVESTIGATOR: Finish your thought. What was Maury doing?

THORN: He was doing something on his phone. And then
                  he interrupted us, and showed us this brand-new
                  tweet from MET.

INVESTIGATOR: You didn't see what he was doing on his phone?

THORN: Oh my God. I'm such an idiot.

INVESTIGATOR: Eric?

THORN: That whole time... He did it right in front of my
                  face. How could I not see it?

INVESTIGATOR: How could you not see what, Eric?

THORN: MET! MET's been fangirling over me since my
                  YouTuber days. Before I had a record deal. Before
                  Clint. Before Katrina. Before everyone on my
                  crew...except for him.

19

HIM

"PUT HER ON the bed, Clint. Tie her wrists."

Maury leaned against the windowsill in Eric's master bedroom, with his hands in his trouser pockets. He looked down at his watch. "Don't scream, or he'll gag you."

Tessa let out a muffled yelp as the bodyguard yanked her arms behind her back. She didn't resist his movements, too stunned to put up a struggle. Clint used a plastic zip tie to secure her wrists to the bedpost.

He had one beefy hand pressed over her mouth, cutting off all oxygen. She needed to take a deep breath. The edges of her vision were clouding over again, in spite of the medication. Tessa sank back against the headboard and let her body go limp.

"Good girl," Maury said.

Clint let go of her mouth, and Tessa gasped for air. For a moment, she closed her eyes, concentrating on her breathing.

Deep breaths. In and out. Eric one…Eric two…Eric… What came after two?

She couldn't go back into panic mode. She needed to keep her senses intact. Tessa sucked in a lungful of air and held it. Her eyes reopened, but she didn't speak. She looked from Maury to Clint and back again, searching frantically for answers.

Maury must have sensed her confusion. He stood up from the windowsill and gave an exaggerated shrug. "Someone has to take the fall, Tessa. A woman is dead. The police need to pin that on someone."

Tessa blew out the air she'd been holding, along with a hoarse response. "I had nothing to do with it."

Maury nodded. "True, but it's either you or Eric. I've worked too long to let him go down over some trumped-up murder wrap."

"But—" Tessa broke off. Her mind was spiraling again. *Eric hadn't really killed someone. Had he?* "No!" she exclaimed. "Eric couldn't. Maybe he was sleeping with Katrina, but he would never—"

"Katrina?" Maury gave her a funny look. His eyes flicked over to Clint.

"I don't think she knows, boss."

"The police didn't tell her?"

Tessa blinked rapidly, struggling to keep up. "Katrina Cortez," she said. "There was something going on between her and Eric."

Maury tilted back his head and let out a peal of laughter. "Katrina Cortez from wardrobe?"

He looked at Clint. The bodyguard's shoulders were shaking. "Got ourselves a real criminal mastermind here."

"Tessa, dear." Maury grinned broadly, baring his teeth. "Katrina Cortez is not sleeping with Eric. Trust me. She lives over by Venice Beach with her lovely wife and two kids."

Wife?

"Wait. She's… But…she isn't dead?"

Maury snorted. "Where do you come up with this stuff?"

"The police said it was a woman!" Tessa protested. "Eric went to the hotel to meet a woman."

"I think the cops were having a little fun with you, kid." Clint snickered as Maury went on. "Let me spell it out. The woman Eric found in the hotel was a good friend of yours. You remember dear old Dr. Regan."

Tessa froze. *Had she heard that right? How would Maury even know about…*

Maury took a step toward the bed. "I flew her out here. First class too. Out of my own pocket." He turned to address Clint. "Never tell me I'm not generous. Generous to a fault, if you're loyal to me. Isn't that right, Clint?"

"More than generous."

Clint smirked, and Maury turned his poisonous smile on Tessa's face. "Thank you. Glad *somebody* around here appreciates it."

Tessa gulped for air. The blackness at the edges of her vision had receded, but her mind still scrambled to make sense of Maury's words. "But why…" she stammered. "Why would you fly Dr. Regan to LA?"

"To see you, obviously."

"But—"

"Let's just say Clint and I were concerned about the state of your mental health."

Tessa shot a glance at the bodyguard. Clint had seen her succumb to a panic attack at the award show, but surely that wasn't what Maury meant…

Clint winked at her playfully, and Tessa's tongue went thick inside her mouth. She couldn't seem to form the questions into a coherent sentence.

"But…but… Then why… How…"

Maury finished for her. "How did the good doctor wind up dead?"

Tessa nodded mutely, unable to summon a response. Her brain, so used to fight-or-flight mode, couldn't control the racing thoughts now that she found herself in actual danger.

She could tell from the way Maury and Clint bantered that they felt absolutely zero guilt. All that laughter covered up a total lack of human emotion underneath. Her stomach rolled. She turned her head, afraid she might throw up, and her hair covered her face.

Maury shrugged. "It's too bad. That wasn't supposed to happen. She'd still be alive if she didn't have such a stick up her ass." He tugged on one of his latex gloves, pulling the rubber tight. "What can I say, Tessa? I'm the cleanup crew. Sometimes I gotta get my hands dirty."

Tessa didn't understand. She tossed her head to get the hair out of her eyes. Maury approached the edge of the bed, observing her, with his thumbs tucked into the vest of his pin-striped suit. "You mean…" she whispered. "You? You killed her? It was you?"

Maury's smile faded. He glared at her down the bridge of his nose. "See, that's the difference between you and me, Tessa."

"What is? That you're a murderer?"

"No. The difference is that you, my dear, are expendable." As he spoke, he shifted position, settling his weight beside her legs on the edge of the mattress. "Eric doesn't need you. He can always get another girl. I'm the one he can't live without. He may not even realize it himself, but I'm the most important person in his life."

It didn't make sense. Tessa couldn't keep up with Maury's logic. The look on his face seemed so unlike him. Not the usual Maury with his jolly mask—having fun, cracking jokes.

Hatred, Tessa realized. That's what she saw when she looked at him. The pure and simple wish that she would disappear.

She'd watched that expression cross Maury's face once before. That day in Eric's dressing room… She'd expected Maury to start guffawing about Emoji-Gate. Instead, for one fleeting moment, she'd seen that same ugly sneer twist his mouth.

Was that the real Maury?

A cold terror swept through her. Tessa kicked her legs, but

Maury saw it coming. His hand darted out and grabbed her shin before she could make contact. He cocked his head at Clint, and the bodyguard secured another zip tie around her ankles.

"Not nice, Tessa." Maury clicked his tongue. "And not necessary. Be a good girl, please."

Tessa's gaze flitted around the room. It was sparely furnished, aside from the massive California king-size bed. Eric didn't spend a lot of time here, and it showed. The bedside tables were mostly empty, aside from the large remote that controlled the blinds and the entertainment center. The walls were just as bare. No artwork. Only the wall-mounted flat-screen TV that faced the bed, with a little red light flashing on and off by the power button.

Tessa's wrists strained behind her. She could feel the pins and needles in her hands as the plastic cut off her circulation. There was no way she could slip free. Her only hope was to signal for help somehow…

But how? She didn't have her phone. Clint had confiscated it in the car on the way over. There was no way she could've placed a call anyway…and no way anyone would hear her if she screamed.

Maury ranted on, but she barely comprehended the words. The sound of his voice went fuzzy, drowned out by the rising volume of her own panicked breathing.

"…Eric Thorn wouldn't even *exist* without me. That's what you kids don't seem to understand. I made him. I spent four years manufacturing him out of thin air…"

Tessa shot a look toward the large picture window, but she knew it was pointless. She wouldn't be able to signal to a neighbor, even if they hadn't shut the blinds. This room was designed for privacy and security. No sight lines for paparazzi to capture clandestine pictures of Eric while he slept. The window faced out above a steep overlook with a multimillion-dollar view of the Hollywood Hills. The next house was set far down the slope below, with only its red roof tiles visible.

"You know what he was before I found him?" Maury's voice dropped lower. He brought his face close enough that Tessa could smell his breath. Minty, but with a hint of something rotten underneath. "A pencil-necked little pipsqueak with a guitar…"

Tessa blinked. Behind Maury's hectoring voice, her ears had registered another sound. She wasn't imagining that, was she? That gentle *swoop-swoop-swoop* of a helicopter, growing stronger by the second.

Was that the police? Searching?

Maury and Clint had said something earlier… The police were looking for a car. Maybe they knew she was in trouble. Maybe they were out there looking for her now.

Tessa sat up straighter, concentrating on the sound. She couldn't give in to the suffocating fear. She'd been in this situation before, and she'd gotten herself out of it. *You can do it again*, Tessa told herself. When push came to shove, she was strong. And she was smart—a hell of a lot smarter than Maury realized.

She needed a plan. Her best option right now was to play for time. Keep him talking…

And pray the police arrived before he grew tired of the sound of his own voice.

Tessa forced herself to focus on Maury's face. "…and I took him into my hands, and I molded, and I polished, and I made him into a star. *I* did that. Not Eric. And definitely not some fangirl he picked up over Twitter."

"But I'm not just some fangirl," she replied, striving to keep her voice calm. "Eric loves me. He'll kill you when he finds out about this."

Maury leaned closer, bringing their faces level. They were eye to eye, and Tessa steeled herself to meet his withering glare. "You know, we could've been friends," he said softly. "We could've gotten along dandy. But you just couldn't share."

"I've done everything you asked of me," she whispered.

He poked her in the shoulder, hard enough to make her flinch. "You wanted him all to yourself. The minute you got your hooks into him, all of a sudden he's lying to me. Making fake accounts. Running away… You're the one who put that garbage in his head. After all the time I invested—"

"I'll share!" Tessa cut in. "I promise. I'll go back to Texas. I'll do whatever you want!"

Maury's face went rigid. The mattress groaned as he stood and turned his back. "Clint? Do something, would you? She's giving me a headache."

"Got it, boss."

The bodyguard stood in the threshold between the bedroom and master bath. For a moment, he disappeared into the bathroom. Then he reemerged with a roll of duct tape in his hands.

Tessa sucked in her lips, and her teeth clamped down involuntarily. *Not duct tape. Not again.* If they gagged her… If she couldn't even speak…

Then she'd be completely helpless.

The tape rasped as Clint unrolled it and grinned across the bed at Maury. Tessa couldn't believe how badly she'd misjudged him. At the award show in March, she'd felt reassured by Clint's hulking presence. Eric had ordered him to watch over her. Eric trusted him. But now Tessa saw her mistake. Clint didn't take orders from Eric. He belonged to Maury. His loyalty had been bought and paid for long ago.

The sound of the chopper intensified, filling Tessa's ears. They were so close… And yet, Tessa had the sinking feeling that they wouldn't get to her in time. She was out of allies. Out of stalling tactics. She only had one move left to her as Clint lumbered toward the bed.

Tessa squeezed her eyes shut and opened her mouth to scream.

THE INTERROGATION (FRAGMENT 11)

May 1, 2017, 3:24 p.m.
Case #75932.394.1
OFFICIAL TRANSCRIPTION OF POLICE INTERVIEW

—START PAGE 8—

THORN: Wait a minute. I know where they're headed!

INVESTIGATOR: Eric?

THORN: Tijuana! We were there in-in-in…February! That place on the beach. Maury was there too. That's got to be it!

INVESTIGATOR: Eric, take your seat, please.

THORN: It was called the-the Playa…Playa something or other. Crap! I forget. I can't think!

INVESTIGATOR: Easy now. Take a breath.

THORN: It's on my phone. Hold on. Dorian Snapchatted it to me!

INVESTIGATOR: I'm not sure it's relevant. We've stopped the car at the border.

THORN: Wait. What the… Where is it? His Snapchat. It's gone.

INVESTIGATOR: Snapchat conversations are automatically deleted.

THORN: No, the whole account is gone. Show you the door... [pause] That's so weird. Do you think he deleted his account? Before he went to jail?

INVESTIGATOR: Who went to jail? Are we talking about Blair Duncan again?

THORN: No! Dorian! Dorian Cromwell!

INVESTIGATOR: Dorian Cromwell from the boy band? What does he have to do with—

THORN: Listen to me! I'm telling you, it's connected. Somehow. Tijuana. Dorian. There's some kind of conspiracy.

INVESTIGATOR: Eric—

THORN: I know I sound paranoid. Just hear me out! Dorian was trying to warn me. About something. Some conspiracy. Something big. He said it went too high up to tell me over cell phones. He was supposed to come meet me in Tijuana, but then... [pause] Where is it? Do I have the username wrong?

INVESTIGATOR: ShowYouTheDor is a Snapchat username?

THORN: Yes! Dorian's private account. Where's the Snapcode? I thought I saved it to my camera roll.

INVESTIGATOR: When did this exchange take place?

THORN: I don't know. It was right after Dorian gave that

press conference. He asked me to get in touch. And then I went on Twitter. And someone... someone tweeted...

INVESTIGATOR: Eric?

THORN: Oh my God.

INVESTIGATOR: Eric, what is it?

THORN: That's how he found us. He must have been watching the press conference!

INVESTIGATOR: Slow down, son. Who found you?

THORN: All that stuff about Horian Cromuelson... Of course that wasn't real. That whole conversation was ridiculous. It was just him cracking jokes!

INVESTIGATOR: You lost me. Who is Horian Cromuelson?

THORN: It's a ship name. The Fourth Dimension fandom... Never mind. The point is the account that tweeted his Snapcode to me. I just remembered who it was.

INVESTIGATOR: Let me guess.

THORN: He catfished me. I never even talked to Dorian. It was Maury the whole time.

INVESTIGATOR: Eric, the account that tweeted you the Snapcode. Was it @MrsEricThorn?

REMOTE CONTROL

TESSA'S JAW POPPED as she strained against the duct tape seal. She clamped her eyes closed, concentrating on keeping the nausea at bay.

At least that dose of phenobarbital had a dampening effect on her morning sickness. She didn't think she would throw up. Tessa didn't know what the drug might do to an unborn baby, but she couldn't think about that now.

Later. After she got out of this...

If she got out of this...

She could hear the laughter in Maury's voice. "You think Eric's going to save you? Eric's a puppet. Talented kid, but not so gifted in the brain department."

The queasiness passed. Tessa opened her eyes. Maury had picked up the remote control and aimed it at the big-screen TV.

"I know all his buttons." He pressed down with his thumb. The little light on the TV stopped flashing and turned solid red. "It's a pretty neat trick," Maury went on. "Just keep plant-ing some new paranoia in his head. I've been doing it for years. Years! You know what I'm talking about, Clint."

Tessa darted a look at the bodyguard. His face was serious, but she could see his mouth quivering. "The best was that time we snuck the girl onstage at his show." Clint pitched forward and slapped his knee.

Maury chuckled. "Seattle? With the fake knife?"

"Oh man! You got him good with that one, Maury."

"One of my finer moments, I'll admit." Maury snapped his fingers. "Every news station picked that story up. PR gold mine!"

Tessa felt her nostrils flare. Did she understand that right? Maury plowed on before she could stop to think.

"Listen, Tessa. I tried my best with you. I would've made you Twitter-famous, if you'd gotten with the program. But it was never enough. You wanted him all to yourself. First, with all that EricThornSucks nonsense." He let out a loud sniff. "You think I didn't know about that? You think I don't monitor every single word that passes through Eric's phone?"

Tessa blinked. *Eric's phone…monitored…*

"I should have nipped it in the bud," Maury continued. "I let that go on way too long. I even let you two have your little fling in Mexico. And you still weren't satisfied!"

"Selfish," Clint contributed.

Maury nodded in agreement. "That's what it is. Selfish. Eric has 35 million Twitter followers. I can't allow him to waste every waking moment on one."

"Boss, clock's ticking."

"OK, Tessa," Maury said. "Time's up."

He fished for something in his pocket. Tessa heard the familiar rattle as he pulled the object free.

A pill bottle.

Eric stood over the interrogation table with his weight balanced on his fists. He looked down, watching in silence as his knuckles turned milky white.

Detective Stevens held Eric's phone. He slid it back across the table as he spoke in a low tone. Eric didn't hear the detective's question. He could only hear the crash of his own pulse reverberating inside his skull.

Maury…

Eric hadn't fully trusted Maury for a while now, but he'd obviously underestimated his manager's capacity for deceit.

A white-hot rage flashed through him. Eric sank down in his seat. The detective was saying something else, but Eric merely shook his head. His T-shirt clung to his chest, damp with perspiration, like it did after one of his marathon workouts with his trainer.

Maury… Was Maury behind the workouts too? Three hours a day of cardio and weights? His manager always blamed the record label, and Eric hadn't questioned it. But could he trust anything that Maury ever told him?

The door of the interrogation room flung open, interrupting Eric's thoughts. He looked up to see the second police detective entering the room. The man placed a beat-up black laptop computer on the table. Detective Morales. His ID badge dangled, glinting in the light, as he bent to mutter something in his partner's ear.

"What is it?" Eric asked. His voice sounded strange somehow. Muffled. Disembodied. Like time itself had slowed to a standstill, and he was watching this whole scene unfold from somewhere far away.

Eric remembered that sensation. He'd felt it once before. That time in Seattle… The concert when that girl jumped him onstage, and he felt nothing but disorienting numbness as his worst fear in the universe came true.

He snapped his head back and forth to clear his mind. *Wake up*, he chided himself. He pounded both his fists against the table.

"What is it?" he demanded when the detectives looked up at him. "Tell me!"

Detective Morales spun the laptop around. "We just saw this. Dispatch picked it up."

Eric squinted at the screen. It took him a moment to register what he was seeing. He normally used Twitter on a cell phone. He could count on one hand the number of times he'd logged in over a computer.

LAPD Communications @911LAPD

The Official Twitter feed of Communications

Division of the Los Angeles Police
Department. This is not monitored 24/7. If
you have an emergency dial 911.

FOLLOWING   FOLLOWERS
235   **53.7K**

Eric groaned. "Not another Twitter account. Please, for the love of God…"

He pushed the laptop away, but Detective Stevens stopped him. "Eric, if you want to help find Tessa, then you need to take a look."

"Why?" Eric shook his head dully. "What is this? You can *tweet* 911 now?"

"It's not monitored like the phone lines," Morales told him. "But yes, we do occasionally receive tips—"

"Wait, did you get something?" Eric interrupted. "About Tessa? Was it from @MrsEricThorn?"

He slid into his seat as the detective clicked a link. "No," Morales said. "Different account. It's been tweeting at us for the past half hour. Do you recognize this handle?"

Eric's eyes followed the cursor to the account name on the screen. His heart stopped beating for a moment as his mind flew backward. Back to the beginning. Back to the day he'd sealed his fate—and Tessa's too—clicking through the prompts to create a new account.

Name:

Username:

Password:

Eric clapped his hand over his mouth. The sound of the policeman's voice faded from his ears. His mind ceased functioning completely, and only a single thought remained, filtering through the haze:

This must be how it feels to die and then come face-to-face with your own ghost.

Detective Stevens narrated into the recorder in his slow, steady baritone. "Let the record show that we're looking at a series of tweets directed at @911LAPD. The tweets originated from a Twitter user listed under the name Taylor. The username on the account is @EricThornSucks."

Tessa fought the rising tide of dizziness threatening to engulf her senses. She remembered this feeling...spacey, zoning in and out. It had happened last time with Blair. How was it possible that she was back in this position once again?

It wasn't like a typical panic attack. She'd blacked out from those before. But this...this was more like static. Gray and fuzzy. A radio station losing its signal. Her mind's attempt to disconnect from reality when confronted with her worst fears come to life.

Tessa resisted the feeling. As much as she longed to escape into that nothingness, she needed to stay alert. She bit the inside of her cheek and focused on the pain.

Maury set the pill bottle down on the bedside table. Tessa turned her head to read the label, but she already knew what it would say:

PHENOBARBITAL

"It's too bad," Maury said. "Neither of you had to die."

Neither of you?

"I didn't bring her to LA to kill her. OK sure, maybe I slipped her a little something to loosen her up. But it's not my fault she fell down and bashed her head in."

Maury rambled on, talking to himself more than her. Tessa struggled to keep up. Was he talking about Dr. Regan? Was that how she had died?

"I just needed the good doctor's help," Maury said. "It was your mother's idea."

Tessa's head snapped round to look at him.

"That got your attention." Maury cracked a grin. "We had a nice heart-to-heart, Tessa. Your mother and I agreed this was not a healthy lifestyle for someone with your disposition."

Tessa felt another wave of nausea at the look of mock-concern on his face.

His eyes hardened. "I tried to get rid of you the nice way. I swear, if you had half a brain, you would've gotten the message."

"That's true," Clint added from his side of the room. "I thought for sure we'd seen the last of her after the YouTube Awards. I mean, what kind of 'publicist'"—he made air quotes with his hands—"gets anxiety attacks from being out in public?"

Maury rolled his eyes. "Any reasonable person would've left."

"But she's in love," Clint said with a snort. "You saw the pics, boss."

"I *took* the pics, Clint."

The bodyguard pointed a finger in Maury's direction. "I swear, you missed your calling. You should've been a pap."

Tessa's head swiveled back and forth between the two of them. *Maury* had taken those pictures in the hotel room that night? But then…Blair…

Her head was spinning. She could've sworn that Blair was involved.

Her eyes went round, examining Maury's face. For a moment, he stared back, and then he mimicked her incredulous expression.

Clint rewarded him with a hoot of laughter. "Look at her. She still doesn't get it!"

Maury shook his head. "Should I explain?"

"Nah. What's the point? Just finish the job. Tick-tock."

Maury glanced at his watch, and Tessa knew she'd run out of time. Even if she could somehow keep them talking, she hadn't heard the helicopters outside for quite a while. They must not have been looking for her after all. Surely, they would've searched Eric's house.

"Grab me a pen and paper, would you?" Maury said to Clint. "I need it for the note." He opened the pill bottle and poured the contents out onto the bedside table. Tessa could hear Maury counting the tablets under his breath.

"Five…ten…fifteen…twenty…twenty-five… Should be plenty, right?"

Tessa's blood turned to ice inside her veins. She knew what he planned to do with all those pills.

He couldn't… There had to be a way…

There was only one hope, she realized. One piece of information that had never passed over any cellular network. One tidbit of data that Maury, with all his surveillance, couldn't have possibly intercepted.

She had to tell him. He couldn't force her to swallow anything without removing the gag. That would be her chance. She just needed him to take off the duct tape.

Tessa allowed her weight to slump backward against the headboard, and her eyes fluttered closed. She heard Clint's heavy footfalls on the carpeting. "Done already?"

"Not yet," Maury replied. "I think she fainted."

Tessa willed herself to keep completely still. She pulled in one last deep breath through her nose. The duct tape tore at her skin as Maury peeled it back, but she didn't react to the pain. She didn't move a muscle until her lips were free.

Her eyes popped open, and she sat up straight. "Wait!" she panted. "Don't do it. There's something you don't know!"

Maury loomed before her with a handful of pills cupped in

his palm. His breath freshener had worn off. Tessa could smell the rancid air that escaped his lungs—the unmistakable aroma of his putrefying core. "Let me guess. Eric loves you? He wrote a song about you?"

"Yes," Tessa replied. She willed her voice to remain steady—to reflect a firm resolve that she didn't quite possess.

"Trust me, Snowflake, he'll get over it. You're not that special."

Maury sneered, but Tessa met it with a smug look of her own. "Maybe I'm not," she told him. "But I'm not the only one you're killing."

Her eyes sank to her belly, and Maury followed her gaze. His knowing smirk faded, and Tessa almost could have laughed as comprehension flashed across his face. Maury Gilroy, the master manipulator, outmaneuvered in the end by something so predictable. So hopelessly clichéd. Two *typical* teenagers, a bed, and a faulty condom.

"Eight weeks and three days," she confirmed when he lifted his eyes at last. "I'm pregnant."

THE INTERROGATION (FRAGMENT 12)

May 1, 2017, 3:24 p.m.
Case #75932.394.1
OFFICIAL TRANSCRIPTION OF POLICE INTERVIEW

—START PAGE 9—

INVESTIGATOR: Let the record show that we're looking at a series of tweets directed at @911LAPD. The tweets originated from a Twitter user listed under the name Taylor. The username on the account is @EricThornSucks.

THORN: What the hell? That account was deactivated.

INVESTIGATOR 2: You're familiar with this Twitter account?

THORN: The FBI shut it down after Tessa murdered me.

INVESTIGATOR: It appears that it's been reactivated.

THORN: How?

INVESTIGATOR 2: Once the FBI took it off the hold list, anyone with a password could have—

THORN: The password was "password." I never changed it.

INVESTIGATOR: Who else knew that password?

THORN:	Me. Tessa. The Midland Texas Police Department. And Blair.
INVESTIGATOR:	Blair Duncan?
THORN:	Yes. This is the account I was telling you about. The one he hacked before!
INVESTIGATOR:	Interesting. Eric, I'm going to read these tweets into the record, and I want you to tell me if anything jumps out at you. These tweets commenced approximately twenty minutes ago at 4:29 p.m. The first one reads, and I quote: "@911LAPD Crime in progress. Send police to 83 Kirkwood Drive in Hollywood! Hurry!"
THORN:	Wait a minute. That's my house. That's my address!
INVESTIGATOR:	We're aware of that. We have units responding.
THORN:	You're just responding now? Someone sent this twenty minutes ago!
INVESTIGATOR 2:	As I said, the @911LAPD Twitter account isn't monitored in real time. The dispatcher happened to notice—
THORN:	What else did they say?
INVESTIGATOR:	The tweets continue every few seconds. There are quite a few of them. I'll read the most relevant ones into the record as I scroll through. Time stamp 4:33 p.m., and I quote: "@911LAPD Tessa Hart has been taken to 83 Kirkwood Drive in

Hollywood. She's with two men. The big one just tied her up."

THORN: Two? Two men?

INVESTIGATOR: Time stamp 4:35 p.m., and I quote: "@911LAPD It's a short guy in a navy pin-striped suit and a HUGE one in gray pants with a black blazer. They're both laughing."

THORN: That's Maury and Clint!

INVESTIGATOR: Clint?

THORN: Clinton Darrow.

INVESTIGATOR: The football player?

THORN: Retired. He's my bodyguard now. Maury hired him last year for extra protection.

INVESTIGATOR: OK. I'm continuing with the messages. Time stamp 4:36 p.m., and I quote: "@911LAPD They're talking about some woman being dead. The sound isn't very good." Time stamp 4:36 p.m.: "@911LAPD I think the short one just said he did it." Time stamp 4:37 p.m.: "@911LAPD He just told Tessa that someone has to take the fall."

THORN: Maury. Maury did it. He's framing her!

INVESTIGATOR: Time stamp 4:37 p.m.: "@911LAPD She's screaming. TESSA'S SCREAMING FOR HELP. POLICE! WHERE ARE YOU? PLEASE HELP HER."

THORN: Oh my God.

INVESTIGATOR: Time stamp 4:38 p.m.: "@911LAPD The big one just gagged her with duct tape."

THORN: Please tell me this is a hoax. Please tell me this isn't real.

INVESTIGATOR: Time stamp 4:39 p.m.: "@911LAPD The big one left the room. I can't see what he's doing. The short one is playing with the TV remote." Time stamp 4:40 p.m.: "@911LAPD HELLO? IS ANYONE THERE? IS ANYONE READING THIS?"

THORN: That one was ten minutes ago. Did someone go to the house?

INVESTIGATOR: Hold on. I'll ask dispatch for an update.

THORN: What else? What else does it say?

INVESTIGATOR: Roger that.

THORN: Can I see the laptop?

INVESTIGATOR: [unintelligible]

THORN: No. No, no, no. It just says he lost the video feed. Maury turned it off somehow.

INVESTIGATOR: I see. Which hospital?

THORN: What? Tessa? Did they find her?

INVESTIGATOR:	I'll tell him. Over and out.
THORN:	Tell me!
INVESTIGATOR:	Eric, I think you better sit down.
THORN:	Just tell me! Is she OK? What happened to her?
INVESTIGATOR:	Officers responded to 83 Kirkwood Drive in Hollywood at approximately 4:49 p.m. Ms. Hart was found unresponsive in the upstairs bedroom. She appears to have ingested a large dose of phenobarbital.
THORN:	No.
INVESTIGATOR:	She left an apparent suicide note on the bedside writing pad that stated, and I quote: "Tell Eric I'm sorry. Good-bye."
THORN:	What? No, that was fake. They forced her. Please, please tell me she's not—
INVESTIGATOR:	She's been rushed to Cedars Sinai Medical Center.
THORN:	She's alive though? Is she going to be OK?
INVESTIGATOR:	She's in the ambulance now. They're doing everything they can.

21
SAY SOMETHING

TESSA FLOATED IN the darkness, her head swimming with disjointed thoughts. She remembered that there was something she needed to do. Something important. Something she needed to tell someone… But what? Her mind wasn't working properly. From somewhere far away, she could hear a voice, but she couldn't understand what it was saying.

"*Tessa…*"

Her head began to throb. She moaned low in her throat.

"*Tessa, can you hear me?*"

Who was that? Why wouldn't he let her sleep? Her limbs felt like she'd been weighted down with rocks. Like she was sinking. Slowly. Down, down, down through the depths of a bottomless ocean. So deep that she might never return to the surface. The weight of the water so heavy that it took a monumental effort to draw a single breath. But the weight felt strangely comforting, even as it crushed her. It would be so easy to let go. Stop breathing. Stop trying. Stop fighting and be at peace…

But she could hear his voice, calling her back.

Eric. That was Eric's voice. The pressure of Eric's palm squeezing her hand.

"*Tessa, please wake up. Please. Please don't go…*"

There was something else desperately important. Something she needed to tell him.

Eric sat at Tessa's bedside and stared into her face. She looked so peaceful. It was hard to believe that she was fighting for her life. He willed her to show some sign that she could hear him.

The nurses had removed the network of wires that had cocooned her last night. No more tube down her throat. She still had an IV poking out of her arm, but she looked fully human again. They'd filled her stomach with charcoal to soak up most of the drug before it hit her bloodstream. The doctor had seemed pleased when he'd emerged into the waiting room this morning.

"*Vital signs look good… Kidney function intact…*"

Eric had tuned most of it out until the doctor said the words that he'd been waiting for all night.

"*You can see her now.*"

He'd taken up his vigil at her bedside two hours ago. So far, she hadn't responded. With each passing minute, Eric felt his worry grow. He spoke to her again, his voice hoarse from lack of sleep. "Tessa, I love you. Please open your eyes. That's all you have to do. Just open your eyes."

What if the doctor was wrong? What if they'd missed something? Eric couldn't escape the thought that she might never answer him. She might stay like this, unconscious—or slip away for good.

He would never forgive himself if that happened. It was all his fault. Everything bad that had ever happened to her, he'd done to her himself. He'd put her in harm's way, not once but twice. He led Blair to her doorstep through his carelessness last winter… And he'd left her vulnerable to an even more insidious predator this time around.

Maury. The worst kind of enemy. The kind that smiled like a friend.

How had he not seen it sooner? His manager had been double-dealing the whole time. It blew Eric's mind when he thought of all the privacy lapses over the years. Pictures that mysteriously went viral…songs that popped up on SoundCloud before the official release…

Eric had always blamed the paparazzi and the fans, but he'd missed the truth staring him in the face. It was all Maury. The pictures in the *Daily Mail* were merely the latest example. His manager had acted like he supported Eric's relationship with Tessa—but the whole time, he was secretly undermining them. Leaking pictures. Putting Tessa in the public eye. Playing on all her fears.

Eric saw the truth now. Maury wanted Tessa gone. Eric had finally found a girl he could trust, and his manager couldn't stand it. Some girl who couldn't be bought? Who had more influence over Eric than Maury himself? No way. He'd done everything in his power to drive Tessa away.

Eric jammed his hands in his armpits to stop them from shaking. The more he thought about it, the deeper the betrayal went. But was Maury really capable of murder?

Impossible.

And yet the evidence lay before his eyes. Tessa. So pale. So fragile. Barely hanging on to life by the slenderest of threads. Maury was the one who had put her in that hospital bed. And there was nothing Eric could do about it but sit here and whisper words that she probably couldn't hear.

"Tessa, please. There's so much I need to tell you. Please wake up so I can tell you."

She was lucky to be alive. Once she swallowed the pills, it was a race against time to empty her stomach. If the paramedics had arrived five minutes later, it would have been too late.

Eric pressed his eyes closed and wiped a weary hand across his lids. He hadn't slept at all last night. She had still been in the ER when he'd arrived. He'd only snatched a glimpse of her hooked up to all the machines before they whisked her out of sight. He'd sat in the waiting room for hours, with no news on her condition. It was midnight before he'd finally gotten some secondhand information. Tessa's mother had flown in, and the doctors had addressed their updates to her. Eric hoped he'd done the right thing by notifying her. He wasn't exactly sure where things stood between Tessa and her mother, but it didn't matter anymore. It all seemed so trivial.

As if on cue, the door of the hospital room creaked open. Mrs. Hart shuffled in, carrying a cup of coffee and a box of Krispy Kremes. Eric studied her in silence. She looked like Tessa, with the same heart-shaped face and almond eyes, although Tessa didn't have those bags beneath hers—or that sullen set to her mouth.

Then again, Eric thought, *he probably didn't look his best either after the hellish night he'd had.*

Mrs. Hart set the doughnuts down with a thud, addressing him over her shoulder. "Why are you still here?"

Eric looked up, startled, and his long side-swept bangs fell in his eyes. He pushed them back behind his ear. "Tessa needs me."

"She needs you like a hole in the head." Mrs. Hart pointed a finger toward the door. "Go. You've done enough."

Eric opened his mouth to protest, but no words came out. He couldn't argue. Tessa's mother had a point. Tessa would still be safe at home in Texas, if @EricThornSucks had never tweeted his way into her life.

But he couldn't abandon her now. He skidded his chair a half inch closer to Tessa's bed. "Mrs. Hart, I just want to say… I want you to know that I care about your daughter. Very much. I'm so sorry this happened to her. This is all my fault."

She turned away and went to the window, pulling open the blinds with a jerk. "You're right. This is your fault."

"I'm sorry."

The window looked out over a parking lot, with the sun-drenched mansions of Beverly Hills rising in the distance. "She never should have been here. She wasn't well. She needed treatment. I tried to get through to her. I tried to tell her…" She set down her coffee and buried her face in her hands.

Eric frowned. "No, she was doing better."

"You call that better?" She lifted her eyes toward the bed. "She was off the rails. And you encouraged her! Social media consultant…" She shook her head. "I knew she spent too much time online, but it wasn't an addiction until you people hired her."

Eric's mouth dropped open. *Addiction?* "Wait. Hold up a sec—"

Mrs. Hart rattled on as if he hadn't spoken. "Internet addiction… I should have seen it sooner. It was bad enough when she stayed holed up in her room on Twitter all day long."

"Because she was being stalked!"

"Is that what she told you?"

Eric rose halfway from his chair, leaning toward her. He didn't know which misunderstanding to clear up first. "Mrs. Hart, don't you know? She was being stalked the whole time."

"Maybe that's what she said, but you can't take the word of an addict."

"No!" Eric argued. "Listen to me. I saw him with my own eyes." He gripped the arms of his chair and stared at her intently, waiting for her to return his gaze. "Blair is one hundred percent real. Tessa might have been too afraid to talk to you about it, but she's not… Hell, she barely even goes near Twitter anymore! It makes her anxious. She has an anxiety disorder, not an Internet addiction."

He could see from the tiny tic in her cheek that his words had come as a shock. Suddenly, the whole rift between Tessa and her mother made more sense. Tessa had never confided about Blair—or about her relationship with Eric either, apparently. No wonder her mother thought she needed that Chalet Santé place.

Hit Refresh…on your life.

Inpatient treatment in a technology-free setting.

It was a treatment program for Internet addiction!

Eric could almost laugh at the sheer absurdity. It was all a mix-up. A failure to communicate. It would all be cleared up once Tessa and her mother were talking again. Once Tessa woke up.

If Tessa woke up…

He looked down into her sleeping face and squeezed her hand for the hundredth time that day. "Come on, Tessa," he whispered. "Please come back."

🔁

Tessa could hear his voice more clearly now. Was he arguing with someone? He sounded so tired. Exhausted. His voice was all gravelly, the way it got when he spent too many hours in the studio.

"*Come on, Tessa. Please come back.*"

She heard the plea in his voice. Didn't he have anyone here with him? He sounded scared. He needed somebody. Somebody to hold him. Somebody to tell him…

Tessa felt tears well up beneath her lids. One by one, they slid down through the fringe of her lashes and made their way across her cheeks. The tears formed two long streams, and she heard him gasp as his fingers brushed the wetness from her face.

"Tessa? Tessa, are you there?"

He gathered her into his arms. She felt herself pulled upright, her head limp against his shoulder.

And then she remembered.

Tessa knew what she needed to say to him. With a monumental effort, she pulled in a shuddering breath.

"Tessa," he whispered. He pressed his lips against her lids, kissing away the dampness. "Tessa, open your eyes."

She couldn't find the strength to make her eyelids move, but she slowly raised her hand. She let it rest against his cheek, coarse with stubble and wet with tears. Her tears or his own?

He gripped the nape of her neck and turned her face toward his. Tessa blinked. Her vision was blurry. She could only see his eyes, ice blue but rimmed with red, as his forehead came to rest against hers. "Tessa," he said softly. "Say something."

She whispered her reply, barely louder than a breath, desperate to get the words out before she forgot them again.

"Eric, what happened to the baby?"

22

BABY

ERIC WATCHED TESSA'S eyelids flutter open. He let out a strangled noise somewhere between a sob and a laugh. Her lips moved, but her voice was too soft for him to hear beneath the incessant hum of the hospital equipment.

He thought she said his name. And then something else. *What happened, baby?* Was that it?

It didn't matter. At least she was awake.

He cupped her face between his hands, waiting for her to speak again. Only a sigh came forth before her eyelids drifted closed. Eric dropped his hands to her shoulders and gave a gentle shake. "Don't go!" he gasped. "Stay with me. Come on. Don't go back to sleep."

He felt a shudder run through her. Then her eyes reopened, blinking rapidly this time.

"That's it. Wake up."

"I'm trying, Eric."

At least she knew his name. That had to be a good sign, right?

Tessa's mother came to the other side of the bed. She reached out toward Tessa for a moment, but she let her hand drop. She flicked the button to call the nurse instead.

Had Tessa noticed her mom standing there? Her eyes were fixed on Eric's face, but she still looked half-asleep.

Eric rubbed his hands vigorously up and down her arms. "Just talk to me," he said. "Keep talking."

She nodded as her chest rose and fell. "Eric, did you hear me? What happened—"

Before she could finish, they were interrupted by the hospital room door. A nurse bustled into the room. "Look who's awake!"

Tessa looked around at last, and she shrank against him. She'd finally noticed her mother, standing awkwardly on the other side of the bed. Tessa hid her face in the hollow of his neck. "No," she said. "I don't want to see her. Make her go away."

"Wait a minute. Are you two…" Mrs. Hart pointed back and forth between them, meeting Eric's eyes. "I thought she worked for you. What is this?"

Eric didn't answer. He could feel his girlfriend trembling, and he pressed a kiss into her hair. "It's OK. Your mom's here for you. She came all the way from Texas."

Tessa burrowed against him even closer. He strained to make out her words, muffled against his chest. "She wants to send me to some rehab center for Twitter zombies."

Mrs. Hart took a step toward them. She let her hand come

to rest on her daughter's shoulder. "Sweetheart, let's talk about that later."

Tessa shrugged her hand away.

"Tessa," her mother tried again. "I'm worried about you. I'm not the only one."

"What do you mean?" Tessa shrank away, looking from her mother to Eric. "You too?" she asked, searching his face.

He shook his head, confused.

"Not him," Mrs. Hart explained. "That manager. Mr. Gilroy. He was concerned enough to track me down and call me."

Eric's head jerked up. Maury? How did Tessa's mother even know his manager's name?

Mrs. Hart reached for her purse. She fished out a cell phone and pulled up a photo on the screen. "He called me a few weeks ago. He sent me this."

Eric took the phone and tapped to enlarge the picture. He recognized the sleek leather seats of his private jet. It must have been taken when they were flying home from Las Vegas after the award show. Neither of them had slept much the night before. He and Tessa had both conked out on the plane. Tessa lay asleep, with her mouth hanging open and her cell phone gripped in her hand, casting her face in an otherworldly glow.

"Sweetheart," her mother continued. "Mr. Gilroy told me you weren't coping well. Obsessing. He thought you needed treatment. He wanted to help."

"Wait," Eric said slowly. "Was Maury the one who told you she had an Internet addiction?"

Her mother nodded. "He felt bad about hiring her. He found a treatment program and offered to pay for it." She slipped the phone back into her purse. "Tessa, he was really concerned about you. He even convinced your old therapist to come out here and talk to you about it."

"Dr. Regan?" Eric said. "That's why she came to LA?"

Tessa looked dazed. "He told me that," she said slowly. "Right before he drugged me."

Mrs. Hart did a double take at her daughter's words.

She doesn't know, Eric realized. The police hadn't spoken to her yet. All he'd told her on the phone was that Tessa had overdosed. Mrs. Hart had no idea that Maury was the one who'd put Tessa in this hospital bed.

"Maury did what now?"

Eric spoke rapidly to fill her in. "He's been manipulating all of us. He killed Dr. Regan, and he tried to kill Tessa to frame her for the murder. He's the one who drugged her!"

"It wasn't a suicide attempt?"

"No, Mom! I'm not suicidal. I'm not an addict. I have anxiety. That's it! I keep telling you, but you won't listen—"

"OK." Eric cut her off. He made a time-out sign with his hands. "She believes you now. Right, Mrs. Hart? You believe her."

Tessa's mother nodded. "Of course I do." She remembered the carton of doughnuts she'd set down on the countertop. She picked them up, waving them in Tessa's direction. "Look what I found down in the cafeteria. Are you hungry?"

But Tessa turned her face away. "I don't want her here."

"Tessa, your mom loves you."

"I know what she's going to say," Tessa whispered. "She's just going to look all smug and say she told me so."

Mrs. Hart cast the doughnuts aside with a frown. "No, Tessa. Why would I say that?"

Tessa didn't answer. She let out a low moan. Eric wasn't sure what she meant either, but his attention was distracted. Her doctor had entered the room.

"Good to see you awake, Tessa." He scanned their faces, getting his bearings, and his eyes came to rest on Mrs. Hart. "Mom can stay," he ordered. "Boyfriend needs to clear out of the room while I examine the patient."

Eric started to rise, but Tessa grabbed his hand to hold him in place. "No!"

"I'm sorry," the doctor said. "Next of kin only. It's hospital policy."

"He *is* next of kin."

Eric hesitated, eyeing her curiously. Her face had gone a shade paler. She pressed her lips together for a moment, and then she chewed at them as if she might gnaw them right off her face.

"This isn't how I wanted to tell you," she said softly.

"Tell him?" her mother asked from the other side of the bed. "Tell him *what*?"

Tessa didn't answer. She rested her hand on her stomach, and her eyes locked with Eric's. He could see the tears forming in the corners. All the air left his lungs in a sudden outrush as he realized what she meant.

She turned her face to the doctor, and her voice wavered as she spoke. "He's the father," she told him. "Is there any way my baby's still alive?"

Tessa heard Eric's sharp intake of breath, but she didn't look at him. She couldn't bear to see him shrink away—or to see the knowing look on her mother's face.

Her eyes went to the doctor. He was the only one there who might ease the fear that stabbed at her from the inside out. This baby's existence had been the source of constant anxiety for weeks—but now, the thought of losing it made her heart shatter into a thousand shards of glass.

It felt strange to say it out loud. *The baby.* She'd kept those words to herself all this time, too scared to speak. Week after week had rolled by, and she'd told no one.

No one except for Maury, in that final desperate plea as he stood counting out the pills.

Five…ten…fifteen…twenty…

Maury had barely paused when he heard the news. He'd looked askance at her for a moment, and she thought she saw a trace of regret on his face. But then his eyes went cold again. *"You should've gone when you had the chance. You know I can't let you walk out of here alive…"*

Tessa wasn't sure how many pills he'd stuffed down her throat or how long they'd been in her system. By some miracle, help had found her in time, but the tiny life inside her was only eight weeks old. How many doses of phenobarbital would it take to stop that tiny beating heart?

She could tell from her mother's pinched expression that she was thinking the same thing. Tessa felt the gorge rise in her throat. Morning sickness? How long did pregnancy symptoms last after...after...

Eric put his arm around her shoulders. She looked up at him, but he didn't speak. His mouth opened, but he let it drift closed without uttering a sound. He didn't know the right words for this situation, and Tessa didn't blame him. What was there to say?

The doctor approached her bedside, leafing through her medical chart. "That's odd. Didn't they run an HCG?" He clucked his tongue and then he looked at her, his voice growing gentler. "It all depends how much of the drug hit your bloodstream before we pumped your stomach. Do you know how far along you were?"

Were, Tessa thought. She didn't miss the past tense.

Maybe it was for the best. She wasn't ready for a baby. She could barely take care of herself. She knew what her mother was thinking. Her mom still hadn't said anything, and Tessa couldn't bring herself to meet her mother's eyes.

She rubbed away her tears. "Eight weeks," she told the doctor. Her eyes dropped to the thin, blue hospital gown, bunched around her waist. Tessa pulled it taut over her belly. She could feel Eric's gaze following hers. "I wasn't showing yet," she said in a halting voice. She made a small O with her thumb and index finger, and pressed it against the gown. "It's the size of a raspberry this week. I looked it up online."

Eric shook his head slowly back and forth. He still hadn't spoken. The doctor filled the silence instead. "Let's take a listen."

He inserted a stethoscope in his ears and pressed it through a gap in Tessa's gown. She held her breath. The doctor's forehead creased with concentration as he shifted the stethoscope around. Finally, he looked up. His grim expression hadn't changed.

"Well?" her mother asked.

The doctor shook his head. "I can't find a heartbeat," he said. "But that's not a reliable indicator in the first trimester. She'll need blood work and an ultrasound to be sure." He inclined his head toward Tessa. "Have you started prenatal care anywhere?"

"No. Not yet." She rearranged her gown to cover herself and pulled the hospital blanket up to her waist.

The doctor patted her shoulder. "I'll call for a consult. Then we'll know for sure." He picked up the chart at the foot of Tessa's bed and made a note.

Tessa's eyes filled with tears again. She didn't need a consult. She knew the truth. She could feel the hollow place in the pit of her stomach. Empty.

The doctor turned to leave, and Tessa's mother followed him out into the hall. Eric shifted beside her. He'd been sitting in a chair, but he rose and settled his weight on the edge of her bed. She inched sideways to make room as he looped his arm around her and buried his face in her hair. He held her there for a long moment. Tessa closed her eyes, bracing for his reaction.

"Why didn't you tell me?" he said at last.

A tiny sob escaped her throat. She didn't know how to answer, other than the truth. "I meant to. I was scared."

He placed a finger beneath her chin and tilted her face upward. "Scared of what?" he asked. "Of having a baby? Or of me?"

Tessa's face crumpled. He looked so hurt. She couldn't bear to tell him the rest. How she'd convinced herself he would leave her—concocted a whole elaborate story in her head about him fooling around with another girl.

She looked away. He didn't need to know all that. Some secrets were better left untold. She sniffed loudly, wiping her nose with the back of her hand. Eric fished in his pocket and handed her a tissue.

"Tessa," he said gently. "Don't you trust me?"

Trust me. Tessa felt her eyes refilling. If only it were that easy. She wanted to trust him. She needed to trust someone, and Eric's arms felt so strong. So secure.

She blew her nose noisily, avoiding his eyes. At least she knew he wasn't cheating on her. Not unless he'd been having a secret fling with Dr. Regan…

Tessa balled up the damp tissue in her hand. That idea would have made her laugh under other circumstances. It still hadn't sunk in that her therapist was really dead. The shock would probably hit her later.

For now, Tessa couldn't quite bring herself to care.

Not about Dr. Regan or Maury or the policemen who would probably show up soon with their endless string of questions. Tessa shoved all of it into some dark corner of her mind. She'd unpack it later. Right now, her only thought was for the baby. She pressed a hand below her belly button and held it there, as if she could cradle it. Comfort it. Keep it safely tucked inside where it belonged.

Was there still something in there, fighting for its life? The doctor hadn't sounded completely hopeless…

Eric placed his hand on top of hers. Their fingers intertwined. Tessa looked up and met his eyes.

"I love you," he whispered. "Baby or no baby. We'll figure it out. Together."

23

QUESTIONS AND ANSWERS

ERIC DISENGAGED HIS hand from Tessa's, careful not to wake her. She'd dozed off again, and the nurse said to let her rest.

She shifted in her sleep, rolling onto her side, with her hand still cradling her abdomen. Eric pushed back his chair and stood to stretch his legs.

This isn't how I wanted to tell you...

She'd known about the baby for weeks, and she hadn't breathed a word. It blew his mind when he thought about it. When exactly was she planning to fill him in?

Eric crossed the room to the pastry box her mother had left. He stuffed a doughnut in his mouth, but he didn't taste the sugary glaze. His mind was in a million other places. A baby? Fatherhood? How was he supposed to process it when he didn't even know if the baby was alive?

He chewed slowly and forced himself to swallow. He couldn't think about it now. Later, he vowed. For now, his mind buzzed

with questions. Like whether his manager had been arrested
yet…and exactly how many different forms of torture he should
inflict when he next found himself and Maury face-to-face.

Eric set the doughnut back in the box, half eaten. He didn't
have the stomach for it. He needed coffee…or sleep.

Or neither, he thought with a stifled yawn. Maybe what he
really needed were some answers.

He drifted toward the door and poked his head out, search-
ing for any sign of a baby doctor or an ultrasound machine.
How long did it take to get a consult? He caught sight of Mrs.
Hart by the nurses' station, with her hands on her hips. *Good.*
Let her take charge of nagging the hospital staff. His job was to
sit by Tessa's side and hold her hand.

Eric moved to shut the door, but a different voice distracted
him from the opposite direction. He recognized the familiar
baritone, filtering in from somewhere down the hall.

"*Is she alert? Competent to answer questions?*"

Eric stepped out of the room. He eased the door closed
behind him just as the two LAPD detectives turned the corner.
Detective Stevens raised a hand in greeting.

"How is she?"

His suit looked less crisp than yesterday. His eyes were
bloodshot, and his partner didn't look much better. The two
of them must have been up all night, putting the pieces of this
tangled mess together.

"She's sleeping," Eric said. "You can't talk to her now. It's not
a great time."

Detective Stevens drew a small notebook from his breast pocket. Morales held a tablet and stylus.

Eric stuffed his hands in his pockets. Suddenly light-headed, he leaned against the wall beside Tessa's door. "What's going on?" he asked. "Has Maury been arrested?"

"Not yet." The lead detective cleared his throat. "Suspects Gilroy and Darrow both fled the scene before officers arrived."

Eric scuffed his shoe against the floor. "You have enough to charge them, right?"

"That's why we need to speak to Tessa." Morales took a hesitant step forward, holding out the tablet before him like a shield. "We have partial video footage of the incident, but there are still some holes."

Video footage…

Eric swallowed. He'd almost forgotten about that part. Detective Morales pulled something up on the screen and angled it so Eric could see. "The video file was uploaded and tweeted to us last night."

> **Taylor** @EricThornSucks
> @911LAPD Tell Tessa I love her. If they hurt her, make them pay. #KeepingWatch #GuardianAngel

The tweet was followed by the opening frame of a video, and Eric recognized the scene in black and white. His bedroom. His own four-poster bed.

He didn't want to see it. He pushed the tablet away.

"You can't show that to Tessa," he said. Talk about a trigger... Blair watching while they both slept. It was enough to give Eric nightmares. He couldn't imagine what it would do to Tessa's head. "How did he do it? How did he have a camera in my house?"

Morales tucked the tablet away. "Your TV had a hidden camera installed in the power panel. When the TV was powered off, it fed surveillance footage to a remote location."

"That CIA shit? From Wikileaks?" Eric could feel the color draining from his face. He'd read an article about it back in March. Laptops...TVs... He'd unplugged the microwave in his backstage dressing room, and Maury had laughed in his face.

"It's unclear how long the device was in place or how many people had access to the feed."

Eric made a fist and pounded it against his thigh. "I knew it. I friggin' *knew* it!" He pressed his shoulder blades against the wall for support. His pulse thundered in his ears, and he felt every muscle of his body convulse. His insides loosened, while his chest clenched so tight that he thought he might implode. Was this how Tessa felt when she was panicking?

"Eric?" Detective Stevens's voice penetrated from some far-off, foggy place. "Eric, are you listening?"

He looked up. The lead detective hovered in front of him with his head tipped to one side. "Son, do you need to sit down?"

Eric shook his head. If this was panic, then he knew what to do. He'd watched Tessa calm herself down a million times.

Deep breaths. Count to five. She'd explained to him how she counted people's names inside her head. *Whose names? Did it matter?* She hadn't specified. He couldn't worry about that now. Any names would do. Eric inhaled slowly, ticking through the mental list of people he'd like to strangle with his bare hands.

Blair one…Maury two…Clint three…

"Eric," the detective interrupted. "The video recording cuts off after a few minutes. We need Tessa to complete her statement."

He held a stack of papers. It rustled as he extended it in Eric's direction. Eric took it, spreading the sheets before him like a fan. His vision blurred at the sight of the black ink swimming across the pages.

Case #75937.394.1
OFFICIAL TRANSCRIPTION OF POLICE INTERROGATION

"These are the relevant sections from the interviews conducted yesterday," the detective explained.

Eric let the air out in a rush. It actually helped—the breathing exercise. He felt a little steadier. He let go of the wall and stood up straight.

He'd be damned before he let them talk to Tessa. Not today. Not with everything else she had on her mind right now.

He dug his heels into the floor and squared his shoulders, blocking the policemen's path to Tessa's door. "You're not going in that room," he said, meeting Detective Stevens's eyes. "But go ahead. Ask your questions. You can talk to me."

Blair turned sideways in his chair, presenting the stroller mom on the other side of the table with a view of his shoulder. He hated being back here in this overcrowded coffee shop. He thought he'd seen the last of this dump.

But here he was again. He'd blown every penny he possessed on a remote connection to a hacked big-screen TV—a useless piece of scrap metal that now graced the inside of a police evidence locker.

What an astronomical waste of money. Blair had actually thought he might be getting somewhere when he stumbled on that DNM posting. Dark net markets were mostly populated by lowlifes selling drugs and fake IDs—but you never knew what you might find lurking in the underbelly of the Internet. Blair had only needed to cough up the cash, and voilà! Like ordering off a menu, only the main course was a peep show into Eric Thorn's master bedroom.

The key was to avoid spooking the guy on the other end of the transaction. Blair had made it a point to steer clear of annoying questions. Like, how did you get access to this video feed? And who installed a spy cam in that TV panel to begin with?

Blair hadn't asked a thing when he met the seller in March. The guy claimed that Eric Thorn put the hidden camera there himself. Heck, maybe that was true. That asswipe probably used it to record all his sexcapades with his latest fangirl flavor-of-the-month.

Poor Tessa. She had no idea. Blair didn't feel a shred of guilt for looking in on her. It was Eric's fault if he chose to parade around his bedroom in front of a camera every night. Why should it be Blair's responsibility to look away?

In any case, it didn't matter now. It was all over. Blair had tipped off the police to the camera's presence the moment he directed his first tweet at @911LAPD.

Taylor @EricThornSucks

@911LAPD Crime in progress. Send police to 83 Kirkwood Drive in Hollywood! Hurry!

He'd hesitated before he sent it. He knew he was putting his neck on the line. His finger had hovered over the tweet button, watching and waiting, until he knew with absolute certainty that Tessa was in trouble. Once they threw her on that bed and tied her up, Blair didn't have a choice. He had to pull the trigger. He couldn't sit there on his hands and watch the girl he loved get hurt.

The girl he loved… What a joke.

What was wrong with him anyway? Maybe he really was delusional, like she'd claimed to those cops in Texas. He probably should cut his losses. They were never getting back together, and Tessa Hart was way more trouble than she was worth. Beautiful, yes. But so incredibly messed up…

Blair's head throbbed. He hadn't slept last night, and he dug the heels of his hands into his eye sockets. He needed to let it go. Forget Tessa. Move on.

But he couldn't do that. Not now! Not after the scene he watched unfold yesterday in real time. He still had no way of knowing how she was doing. He'd called the hospital to check, but they would only tell him that her condition was stable.

At least that meant she was alive.

Thanks to him, Blair thought. She was damned lucky she had him. Blair couldn't really regret all the money he'd blown on the surveillance feed. If he hadn't been keeping an eye on her, no one would have. Certainly not that self-obsessed goon she called a boyfriend. Talk about a dysfunctional romance. He was too busy prancing around in his music videos…or working on his abs.

Blair sighed. He knew he should let it go, but a part of him still clung to some tiny molecule of hope. Maybe the near-death experience would wake her up. Maybe Tessa would finally see where she belonged. Hadn't he done enough to prove himself? Hadn't she tortured him sufficiently? Rejected him. Hid from him. Pushed him off a deck. Gotten him thrown in jail for a week before the police dropped the charges…

Surely, she would see the truth now. She would figure out who really cared about her.

With a sniff, Blair clicked onto his camera roll and scrolled through the old photos. He stopped at random and gave a little start when he saw the picture that came up. Out of all the thousands of images, this one was one of a kind. Not Tessa by herself. She was dancing in a crowd, arm in arm with a group of friends. Happy. Full of laughter. Tessa, the night he met her— before she hid herself away.

Blair smiled.

Someday, she would dance with him again. It was only a matter of time. He needed to be patient. Let her come to him. He understood that much about her by now. The more he chased, the more she ran away.

So he wouldn't chase any longer, he decided. Tessa knew how to find him. She'd come crawling back into his Twitter mentions one of these days. He'd saved her life after all. The least she could do was thank him.

Maybe she was tapping those words into her phone right this very instant. Blair wiggled his fingers at the thought and logged on to the Twitter account to check:

> Username: **EricThornSucks**
> Password: **password**

The home screen came up, and his smile faded.

No new messages. No new notifications. Nothing to do but wait.

And refresh…

And refresh…

And refresh…

A hand clapped him on the shoulder. Blair shoved the phone into his pocket. Who was bothering him now? Hadn't anyone in this godforsaken coffee shop heard of privacy? He jerked his shoulder out of range and opened his mouth to snap at whoever had crept up behind him.

But the words died in his throat. The stroller mom in her yoga outfit gaped from the other side of the table. She grabbed her baby and scurried off, leaving the stroller behind in her haste to get away. Blair grimaced when he realized what must have freaked her out.

He turned around slowly with his hands raised in the air. *Oh great*, he thought. *Here we go again.*

"Blair Duncan, you have the right to remain silent. Anything you say can and will be used against you in a court of law…"

24

THE MIND PERCEIVES

ERIC RAISED HIS chin, locking eyes with the tall detective. He wondered if he'd overplayed his hand. Was it a crime, blocking Tessa's door? Obstruction of justice?

He wouldn't back down. They'd have to drag him away in handcuffs before he let the girl on the other side of that door face another round of interrogation.

The detective edged closer. Eric braced, waiting for the order to step aside. Instead, Detective Stevens reached out and patted him on the shoulder. "You're a good guy, Eric. She's lucky to have you." He flipped his notebook open and cleared his throat. "I've got more questions for you too as long as we're here."

Not under arrest, then. Eric swallowed, suddenly aware of how dry his mouth had gone. "You're not going to record me, are you?"

"We can if you like, but we'd have to take you back down to the station."

Eric shook his head. No way. He'd be perfectly happy if he never set foot in a police station again.

Morales approached and whispered something in his partner's ear. Detective Stevens nodded. "We're still nailing down Maury Gilroy's motive. Can you shed any light on why he brought Dr. Regan to that hotel room the night she died?"

Questions, Eric thought. Still so many questions, flooding his mind, drowning out his ability to think straight. At least that one he could answer. "Chalet Santé."

Detective Stevens cocked an eyebrow.

"Google it." Eric pointed to Morales. "There's a website. Look it up." He waited for the policeman to pull it up on his tablet. "'Hit Refresh on your life.' It's a treatment center for Internet addiction."

Morales nudged his partner, reading from the screen, as Stevens jotted notes. "Ninety-day voluntary lock-in… Secluded setting… No access to electronic devices of any kind…"

Eric waited for them to catch up, bouncing on the balls of his feet. "Maury told Tessa's mom that she had an Internet addiction! He totally lied to her. He must've told Dr. Regan the same story."

Detective Stevens stopped writing and squinted at the tip of his pencil. "Why?"

They still didn't get it. He wasn't making sense. Eric pressed his hands against his legs, gathering his scattered thoughts. "Maury was trying to break up Tessa and me. He wanted Dr. Regan to talk Tessa into going to that place. That way she'd disappear. *Poof!* No phones. No Twitter. No Snapchat. It would look to me like she totally ghosted!"

He paused a moment, thinking. It was all starting to make sense. He felt like the truth was right in front of him, just out of reach, like a word on the tip of his tongue that he couldn't quite remember. "There's something else," Eric said slowly. "That DM yesterday. The one from @Snowflake734. Did Maury send that?"

Detective Stevens met his eyes. "He must have. Who else could have done it?"

"But how?" Eric asked. "I was so careful. No one could have guessed that password!"

The lead detective stood silent, tapping his pencil eraser against his chin. It was his partner, Morales, who chimed in. "I could venture a guess. Can I see your phone?"

Eric glided it out of his pocket in its custom titanium case. He entered his passcode, and then he stared at it with widened eyes. *No*, he thought. *No way...* Morales plucked it from his hand, but Eric already knew what the detective would find. "Maury programmed that phone. It came in my swag bag at the YouTube Awards."

Morales handed it back to him with an app on the screen that must have been hidden from view until now.

iMonitor

"Spy software," Morales explained. "He had access to every keystroke you made. Your passcode. Passwords to all your accounts. The works."

Eric exhaled slowly. He could feel all the blood in his body rushing to his head. His legs had gone rubbery. He needed to sit down, but he couldn't think about that now. "That's why," he whispered. "Maury wasn't expecting me to show up at the hotel. He thought it would be Tessa. Because that night when I set up the meeting with MET, I was using Tessa's phone!"

"You catfished the catfish." Morales eyed him thoughtfully. "You're lucky. He might've gotten away with it if Tessa had shown up."

Detective Stevens frowned. He'd been writing frantically, but he looked up from his notes. "I still don't understand why Gilroy brought the psychiatrist and the mother into it. If he wanted to get rid of Tessa, all he had to do was get her alone and stage a suicide."

Eric closed his eyes. He had a headache coming on. A bad one. He pressed his temples between his hands. He could have lost Tessa so easily—and he never would have known where she had gone. It was too much to process. He sucked in a ragged breath and held it.

Maury one…Maury two…Maury three…

Morales answered his partner. "I don't think Gilroy initially intended to kill anyone. He was hoping Tessa would leave willingly. He said so in the video, didn't he?"

Stevens flipped backward in his notebook, searching. "Here. Suspect was asked why he killed Dr. Regan. He responded, quote, 'That wasn't supposed to happen. She'd still be alive if she didn't have such a stick up her ass.'"

"Dr. Regan must have spoiled his plan somehow."

Eric held up a hand. A memory came to him, jarred loose by the cross talk between the two detectives. "Tessa always used to complain about her…how she was so rigid. Always by the book."

"Maybe he tried to pay her off, but she insisted on evaluating Tessa herself."

That made sense, Eric thought. Obviously, once Dr. Regan talked to Tessa, she would have seen that the so-called "Internet addiction" was a load of BS.

Detective Stevens scratched his nose. "So he dosed the doctor's drink with phenobarbital. Only he overdid it. She must have gotten dizzy and hit her head."

"And then he had a real mess on his hands," Morales added. "He needed to pin that dead body on someone. Probably intended to stage it as a murder-suicide then and there."

Eric nodded. "Only Tessa didn't show up. I did."

"Right," Morales agreed. "At which point, the whole plan was shot to hell. He had to wait and finish the job on Tessa the next day."

Eric gritted his teeth. He could feel the weight of his cell phone in the front pocket of his jeans, pressed against his thigh. He was surprised the detectives had let him keep it. They would probably need it for evidence, and Eric wouldn't mind handing it over. He never wanted to touch his phone again. In fact, he might be ready to wash his hands of personal electronics altogether.

"The TV," he said slowly. "In my bedroom. With the secret camera… Was Maury the one who put it there? Or Blair?"

Detective Stevens closed his notebook and stuffed it in the pocket of his suit jacket. "We should know more soon. Blair Duncan was picked up by agents this morning for violating federal wiretapping laws."

Eric nodded. *Good.* At least that was one less cyberstalker to worry about.

"But, Eric, that's why we need to talk to Tessa. We need to hear from her if she wishes to press charges."

"Of course she does. Why wouldn't she?"

"Blair Duncan saved her life." Detective Stevens gestured past him toward the entrance of the room, but Eric didn't budge.

"You can't talk to her," he said. "Not today." Not while the biggest question of all remained unanswered.

Tessa woke disoriented. It took her a moment to remember where she was.

The hospital.

The baby.

She pressed her hand to her belly. How long had she been sleeping? Where was everyone? She sat up, but the room was empty. The door was propped open a crack, and she heard voices coming from the other side. Was Eric out there? Who was he talking to?

"Blair Duncan saved her life…"

Tessa froze.

Did she hear that right? Her mouth dropped open, but otherwise, she sat perfectly still as the words reverberated inside her skull.

She'd been looking at her lap. Her eyes remained fixed in place, but she no longer saw the sheet covering her legs. She couldn't hear whatever words Eric said in reply. She ceased to follow anything going on around her. She only heard the thrum of her own heartbeat, whispering that name inside her ears.

Blair.

Blair.

Blair.

Blair…

"Tessa?" Someone was shaking her arm. Tessa looked up, confused. How long had she been out of it?

Eric's hand rested on her shoulder. He bent close, examining her face. "Tessa?" he said again. "Earth to Tessa."

She must have missed something. The hospital room door stood open. A woman in scrubs had entered, wheeling a machine before her.

"What happened?" Tessa blinked, trying to get her bearings. Her hand lay in her lap, gripping a damp tissue. Or not just damp, she saw. The bloodred stains stood out against the white. She'd clutched it so hard that she'd dug holes in her palm with her fingernails. The sight of the bloodstains made her panic worse somehow. Maybe it was the fact that she hadn't even felt the wounds as she'd inflicted them.

Tessa thrust the bloody tissue beneath her sheet before Eric could notice.

"Tessa," Eric said. "Did you hear her?"

She shook her head. Her eyes went to him, and then to the woman pushing the machine.

"Tessa, I'm Dr. Keller," the woman said. "Someone called for a maternity consult?"

Tessa's mother stalked into the room, and Tessa slumped down in the bed. She couldn't face it. The anxiety consumed her, sucking her down like quicksand. She couldn't escape its pull, no matter where she turned her thoughts. Maury. Blair. The baby...and somehow, her mother's presence made it infinitely worse.

Tessa closed her eyes. Her hands were shaking. Why didn't any of them say anything? Couldn't they see she was suffocating right before their eyes? Instead, they all ignored her, talking to each other. The doctor explained something about the machine and how it worked. Tessa couldn't even understand what she was saying. It was like her brain had forgotten how to comprehend the English language.

She needed to hold it together. *Focus!* Forget everything except the one thing that mattered.

The baby.

Tessa nodded to herself. She could do this. She didn't have a choice. She pushed the blanket down to her hips and hiked up the hospital gown high enough to expose her abdomen. The doctor pulled up a rolling chair beside her. The ultrasound wand made contact, and Tessa sucked in her stomach, chilled by the sensation of the gel that spread across her skin. The room fell silent aside from a low whooshing sound that came from the machine.

Her mother's voice broke through. "What's that? Is that a heartbeat?" She pointed at something on the monitor, gray and pulsing rhythmically.

The doctor shook her head. "That's Tessa's heartbeat."

Tessa's eyes flew to her mother's face. She'd heard the way her mom's breathing had quickened just now. *Hoping*, Tessa realized. Her mother was *hoping* they found a heartbeat.

Could that be? Could Carla Hart—queen of the safe-sex lecture—actually want this baby to live? It went against everything Tessa thought she knew about her mom. And yet, she could see the evidence all over the older woman's face.

Tessa's eyes widened with a sudden flash of insight. She understood exactly how her mother felt. Tessa knew firsthand how a baby could be unplanned and poorly timed—but still wanted. Still *loved*.

The thought made Tessa's eyes flood with sudden tears. She clamped her hand across her mouth to stifle the sob that threatened to escape. Eric moved to stand beside her, and Tessa slipped her hand in his. His grasp felt firm, and it helped ease the hollow pain inside her chest.

The doctor pursed her lips. Her eyes never left the

rectangular screen that sat atop the rolling cart as she slowly moved the wand across Tessa's skin. "And you're how far along? Eight weeks? Are you sure about that timing?"

Tessa felt the color rise to her cheeks. Maybe she should ask her mom to leave. Not that it would really come as a surprise to her mother when she heard Tessa's answer. Her mom had predicted it all along.

"It was the first time," Tessa answered in a halting voice. "The first time I ever...we ever..."

Even as she spoke, she could hear her mother's voice inside her head. *You're a Hart, Tessa. It runs in your blood...*

The doctor pulled the wand away and wiped Tessa's stomach with a towel. "You can lower your gown," she said. She picked up the medical chart and scribbled something at the bottom.

Eric rose to his feet and took a step in her direction. "But what did it show? What did you see?"

The doctor shook her head. Her face was blank, her voice matter-of-fact. "I need to call for a consult."

"Another one?" Tessa could hear Eric's frustration. "Why?" he asked, peering over the doctor's shoulder. "Can't you tell? Isn't this supposed to be your specialty?"

"I'm an ob-gyn," she replied. She looked up, but her eyes went past Eric, seeking Tessa instead. "Ms. Hart, would you prefer to speak privately? I can have your family clear the room."

"No," she whispered. Tessa gripped the sheet at her waist. Something in the doctor's face made her tremble. "Just tell me. What is it?"

The doctor smiled at her kindly. She patted Tessa's foot through the blanket. "Do you have a history of anxiety?"

"How is that relevant?" her mother asked. "What's going on? What did you see?"

But somehow, Tessa knew what the doctor was about to say. She could hear the answer in the gaps and spaces—the words the doctor hadn't uttered.

Tessa's mouth filled with the familiar taste of acid burning the back of her throat. Not morning sickness after all. She should have realized... She even knew the name for the cognitive distortion.

"Priming," Tessa whispered. "It was all just priming."

Eric turned toward her. Did he remember what that word meant? She'd explained the concept over Snapchat not so long ago.

The mind perceives what it expects to find, even if it's not really there...

Tessa placed a hand on her belly, still sticky from the gel. Her mother had warned her a thousand times. A million times. *I got pregnant the first time your daddy even looked at me sideways...* Of course her brain was primed.

"Did you take a pregnancy test?" the doctor asked.

Tessa looked away. "I was so sure," she said slowly. "I had all the symptoms. The nausea. I even missed my period. Did I imagine all that?"

"The mind can do all kinds of funny things," the doctor explained. "We use the medical term *pseudocyesis*. Phantom pregnancy."

"Wait." Her mother edged closer. She rested her hand on Tessa's shoulder, and Tessa covered it with her own. "Phantom? You mean…"

The doctor slid Tessa's chart back into its holder. "I've called for a psych consult," she said. She turned to collect the ultrasound machine and wheeled it toward the door. "I see no sign that the patient is currently, or ever has been, pregnant."

25
HIT REFRESH...ON YOUR LIFE

June 2, 2017 (One Month Later)

ERIC SAT BEHIND the steering wheel of the VW van. He hummed softly so he wouldn't disturb Tessa while she napped in the back. His lips mouthed the first verse of his latest single: "Pistols at Dawn."

> *Caught a pair of eyes*
> *Where you know they're not wanted.*
> *Fed up with your lies.*
> *Got my gun. I'm going huntin'...*

Eric bit his lip. He'd been completely fixated on Blair when he wrote those lyrics—so single-minded in his hatred that he'd failed to notice the other enemies surrounding him. Lesson learned.

It didn't matter now. After all the smoke had cleared, it was his career that lay in a bloody heap on the pavement. His label had released the single, but the sales numbers sucked. The fans kept tweeting that it didn't sound like him. Too angry. Too aggressive. Nothing like the sweet, sensitive @EricThorn they knew so well. It must have been ghostwritten by someone else…

He'd seen the hashtag going around yesterday, and it didn't even need a retweet from MET to make it trend.

#EricThornIsOverParty
2.1 million tweets

Eric grinned. They didn't know the half of it.

The music video production had been put on hold indefinitely. The label might edit together the footage they'd already shot, but Eric had a feeling it would never see the light of day. Not without him around to promote it.

It still didn't feel real. After all these years, shackled in an ironclad record contract…a contract he'd never actually read himself. Why would he? He had a manager to handle all the legal stuff.

Eric hummed a little louder, drumming his hands against the steering wheel.

You're going down.
Let's get it on.
I'll lay you out.
Pistols at dawnnnnnnnnnnnnnn.

How had it taken him this long to hire a real lawyer? Eric had set up a conference call with a whole team of them last month, and his head was still spinning from what he'd learned.

"Of course you can take a hiatus," the lead counsel told him. "There's language in place here for you to take up to a six-month leave of absence without facing any penalty."

"But what if I don't want a break?" he'd asked. "What if I want to walk away for good?"

"It's a standard termination clause. Either party can terminate at any time with thirty days' written notice."

He'd only stared at his phone, his mind reeling as he struggled to grasp what the words meant.

"We can draft a letter on your behalf if you wish to terminate the contract."

"That's it? You write a letter, and I'm free?"

"Yes, after thirty days."

"And they can't sue me? They can't sue my family?"

"Your family?" The lawyer sounded bewildered on the other end of the line. "Of course not. What in the world gave you that idea?"

Eric hadn't answered. He'd ended the call abruptly and stumbled out of the van. He'd barely made it outside before the contents of his stomach ended up on the concrete floor of his carport.

How could he have been so naive?

All these years, working like a dog, hating every second of the living hell that his life had become… It was all a lie, designed by Maury to control him. Maury didn't want him quitting show business. He was Maury's meal ticket—Maury's one and only client. And so, his manager had figured out a way to keep Eric bound and gagged for years.

The pure rage would have consumed him whole if not for Tessa.

Eric tossed a backward glance through the gap between the seats. Tessa lay sprawled on the mattress, concealed by a nest of blankets. As the van sped down the freeway, the glow of passing streetlights cast her sleeping form in an alternating flicker of shadow and light.

They'd spent the past month camping out in his carport, but the termination clause had finally kicked in yesterday. They were free to hit the road, and Eric had been more than happy to take the first shift behind the wheel.

The only question was the final destination…

Tessa's mother wanted her to come straight back to Texas, but she refused. "No," she told her mom. "I'm staying with Eric. End of story." Not the warmest mother-daughter chat he'd ever witnessed, but at least the two of them were back in communication.

He and Tessa had returned to his house, but they'd only stayed inside for the first night. She was OK in there as long as they remained downstairs and didn't set foot in the bedroom. It was Eric who couldn't handle it. He finally understood what Tessa meant when she talked about her triggers. He'd spent that whole night curled up in the corner of the couch with his eyes propped open, sweeping up and down the walls. He'd counted and recounted every electronic device in the place, imagining all the hidden cameras lurking within. By morning, he knew they couldn't stay.

He heard Tessa rustle the covers behind him. She made her

way forward and scooted into the passenger seat, yawning and rubbing her eyes.

"Where are we?"

"No clue."

Tessa glowered at him, but he could tell she wasn't really annoyed. "This is why people use GPS apps."

Eric kept his eyes firmly on the road. They'd been over this. He'd trashed both their cell phones on their way out of town—pulled the van over at the first scenic overlook he came to and tossed their phones off the edge of a cliff. "I'll stick with road signs, thanks."

"But you just said you have no idea where we are!"

He waved his hand vaguely toward the wide-open freeway before them. "Pretty sure we're headed the right direction."

They'd finalized their travel plans this morning. Tessa had suggested it, and they both knew it felt right: Tijuana.

They were headed back to their old bungalow at the Playa de la Joya Beach Club. It was the last place they'd both felt safe before Maury busted up their plans. Now they could finally pick up where they left off—and the beach club offered all the amenities they needed.

"Voluntary ninety-day lock-in," Eric had joked, "in a secluded, technology-free setting."

She'd stuck out her tongue at him. "Not funny."

But he saw the laughter in her eyes. It was slowly coming back—the old Tessa, with her inextinguishable positive outlook in the face of all her battles. He hadn't been so sure a month ago. After she heard the truth about the pregnancy, she looked so lost. Silent. Vacant. With that haunted expression—like she'd misplaced something important, but she couldn't remember what it was. Eric still caught her with that empty look in her eyes sometimes, but not so often anymore.

The hospital psychiatrist had started her on an antidepressant, and it definitely helped. Not a total personality transplant, but she seemed better able to cope with each day's ups and downs. He could put the radio on the pop music station without worrying that she might flinch at the sound of Dorian Cromwell's latest hit. He called it "Tell Me No Lies."

> *Boy, you really slay me.*
> *I won't apologize.*
> *Tell me you still love me.*
> *But don't…(oh no, oh no…)*
> *Tell me no lies.*

Dorian's stint in jail had only grown his fan base. Rumor had it he'd written that song from his prison cell and dedicated it to his old bandmate Hugo. Eric called bullshit, but Tessa laughed when she heard the story on TMZ. "Don't be jealous," she scolded. "Ariana Grande's still available."

Eric smiled. He loved it when she teased him. It reminded him of the old days over Twitter. They'd lost that easy banter somewhere in the transition to real life, but he could feel it coming back. They would hit their rhythm again, he felt certain. *Tijuana. They just needed to get to Tijuana…*

Eric darted a glance in Tessa's direction. She'd fallen silent, gazing out the passenger-side window. "What are you thinking about?" he asked.

Her shoulders jumped. "Huh? Oh, nothing."

He could tell that she was keeping something from him. The old Eric would have let it go, but not anymore. They needed to work on communicating. No more secrets. No more half-truths. No more hiding behind typed words and text messages. Real communication. Face-to-face and eye to eye.

"Tell me," he said. "Spill it."

She lifted her thumbnail to her mouth and chewed the cuticle. "I don't want to freak you out."

"I can take it. Go ahead."

She dropped her hand and twisted her fingers in her lap. "It's Maury. MET. I keep going over it in my head. It gets more and more messed up the more I think about it."

Eric knew what she meant. His thoughts kept drifting back and forth through time, retracing every moment of the past four years since Maury entered his life. One thing was clear. His manager had been keeping tabs on his cell phone from the beginning. Maury knew all about Eric's fake Twitter account last summer, and the online friendship he struck up with Tessa. His manager had been watching the whole time.

Tessa's voice cut through his thoughts. "I was remembering the night we met in Midland. I never told you... It didn't seem important at the time."

"Never told me what?"

"MET DM'ed that night. Just before I left my house to go to the private show." Tessa bit her lip. "It was super-creepy. I almost didn't go."

Eric felt the hairs rise on the back of his neck. He shivered, suddenly chilled. He remembered standing in the frigid parking lot outside the club when Maury came outside, doing something on his phone. "He told me you no-showed. He said the gig was canceled."

"He was trying to break us up, even then."

"Unbelievable," Eric said. He supposed their Twitter friendship must have amused Maury at first. But his manager drew the line when Eric decided to meet Tessa in person. And when the two of them ran away, it only cemented Maury's resolve. He'd been trying to get rid of her ever since.

Eric remembered his jam-packed schedule during the first weeks back from Mexico. That was Maury's doing, not the label. His manager wanted Tessa to feel neglected. Overwhelmed. And when that didn't work, Maury merely escalated his efforts.

Eric pressed down on the gas pedal at the thought of his manager skulking in the shadows outside his bedroom door. How had he not seen it sooner? How had he allowed himself to trust that leering face?

He wasn't quite sure he trusted anyone at this point. He had a feeling he would never trust anyone or anything again.

Well, no. That wasn't completely true. No one except this girl sitting in the passenger seat. Eric still had Tessa by his side, more precious to him than ever. Probably the only living soul he would ever trust for the rest of his life.

"Eric? Are you OK?"

"I'm fine." His hands squeezed against the steering wheel, hard enough to turn the knuckles white.

"Pull over," she said in his ear. "There's a rest stop ahead."

"No. I want to make it to the border before we stop." He made an effort to relax his hands, but the more he tried, the harder they gripped. Maybe she was right. Maybe he wasn't fine. Maybe he wouldn't be fine for a long time.

He turned the wheel and glided the van to a stop on the shoulder of the freeway. "I just need a sec," he said, but he could hear the tightness in his voice.

Tessa covered his hand on the steering wheel. "Breathe," she said.

She was staring at him hard now. Eric looked away, ashamed. He didn't want her worrying about him. He was supposed to be taking care of her, not the other way around. She was the one who'd been through an ordeal that nearly took her life.

She disappeared into the back of the van, riffling for something in her duffel bag.

"I don't need my Xanax. I'm fine!" His voice came out more exasperated than he intended. That was one thing he'd realized about himself in the month since he and Tessa took up residence in the van. He'd always had triggers, same as Tessa, but his fear usually expressed itself as irritability and anger. It was only recently—as he wrapped his head around Maury's betrayal—that he fully understood the anxiety that lay beneath.

Tessa reemerged with something in her hands, but it wasn't a pill bottle. Eric recognized the spiral-bound journal that she used to record her thoughts. "Talk to me," she said. "Tell me what's going through your head."

Tessa watched Eric's face, waiting for him to speak. He pinched the bridge of his nose, and his overgrown bangs fell forward into his eyes. Tessa recognized the pose. She'd seen photos of him like that: the tortured artist after a long day in the studio. It would sell a ton of copies if he ever put out an acoustic album with a shot like that on the cover.

Maybe someday. Tessa wondered if he would miss his old life as a musician. She had a feeling he would stage a comeback eventually. But for now, she knew that pose wasn't a performance. He'd been getting his headaches on a daily basis. She couldn't tell if they came from tension or inactivity, spending all day holed up inside a van.

Why did she feel like he was showing signs of agoraphobia? Was she projecting? He wasn't housebound. He was comfortable enough to leave home and drive to Mexico. But Tessa knew agoraphobia could be more subtle than that. She saw him making excuses to stay inside the van with the curtains drawn. He'd spent the past month wrapping up his affairs, and he'd conducted most of the conversations with lawyers and accountants over the phone. The only human being he'd interacted with in person was her. He would listen to the radio, but he refused to go online. And then there was the question of the cell phones he'd chucked off the side of a mountain...

Maybe that's what agoraphobia looked like in the smartphone age.

Tessa sighed. He hadn't answered her, but she could guess what he had on his mind. She wished she hadn't brought up Maury. She knew it would set him off. "Eric," she said softly. "No one's asking you to forgive him."

"I just don't understand." He looked up and met her eyes. "How can you go on, knowing he still exists somewhere in the universe...and not want to hunt him down and bash in his skull with a rock?"

His hands clenched on the steering wheel again. Tessa peeled one hand free and cradled it. She could feel the sweat of his palm—a physiological response, thoroughly predictable. Adrenal glands fired. Palms went damp. "Fight or flight," she said. "You're all about fight, but I'd rather run away. I'd be perfectly happy never to see Maury again."

He shook his head. His voice was low and raspy, but she heard him clearly enough. "I'm not talking about Maury. I'm talking about Blair."

Tessa looked down at her lap. A month had passed since her release from the hospital, and she still refused to speak her stalker's name. Maury, she could talk about. Not Blair. The police kept coming by, asking questions, but Tessa shut them down. They could prosecute Blair without her if they liked. She didn't want any part of it. She didn't have the stomach to sit before him in a courtroom and look him in the face.

Eric knew where she stood. They'd fought about it more than once. Why did he have to bring it up again?

"Tessa, you have to press charges. They'll let him walk!"

She shook her head.

"I don't care if he saved your life!" His eyes went hard. "He's a predator. He doesn't get a free pass."

"I know, but—"

"You have to protect yourself." Eric turned toward her, clutching both her hands firmly in his grasp. "That has to come first, before kindness."

Was that what he thought? Tessa's eyebrows rose. She supposed that used to be her motto.

EVERYONE YOU
MEET IS FIGHTING
A BATTLE YOU KNOW
NOTHING ABOUT.
BE KIND. ALWAYS.

Her entire worldview, summarized in meme form. If only life were truly that black and white. She still believed in kindness, of course. She believed in battles too. It was the "always" part she could no longer stand behind.

She pulled her hands free and looked out through the windshield into the deep, black nothingness around them. "It's not about kindness," she explained. "It's about moving forward."

Tessa understood that now. She could never rely on prison cells and courts of law to keep her phobias at bay. She would never truly be free of Blair Duncan for as long as they both drew breath—not until she found a way to live her life without thinking of him every single day.

She looked at Eric. He pitched forward with his forehead resting against the steering wheel, massaging the base of his skull with his fingers. Tessa reached out to him and pulled his head into her lap.

"Take a deep breath," she instructed, and she felt the inrush of air against her knees. "That's it. Hold it while I count. Tijuana one…Tijuana two…Tijuana three…Tijuana four… Tijuana five…"

His shoulders relaxed as she led him through the exercise and worked her soothing fingers through his hair.

"How's that? Better?"

Eric sat back up, rubbing the back of his neck. "A little."

She'd set her thought journal on the dashboard. Tessa picked it up and dropped it in his lap. Then she jerked her thumb toward the back of the van. Eric frowned at her, confused.

"Go ahead," she said. "I want you to write a journal entry. Write down whatever you're feeling, and then we'll talk about it later."

He wrinkled his nose. She knew what he was thinking. Who was she to dole out secondhand psychotherapy? She had enough to deal with on her own.

But she'd been on this road a lot longer than he had. She'd learned a thing or two about anxiety in the past year. If she could find a way to leave behind Blair Duncan, maybe she could help him shake the specter of Maury Gilroy.

"Writing," she said. "It'll help with the headaches. Trust me. I've been where you are."

He looked at the journal with its well-worn cover. "This seems like it's not your job."

Tessa almost replied with a snarky comeback, half-formed inside her head. Something about iTherapy apps and shattered screens...and boyfriends who made a habit of throwing away people's phones without permission.

But she held the words inside. Eric didn't need a joke. His fears were not the kind that he could easily laugh away.

He needed love.

He needed kindness.

He needed treatment from a qualified professional, and she would talk him into that eventually. But for now, all he had was her.

Tessa turned and ran a finger along his chiseled jaw. *So perfect*, she thought. *And yet so flawed.* "Eric, do you remember what you said the night we met?"

"I say a lot of things. Which part?"

She scooted closer. "We were sitting in my driveway, side by side in a parked car. And I told you what a mess I was, but it didn't scare you off." A lock of hair fell in his eyes, and Tessa swept it away with her thumb. "'I know you.' That's what you told me. 'I know your weaknesses, and you know mine.' And, Eric, that's the heart of it. That's the truest thing you ever said, and it meant more to me than any love song you could write."

Eric caught her hand and pressed a kiss into her palm. "I love you, snowflake," he whispered.

He hadn't called her that in a long time. Tessa tried to go on smiling, but she felt like she might cry. She held the feeling in, buried deep inside. He needed to focus on his own battle. Not hers. She kept her face blank, just the way Dr. Regan used to look at her—the human equivalent of a white noise machine.

"You write," she said. "I'll drive."

Eric chewed his lower lip. He flipped the journal open and shuffled past her old entries until he came to a clean page. "Does any of this therapy crap work?"

"Of course," she answered with a tiny smile. "Look at me. I'm the poster child for mental health."

Eric laughed, but he didn't argue. He plucked her pencil free from its spiral metal cage. Then he crawled backward through the gap between the seats, and Tessa took her place behind the wheel.

ACKNOWLEDGMENTS

Let me begin by thanking my readers. I heard from many of you in the months since *Follow Me Back* hit the shelves: Wattpad followers cheering for me online and new readers who discovered my work in print. Your passionate responses have lifted me up, helped me to grow as a writer, and pushed me to make this sequel the best book it could be. I thank each and every one of you who took the time to reach out, write reviews, share my work with fellow readers, or respond to my words in your own way.

I must also acknowledge the writing community who embraced me as one of their own. I can't tell you how much it means to have dear friends going through the same ups and downs at every stage of this publishing adventure. Thank you to my fellow 2017 debuts and to my family of Wattpad authors for your wisdom and encouragement. To Kayla Olson and Jordan Lynde, who offered critique on an early draft of this book, I hope you know how deeply I feel indebted. I must also say a word of thanks to Anna Todd, Ali Novak, Paula Stokes, Sandy Hall, and Laurie Elizabeth Flynn, whose kind words about my debut novel meant so much to me.

To my agent, Myrsini Stephanides, my heartfelt thanks for taking me under your wing and guiding me through every twist and turn. Without your insight and good humor, I would be lost. I'd also be remiss not to thank my former agent, Lydia Shamah, who saw promise in a first draft by an unproven author and set me on this road to a published duology.

That brings me to my publisher, Sourcebooks, and the amazing group of people who had a hand in the making of this book. Thank you first and foremost to my wonderful editor, Kate Prosswimmer. You have come to know Tessa and Eric nearly as well as I do, and you have helped in countless ways to bring their story to life. I hope you take as much pride as I do in the final product. I am thoroughly grateful as well to the entire Sourcebooks team, including Annette Pollert-Morgan, Elizabeth Boyer, Alex Yeadon, Katy Lynch, Stefani Sloma, Beth Oleniczak, Sara Hartman-Seeskin, and so many others who had a hand in bringing both *Follow Me Back* and *Tell Me No Lies* into the world. I could not be more appreciative of the care you have shown in bringing my stories to the printed page.

Before my words came to a bookstore shelf, however, they first caught fire online within an extraordinary community called Wattpad. I would be nowhere without the incredible people at Wattpad HQ who have opened doors and done so much to amplify my voice. Thank you all, and a particularly hearty thanks to my talent manager, Caitlin O'Hanlon.

Finally, a word of gratitude to my family: Helene, Alex, Ted, Debbie, Allan, Gail, Jeanne, my children, and above all, David. This book would not exist without your endless love, patience, and support.

Thank you for sharing in my hopes and believing in my dreams.

ABOUT THE AUTHOR

A. V. GEIGER is an epidemiologist who spends far too much spare time on social media. By day, she studies women's psychiatric and reproductive health. By night, she can be found fangirling, following people back, and photoshopping the heads of band members onto the bodies of unicorns. Her writing career began with celebrity fan fiction, and her work draws extensively on her own experiences with online fan culture. Her original teen fiction has received millions of hits on the story-sharing website Wattpad, ranking as high as #1 in the mystery-thriller genre. She lives in New Jersey with her husband and twin boys. Visit avgeiger.com.